JONATHAN ADVENTURE

The LOST SCROLLS

MICHAEL J. SCOTT

Ellechor Publishing House, LLC

Ellechor Publishing House
2431 NW Wessex Terrace, Hillsboro, OR 97124

Copyright © 2011 by Michael J. Scott
2012 Ellechor Publishing House Paperback Edition

The Lost Scrolls/ Michael J. Scott.
ISBN: 978-1-937844-90-5
Library of Congress Control Number: 2011945173

Printed in the United States of America

Cover & Interior Design by BookImage Designs, LLC

www.ellechorpublishing.com

ACKNOWLEDGMENTS

Several people contributed to this book who deserve special recognition. Some of them are people I've only met online, and yet their assistance proved invaluable in taking this novel from concept to the book you now hold in your hands.

I want to thank, first of all, those special people at ChristianWriters.com too numerous to list who took the time to review early drafts of the manuscript and offer their comments, encouragement, and especially their critiques. Among them, my comrade in composition, Linda Yezak, deserves significant credit for reviewing and editing the manuscript entirely. I hope someday to get down to Texas or over to an ACFW conference where we can finally meet in person. Due credit also belongs to agent Steve Laube. Although he ultimately turned down representing the manuscript, his comments and suggestions proved invaluable in sharpening the storyline.

Finally, I must recognize my editor and publisher, Rochelle Carter. Thank you so much for taking a chance on me. I hope we're able to enjoy a long and mutually prosperous relationship.

For my beautiful wife, Wendy.
Thank you for believing in me.

PROLOGUE

Within fifteen minutes Dr. Stephen Kaufman would face death. He knew it. His heart pounded the point home. He threaded through the crowded streets of Ankara, Turkey, brushing by pedestrians, thrusting past the busy shops, glancing furtively behind.

Once or twice, he thought he spotted his pursuer. That same face he'd seen after too many turns to be coincidence. But then, he thought he'd seen him ahead, too, nonchalantly bearing down on him, until he realized it was someone else.

He drew his hand across his brow, wiped the sweat off on his shirt, and rushed forward. Along the hurried streets the temperature was a mild ninety degrees. The smell of exotic spices and coffee mingled with the acrid stink of exhaust fumes, and he struggled to breathe.

He ducked into a side street café and out the back door, creeping through the alley until he spied the FedEx shop across the street. Stephen swallowed with relief and crossed to the other side.

Inside the shop, he obtained a box and dropped in the small brass key he'd been carrying on a chain around his neck. A moment later, its fate was sealed. He breathed a shaky sigh and asked to use one of the computers. The clerk directed him toward a workstation in the back of the shop.

The cramped room was dark, lit only by the incandescent bulbs hanging above each workstation. He took his seat at one of the archaic computers and logged onto his email.

Almost nothing had gone according to plan, and he was almost out of time.

But it was worth it. There was no question of that. Worth his life and more. Even worth the life of his beloved sister. God, please don't let it come to that. He saw her dark eyes smiling against her cream-colored skin, her raven locks framing her beautiful face. With a little luck, he just might get them both out alive.

He wrote the simplest message possible, letting the great gulf of the unsaid remain placid and undisturbed. He clicked "Send," logged off, and left the shop. Nothing else remained now, but to wait.

If FedEx held true to their promise, the package would be on a plane tonight. At some point the next morning, it would arrive safely halfway around the world in America. Oh, the wonders of the modern era.

From his left, speakers in a distant mosque blared the long wailing call of the muezzin, announcing Maghrib, the beginning of evening prayer. He glanced toward the mosque.

A shock of pain stopped him cold. The knife pierced his abdomen just below his ribs. Its blade sliced cleanly through his skin and intestines. He felt more shock than pain, and strangely warm. The hand holding the knife pulled free. He saw it was not a hand at all, but a blade seeming to grow straight out of an arm. The notion struck him as absurd, and he laughed. Then his knees buckled, and he fell against his assailant. The man with the knife that was not a knife but somehow an arm said nothing. Instead, he gently laid Stephen in the street. The man bent over him, pawing through his pockets before rising and walking away. Stephen felt his life-blood draining onto the pavement, and he wondered how long until the prayers would be ended, and his own outcry could be heard.

Hamid never looked back as he left the crumpled form of the archaeologist. He twisted the blade free of its cuff and let it fall. It landed on the road with a small clank. In its place he affixed the prosthetic hand he'd worn since adolescence, snapping it in position with a firm click. The authorities might find the knife, but there'd be no traceable fingerprints. He smiled at the irony and turned down a side street. That the Muslim insistence on clinging to ancient standards of justice should somehow deny them the right to modern methods of criminal investigative techniques—even if the Turks themselves were not so barbaric—was deliciously fitting.

Around him, the buildings were the only witnesses to his crime—conspirators complicit in their silence. He slipped through an alleyway between townhouses of beige brick and red tile roofs, making several turns to place himself far from the crime scene. He stepped through an enclosed archway and pulled out a cell phone, speed-dialing the number.

After the third ring, a voice on the other end said, "Yes?"

"It's done."

"Did he have it on him?"

"No. He'd already sent it."

"Are you sure?"

He hesitated. He'd checked the body. He'd seen Dr. Kaufman come out of the FedEx building and assumed the archaeologist mailed the key. He must have!

"Yes," he finally said.

The man swore at him. He winced. None of his Muslim clientele ever used such profanity. Why those in the Christian West insisted upon it was lost on him. Not that he cared either way. As a Kafir—an unbelieving infidel—he'd long ago given up the notion of God.

"He didn't have it. If you don't believe me, you're welcome to check for yourself."

Silence. Then, "Alright. I'll be in touch."

"When you do, remember: my price just went up."

He pictured the man seething, his face turning red, his jaw clenching. He wished he could see it.

"How much?"

He pursed his lips. He'd anticipated some sort of objection when he raised his rates. The simple question suggested he hadn't been charging him nearly enough. "Double."

Laughter. "You're not worth it."

"Then you can find someone else."

The client made a discourteous reference to 'towel-head' and then said, "Ten percent."

He was at least close. "Twenty-five," he replied, if only to show he was willing to admit he'd overshot.

They settled on fifteen, which was considerably more than Hamid had hoped. He closed the cell phone and glanced at the setting sun.

There was one thing left to do. In many ways he enjoyed this part the most. Watching the miserable wretches of this society recoil from his handiwork thrilled him even more than the kill itself. He maneuvered back toward the place where he'd left Kaufman to die. He slowed and came to a stop by a telephone pole on the corner of the street.

Already an ambulance and three white polis cruisers with broad, blue stripes across their sides were parked in the center of the street, their emergency lights reflecting from the windows of the townhouses and shops. Hamid contemplated the expletive he'd heard earlier. The response time was too fast.

Someone must have seen him. He watched as they loaded a stretcher into the back of the waiting ambulance, the oxygen mask clearly visible on Dr. Kaufman's face.

He turned abruptly and walked away. Kaufman wouldn't be going anywhere soon, assuming he survived, and Hamid had a plane to catch.

The Lost Scrolls

CHAPTER
1

Dr. Jonathan Munro staggered into his office with his arms full of papers and a leather satchel slipped over one shoulder. The bag's strap clung precariously to the edge of his jacket, threatening to fall against his overloaded arm and bring the whole stack tumbling to the floor. If he could just get it to the—

He smacked his shin on something and stumbled, yelping in pain. The shoulder bag dropped, dragging him with it. His papers flooded the floor.

What on earth?

He pushed his glasses onto his nose and disentangled his arm from the computer bag. Scooping the papers into a pile, he set them on the desk, and turned around to whatever offending object had derailed his balancing act. A metal stool lay across his path on its side. He furrowed his brow and set the stool upright.

How did that happen? He glanced around. The narrow office was a blend of mismatched bookshelves, two overloaded workstations, a single-cup teapot sitting on a cluttered counter, and a frayed Oriental rug thrown across the floor. There was also a draftsman's table in the far corner with a lamp above it, and a magnifying glass on a boom arm swung around in front of it. Normally the room filled him with a sense of comfort, but in a frumpy sort of way. Now it felt disquieting.

Things were out of place. His fingers left the stool. He scanned the office, taking in the details. The tea box was open. Had he left it like that? The leaves would grow stale and lose their flavor. The light on the draftsman's table glowed brightly, and the magnifier hung over the table, not to one side. Could he really have forgotten to put it away? As absent-minded as he was, he wouldn't have left the light on.

Behind him, the door creaked open. He whirled about as a figure in blue jeans and an olive sweater backed into the room, pushing at the door with his elbow. The man turned, his arms full of more papers, and nearly collided with the computer desk.

"Leon, wait a second. Let me take those from you."

"Oh, thanks," Leon breathed, relieved of his burden. Jon set them down and turned to see Leon grabbing the teapot, ready to fill it with water.

"Were you in my office earlier?"

Leon paused by the door, teapot in hand, and gave him an odd look. "Uh, yeah. I'm in your office all the time. Hang on a sec." He disappeared from the door, returning shortly with the pot full of water. "Why'd you ask?"

"You didn't leave the light on, by chance?"

He pursed his lips. "I might've. Don't think so, though."

"Or the tea box uncovered? Or the stool knocked over?"

Leon glanced around. He looked at the professor, wearing the same concern.

Jon put his hands on his hips. "Someone's been in here."

Now confusion joined Leon's concern. "Don't you keep it locked?"

"All the time."

"You think someone wanted to massage their grades, maybe?"

Jon shook his head. "I don't know. Maybe just a prank. Grades are all on the website. Breaking in here wouldn't do any good."

"Well, it's not like you have anything worth taking."

He nodded. Leon was right. There was nothing at all, except—

"The papyrus!" He leaped for the safe behind the draftsman's table. Leon followed. Jon glanced up at him as he fumbled with the combination. "Call campus security."

Leon picked up the phone. He turned around as Jon pulled two glass plates out of the file cabinet.

"It's okay." Jon set the plates on the draftsman's table and let his fingertips glide over the surface.

Leon put down the phone without completing the call and came up behind him. "Is that what I think it is?"

Jon chuckled. "Yeah. It's had me on edge ever since it arrived." He swept the magnifier over the papyrus, bringing the letters into sharp clarity. Two millennia of wear and tear obscured the text. The ink was faint, faded almost to nothing against the taupe papyrus. Jagged tears lined its edges, and holes pockmarked its surface, rendering some of the Greek lettering illegible. In the center of the fragment was an enormous gash, which made a precise translation impossible. Two glass plates carefully sealed the entire manuscript.

He moved to one side and let Leon take the seat in front. The ancient document clearly intrigued the graduate assistant, as Jon knew it would. The Egerton Papyrus was from an unrecognized gospel of the first century. At least one of the fragments paralleled John's Gospel. Other portions more closely resembled Luke. The fragments consisted only of three leaves from an ancient book purchased in Egypt in 1935. All told, the pages were only about four and a half inches tall, by three and three eighths inches wide.

Jon left the draftsman's table and returned to the stack of term papers he'd brought in. "Do you believe this? 'A Comparative Analysis of the Codex Vaticanus and the Textus Receptus.' Oh Lord, I should give him an F just for the title." He set it to one side and picked up another.

Leon leaned in close over the papyrus, trying to make out the words. "How did you get this?"

"I've a friend in the British Library."

"For real?"

He nodded. "They've brought a good number of their artifacts to the States on tour—raising money for the cause—that sort of thing." Jon scanned the title of the next term paper and set it aside. "Ever since the British treasury threatened to trim their funding, they've been looking for new sources of revenue."

"I thought there was a petition against it."

"Sure, but you still gotta eat." He read the title of the next paper. "'Secrets of the Dead Sea Scrolls Revealed'—what is this? Tabloid graduate school?" He dropped the paper in disdain. "Anyway, I heard they were bringing the religious texts on tour, and I made a phone call. I'm not supposed to have it, but you know someone owed me a favor, so I have Egerton all to myself for at least another two days."

Leon fingered the notebook lying to one side of the table. "You're making your own translation?"

"Working up the transcription, first. Then a translation. The lacunae are particularly bad in the second leaf. A whole wedge of text is missing from both sides."

"Tragedy."

"Mm-hmm." He glanced at his computer. His email icon pulsated. He opened the window and scanned the addresses. There was a notice from the university that the email servers would be offline later. That was no big deal. He had plenty to keep him busy. Several others were from various students sending in their term papers electronically, despite the fact he'd requested they be printed. He'd have to make a note: no more electronic term papers. It was too hard on his equipment to print them, and too hard on his eyes not to. The students could pay for their own ink. It might improve the quality of their research.

One of the emails stood out. Stephen Kaufman. He frowned. He hadn't thought of Stephen and Izzy in a long time, not since—he shook his head. It had taken him a long time to get over Izzy. What could her brother possibly want now? He moved the cursor over the email.

"Do you think it's real?" said Leon.

He smiled and pulled away from his computer, leaving the email unread. Whatever Kaufman wanted could wait. He wasn't about to let a casual electronic hello ruin his day now. He had other things to think about. He sidled up to Leon.

"Oh, it's real, alright," he whispered. "An independent gospel. Not a Gnostic heresy, either." He patted Leon's shoulder. "Would you like to take some time with it? I'll get us some tea."

"Oh, uh—I can't. I was actually supposed to give you a message." He fumbled through his pockets. "Here it is. Your neighbor called. Said it was urgent." Leon held out the pink phone message to him. Jon furrowed his brow and took it. He glanced at the name, barely recognizing it.

"Did she say what it was about?"

Leon was studying the letters through the magnifying glass. He shook his head without looking up. Jon smiled and folded the note into his pocket. As a graduate assistant, Leon was the best he'd ever had. He could as easily get lost in the work as Jon could. He'd been with Jon for almost two years while completing his doctorate. Jon hoped he would remain with the university as a colleague, but that was out of his hands.

It was up to the Director of Antiquities, Dr. Anthony Michaels, to offer him a position, first—and up to Leon to accept it, second. Jon would never stand in the young man's way. He had prospects, whatever choices he made.

Jon left him sitting by the draftsman's table, picked up the phone, and dialed the number. As he listened to the phone ringing, he meandered back to the still unread email. Why would Stephen be sending him a message? They hadn't spoken in ten years, and last he'd heard, Stephen was on a dig in Turkey with his sister, Isabel. On the other hand, if something had happened to Izzy…. He clicked on the icon, and the message opened up before him.

"Jonathan," he read, "I'm so sorry to bring you in on this, but I have no time and no one else—"

A perplexed voice answered the phone. "Hello?"

"Oh, um—yes, Dr. Munro calling. Is this—" he opened the pink phone message and scanned the name, "Vera DiMarco?"

"No. This is her son."

He closed his eyes. *Idiot.* "Terribly sorry. I meant to ask if she were available."

"Hang on," said the man in a disbelieving tone. Jon heard him yell off the phone, "Mom! Phone's for you!"

"If it's a telemarketer, please get rid of him. I have to keep the line clear for Dr. Munro."

"It is Dr. Munro. You said he was smart."

"Harry! He can probably hear you. Give me the phone."

"He thought I was you." There was a loud rustling as the phone exchanged hands.

"Hello, Dr. Munro?"

"The guy's an idiot, Mom. I can't believe you like him."

Jon flushed, and decided to ignore Harry. "Yes," he said, "I'm returning your call."

"I hate to be the bearer of bad news," she hesitated. "It's about your house."

"What about it?"

"Someone broke into it after you left for work. I called the police as soon as I could. There's a detective there now."

"What?"

"I'm sure he wants to speak with you."

"Someone—?"

"Broke into your house. They went through the back door. There's glass everywhere. I didn't go in."

"When?"

"This morning. After you left for work. I noticed it on my way back from my morning walk. Can't say if they got anything or not."

Jon stared ahead in stunned silence. He turned and met Leon's eyes, who'd come to stand beside him.

"You should probably come home," said Ms. DiMarco.

"Idiot, Mom," said a distant Harry. "You can do better."

"Th-thanks." He hung up, sank down in his chair, staring straight ahead.

"What happened?"

"Unbelievable," he muttered.

"What?"

"I've been robbed."

"Robbed?"

"I...I have to go home."

"Seriously? Robbed? Okay, I'll... I'll tell Michaels. I can handle your classes if you want," Leon offered.

After a moment, Jon said, "Yeah. Yeah, okay."

"What do you want me to do about the papyrus?"

"The what?"

"Egerton."

"Uh—oh, right. I can't even think—just keep it safe. I'll..." He rose and grabbed his coat, muttering as he left the room.

When he got out to his car, he slowed, gaping at the driver's side window. Someone had smashed it. Tiny diamonds of glass dotted the parking space, the seat, and floorboards. He fell back and ran his hand through his hair.

Lord, what is going on? First his office, then his home, and now his car? He didn't have anything valuable. Unless this really was about Egerton, and they just missed it....

He whipped out his Blackberry, calling his office.

"Dr. Munro's office, Leon spea—"

"Leon, it's Jon. My car—my car's been ransacked, too." He stopped when his Blackberry chirped. The battery was low. He'd forgotten to recharge it. He swore. "Get campus security to post a guard on my office and notify the police."

"Yeah, I'm on it."

"And get that manuscript in the safe. Don't tell anyone I have it. I don't want to get anyone in trouble, just—I don't want anyone to touch it."

"Okay. Done. How are you going to get home?"

"I—uh..." He grimaced. "My battery's dying. Look, it's just the window. I'll just have to drive carefully."

He hung up and reached for the door, but stopped at the handle. He put his hand in his pocket and opened the door with his coat wrapped around his fingers. Scraping the glass off the seat, he climbed in. The seat had been pushed all the way back, as had the passenger seat. The glove box hung open, its contents spilled across the floor. The charger for his phone dangled from the cigarette lighter, the wires broken and exposed. *Great.* He fished out a pair of napkins and palmed them on the steering wheel. He wasn't about to mess up any fingerprints left by whoever had done this. He turned the key. The Audi's engine purred to life, and he left the parking lot, headed home.

CHAPTER
2

"Brother Demetri, your garden looks well."

Demetri Antonescu glanced up at his unexpected guest, both surprised and pleased to have a visit from the abbot. He immediately clenched his teeth against the surge of pride forming in his heart, and fought for an appropriately humble reply.

"It is the blessing of the Lord that makes it so. He sends the sun and rain, and gives the increase to these simple tomato plants." He fingered a leaf on one of the plants, and then plucked a large, round tomato from the vine. He held it up for the abbot.

The abbot took it with a smile. "You tend it with a faithful hand, Brother."

"Thank you, Father." The sun was bright and not too hot for the black cassock he wore. The breeze blew fresh from the Aegean over the peninsula, gently caressing the leaves in his garden and filling his heart with a warm contentment. "It is my task." He picked up his clipping shears and turned back to the tomato plants.

"I have another for you."

Demetri paused. Something in the abbot's voice splintered the peace in his heart. His fingers tightened on the shears, and for a moment, they felt familiar, reminding him of the gun.

He stood to face the Orthodox monk. Drawn to his full height of six foot four, two hundred and twenty pounds, he towered over the smaller abbot. In his previous life in the Romanian Securitate, he could take a man like the abbot and send him to God with a single strike to the Adam's apple, heart, or any other vital targets on the human body. Such thoughts troubled him now, and why he should have them toward his spiritual mentor—a man who had shown him nothing but kindness—filled him with sorrow.

He'd come to the monastery on Mount Athos two years after Comrade Supreme Commander Nicolae Ceauşescu's execution in Târgovişte on Christmas Day, 1989. It had been more than twenty years since he'd taken a life. He'd spent a decade reliving the faces of those he'd killed—his willfully deaf ears awakened to their pleading. He'd hated himself for the monster he'd become, and he'd marveled at the grace of a God who could forgive such a man as he. His spiritual training at Mount Athos purged him of the nightmares he'd earned enforcing the Romanian dictator's will. But there was a deeper training, one ingrained from years of hunting down dissidents and foreign operatives, which rose to the surface now. The abbot's voice called to it.

"How may I serve?" he asked, praying to God that his instincts were wrong.

The abbot smiled, oblivious to his torment, and invited him inside the *skete*. Demetri swallowed, staring up at the thatched roof and cinder block walls of the *skete*. It had been his home for more than a decade, but now it felt foreign. A fragment of scripture trailed through his mind. *"Eu sînt străin şi venetic printre voi—I am an alien and a stranger among you."* The three pillars of monastic life were poverty, chastity, and obedience. He'd willingly given up material possessions to serve God. He'd never had much to begin with. Long ago, he'd lost interest in sex, except for the occasional indiscretion. On the Holy Mountain, women were forbidden, and he deliberately allowed the feel of a woman's body to fade from his memory. And obedience? His years in the Securitate taught him to obey without question—a virtue here.

And yet, he hesitated.

The abbot poked his head out of the *skete*, a puzzled look on his face. Demetri fondled the clippers, and then flipped them in his hand so he clutched the sharpened blades, with the handles pointed safely downward. He ducked through the door and set them in their place on the shelf, next to his Romanian Bible and a book of prayer.

The abbot checked the teapot hanging over the coals of the fire pit in one corner. He tossed a few more briquettes into the glow and stirred it with the poker by the hearth. Demetri always had a pot warming over the coals for guests, but now he felt more like an intruder than a host. He picked up a pair of cups from the shelf and set them on the low table by the only window in the *skete*. The abbot took his seat across from Demetri, leaving him the chair closest to the door. He sat with his back to it, trying to feel comfortable.

"Where to begin?" said the abbot, folding his hands. "Are you familiar with the *Domo tou Bibliou*?"

Demetri furrowed his brow. He'd heard of it, once or twice in idle conversation—speculation among the monks about relics yet uncovered. They dismissed it as a legend, on par with those who sought the Holy Grail.

"It is a myth," he replied.

"It has been found."

He laughed nervously. "Surely, Father, you have made a joke—a story to play sport with me."

The abbot poured his tea and glanced at Demetri from over the kettle, his eyes veiled by the steam. "Dear Brother,

I would not trifle with you. The legend of the *Domo* is true. Crescens, the bishop of Galatia, entrusted this most holy relic to a simple priest, before he left to join his brothers in glory at the hand of the pagan Caesar Trajan. The priest carried the secret with him to the grave. Even his name has been forgotten. But in nineteen centuries of sleep, he did not fail to keep this sacred trust—until now. A week ago the protus learned an unbeliever has disturbed his rest."

"The crypt has been found?"

"It has."

"Then it is lost?"

"No, Brother," the abbot shook his head. "The Lord has smitten the unbeliever. The man was an archaeologist, he would have told others of his discovery. We must protect it, my friend."

Demetri stopped sipping his tea. He swallowed and set the cup down. His instincts had been right. "You wish me to leave the Mountain."

The abbot nodded. "We have prayed about this mightily, my friend. There is no one else here who possesses the skills needed to accomplish this great work."

"Skills?" He stared down at his hands. "Father, do you know what it is you are asking of me? To go back to that life? To become that which I have crucified? Eighteen years I have tried to forget these 'skills'!" He shook his head. "Long ago I beat my sword into a plow. Please do not ask me to remake it."

The abbot rose and came around the table to place a kindly hand on the monk's shoulder. "Dearest Brother, we would never ask such a thing. If you do not wish this assignment, someone else may go, someone far less likely to succeed, I am afraid, and perhaps at greater cost."

Demetri turned and looked hard at the abbot as he continued to speak.

"Consider this, my friend, with all that you are, and all that you once were, whether or not you were saved for such a time as this. Perhaps it is God's will."

God's will. He picked up his prayer beads, folded his hands, and rested his chin on them. So much he had tried to forget. At the end of his prayer beads, right next to the cross, dangled a handcuff key. He fingered the key – the promise of freedom. Could it be? Might God even redeem his past for His service? His eyes wandered to the window. Outside, the sun shone on the leaves and trees – a field of green rushing endlessly down to the perfect, lethean blue of the Aegean. Maybe he wouldn't have to be the man that he was. Maybe this time would be different. He turned and looked at the abbot, who leaned against the door frame, watching him with silent, patient eyes. When Demetri spoke, his voice was even and smooth—a ready soldier willing to lay down his life for his captain.

"What would you have me do?"

Half a world away, dot com millionaire and venture capitalist Mark Beaufort stared at the line of text scrolling across his computer screen from his Tribeca loft overlooking West Broadway. The text came from one of several internet sources designed to alert him of unique opportunities in which he might invest. He ran a hand through the straight dark hair hanging limply across his face, subconsciously aware there was less of it now than there had been a year ago—much less ten years, when his future seemed bright and the sky the limit. That was before the technology bubble burst, and he'd almost been wiped clean in the resulting crash. His sources had saved him then, allowing him to dump his stocks before the Dow took its plunge. He'd escaped with slightly fewer millions than he'd hoped to make, but certainly far more than he'd have kept had he not sold when he did. It was an ongoing frustration, Forbes leaving him from the list of the ten wealthiest men in the world.

Since then he'd steered clear of anything with a promising tomorrow. The future lies in the past. He repeated this to himself every day as he scoured the internet for suitable opportunities. Two months ago he'd invested in a company supporting a dig near the Temple Mount in Jerusalem. Breaking news that an archaeologist had found an inscribed seal dating to the time of Nehemiah rewarded his investment. It didn't matter to him whether or not the story was true—the web traffic it generated was enough to double his investment. It was simply one of the small ways he had of profiting from antiquities.

His greatest joy, however, came from acquiring the rare artifact, such as the pottery he'd purchased from the Musconetcong River in New Jersey, dated some 12,000 years old. The team excavating the site never suspected the intern he'd co-opted would seize their prize and ship it to him. It only cost him thirty thousand dollars. The artifact would easily catch ten million on the open market.

The announcement on his computer wasn't about another pottery find or chipped flint arrowhead. He leaned in close, studying the text. His heart beat faster. Could this possibly be true? If it were, no amount of money could buy such a prize, though many would try. Some would risk their entire fortunes for this. A few keystrokes sent an encrypted message to his dealer.

R U in possession?
Offer is 4 info only.
He hesitated, then typed, *$?*, and hit send.
$500K.

He typed an exclamation point as the only reply. There was no response from the dealer. He cupped his hands in front of his face. It meant the offer was firm. The information was solid. The dealer wouldn't risk coming to him and asking for half a million if it were otherwise. He had to make a counter offer.

Mark turned, staring out his apartment. The morning light dazzled his window, inviting him into the day. Even from the tenth floor he could hear the roar of the city—the plaintive bleeps of the police cruisers navigating through traffic, the incessant honking of cabbies calling out a New York greeting to one another—like a flock of Canadian geese roosting on the streets below.

If what his dealer was suggesting checked out, it could be greater than the value of the entire city. *Greater than the glory that was Greece and the grandeur that was Rome,* he mused.

Abruptly he returned to the computer. *100K now. 500K more if info checks out.*

There was a long moment, and then the reply flashed onto his screen. It was a bank routing number. He copied it and set about transferring the funds. Within ten minutes, he'd wired the money to the offshore account. He sent the response code back to his dealer. A moment later, the dealer signed off the instant messaging service.

He sat back and vented his breath. He hadn't realized he'd been holding it. Mark frowned. He'd vetted the dealer through numerous sources, and all had given him a green light, yet it was entirely possible the dealer would disappear with his money. It wouldn't make sense for the man to jeopardize their relationship. They'd worked together for a little more than two years now, and Mark had already paid more than a hundred thousand for his services in that time. Still…

He shook it off. These were normal mid-transaction jitters. The exchange wasn't out of the ordinary. Only the product had him rattled.

He pushed away from the desk and stepped to the liquor cabinet on the back wall. He grabbed a bottle of Glenlivet and a highball glass, and poured himself a Scotch. As he lifted the glass to his lips, his computer chirped. He glanced at the monitor in the mirror. The mailbox icon showed new mail. He smiled and tossed back the rest of the drink.

There were no words in the email. Only a PDF attachment. He opened the file, sorting through the scanned document until his eyes caught sight of a hastily scrawled note on the bottom of the page. The lead wasn't much, but it was legitimate.

He picked up the phone. After three rings, his personal assistant answered. "Yes, Mr. Beaufort?"

"Get me Sean MacNeil. I have a job for him."

"Sir? It's 1 a.m. in New Zealand."

"Did I ask for the time?"

"No sir. Right away, sir."

He hung up. All that remained now was to wire the rest of the money. This would easily be the biggest deal of his life.

Father Philip Bellamy sat against the wooden bench with his hands clasped in his lap. He'd smoothed out the folds of his robe until they fell neatly on either side. He supposed he should be praying. He pushed a lock of hair out of his eyes and waited.

In the hallway the late afternoon sun appeared citrine through the open windows, illumining the dust particles floating in its beam with a fiery glow. Outside in Saint Peter's Square, the air was still warm. He stared out at the ancient obelisk standing defiant toward the heavens. The cross atop the obelisk did not change the fact the Emperor Nero erected it for his circus, at which thousands of Christians were martyred following the great fire of Rome in A.D. 64. Tradition held they'd crucified Saint Peter himself upside-down in the square that now bore his name.

Philip pulled out his rosary, patiently mumbling the ancient prayers he'd memorized as he waited.

"Che questo incoraggi i santi, cioè coloro che osservano i comandamenti di Dio e hanno fede in Gesù ad essere costanti, anche nella sofferenza—This calls for patient endurance on the part of the saints who obey God's commandments and remain faithful to Jesus."

A door at the far end of the hallway opened, resounding drum-like through the corridor. He pressed his lips together and rose to his feet.

"Padre Bellamy," said the older man striding toward him. "I am Cardinal Rauschad. We spoke on the phone. I apologize if we've kept you waiting."

Philip guessed him to be about fifty years old. Young, by Vatican standards. He took his hand and kissed the ring. "Not at all, Eminence."

"Your flight went well?" He steered Philip toward the door he'd just left.

"It was acceptable. Much security. I've not had to fly since September 11th."

"Ah yes. I imagine it has changed things."

"It has." He pursed his lips, not quite sure if was time for the question. "I am curious why I was summoned here."

The cardinal chuckled. "I imagine you are. Come." He held open the door for the young priest. Philip walked through.

The room he entered was spacious and well lit. A large window overlooked the courtyard below. In the center of the room stood a very old table with a few chairs around it, and another cardinal sitting at the far end. He was considerably older than Rauschad, with tufts of white hair peeking from his skullcap. He pored over a set of documents laid out on the table.

"Padre Bellamy, let me introduce you to His Eminence, Cardinal Antonio Cellino, chief librarian and archivist."

"Your Eminence," Philip said with a slight bow.

The librarian glanced up. "He neglected to mention I am also the resident fossil."

The cardinal smiled. "Cardinal Cellino has been here longer than anyone."

"And I can't say as I approve of this course of action. Sit down, son, and let me have a look at you."

Philip took a seat diagonally to the librarian. Cellino peered at him from beneath bushy eyebrows, eying him warily like some furtive creature unsure whether to choose fight or flight. Philip wondered what could engender this reaction from someone he'd only just met.

"So," the librarian said. "You're to be our mercenary, eh?"

Philip shot a glance between Cellino and Rauschad.

"Padre Philip has not been told why he's been summoned just yet."

Cellino frowned. "Well, that's a dastardly trick! You could've at least told him before he came all this way."

"I thought it best not to speak of it on the phone."

Cellino frowned deeper, clearly unsatisfied. He said nothing for a moment, and then waved a hand toward Philip, staring at Rauschad. "Well?"

"Padre Philip," Rauschad began, taking a seat on the table itself. "You have a rather diverse background."

"I suppose."

He read from a folder. "You're the son of an American serviceman and a local woman. You grew up here in Italy, but moved to the States when you were fifteen. There you entered the United States Marine Corps before studying medicine, and then law—a somewhat unusual career move."

Philip smiled. "It is no secret I was training for a career with the U.S. State Department when I received my calling."

Rauschad smiled but ignored the interruption. "And you speak two languages."

"Three, actually."

"It is widely believed the 'U.S. Department of State' is simply code for 'CIA,' correct?"

"So I understand."

"And do you still work with the CIA?"

Philip smiled and said nothing.

"But you did work for them."

"I can neither confirm nor deny anything, of course. I consider such things as inviolable as the confessional. But all that was a long time ago."

"Let us hope not too long ago."

"Cardinal, please forgive my boldness, but what do you want? I've left that life behind. I have no desire to return it. It is nothing but lies and deceit. I have been a faithful priest for many—"

"Oh, Don! Quit beating around the bush already!" Both gaped, startled by the librarian's outburst. Cellino ignored their stares. "Philip," he said in a low voice, "have you heard of the *Domo tou Bibliou*?"

Philip frowned. He shook his head. "No. I haven't."

Cellino passed a fragile document over to him. "This is a letter from a fifth century saint, St. Anysius, bishop of Thessalonica. He warns his successor to keep watch over the

Domo tou Bibliou. See here? 'Interred within lies preserved a great treasure which belongs to the Church in perpetuity.' It is the only written account of the *Domo* prior to the eleventh century. At which point we have the account of Godefroy de Bouillon, a crusader from France." He slid another paper over. "He writes how the Seljuk Turks destroyed churches in their assault upon Byzantium, and specifically tells us the *Domo tou Bibliou* has been lost to the sands."

Philip stared at both documents. He cleared his throat. "Well, this is…"

"Ancient history, until two weeks ago."

"I don't understand."

"Philip," said Rauschad, "the *Domo tou Bibliou* has been found. An archaeologist named Stephen Kaufman located it in Turkey, southeast of Ankara." He slid an eight-by-ten photograph of the man over to the priest. "Two days ago, he was attacked and left for dead. We believe his assailant is seeking the treasure St. Anysius spoke of."

Philip stared at both men. "What does this have to do with me?"

Rauschad pulled a thin document wrapped in leather and sealed with wax from his vestments. "This is a Papal Indulgence. It hereby grants you leave to take whatever measures are necessary to retrieve the treasure and return it safely here to the Vatican. Also, a Letter of Recommend. This instructs whatever church with whom you may come into contact to provide you whatever you need. No questions asked." He passed the packet to Philip. "Padre, the treasure of the *Domo tou Bibliou* cannot fall into the wrong hands. It must be secured."

Philip took the letters in hand, feeling the weight. He set them down in front of himself on the table and rubbed his hands on his robe. After a moment he said, "I want to ask, 'Why me?' but I think you've already answered that."

"You are the most qualified candidate on a very short list. No one else even comes close."

"At the same time," interjected Cellino, "you must realize this is voluntary. You are not obligated."

Philip pressed his lips together. "How many names were on that list?"

Rauschad smiled thinly. "Just one," he said.

The Lost Scrolls

CHAPTER
3

Jon's Audi careened around the corner, shoving cold, damp air through the shattered window. Trees flashed past, a blur of green demarcating the borders of the road. Heavy storm clouds, buffeted by strong winds, threatened to break open. Jon grimaced as his foot scraped against the graveled glass. He'd swept most of the fragments from the leather seats, but a few recalcitrant shards hid beneath the seat where he couldn't reach.

As cold as it was, it could've been worse. It could've been raining.

He shook his head. Actually, it was worse. Quite worse. He couldn't help but imagine the mess that awaited him at home. More glass, according to his neighbor. Why hadn't the thief simply pried the door open? At his parents' house, he'd done it himself. When he was a kid, he'd forgotten his key and been stuck outside. A simple shovel from his dad's shed was sufficient to pop the lock on the sliding glass door and grant him entrance.

He dismissed these thoughts as the greater threat weighed in. *Who had done this? And why?* It's not like he'd have kept Egerton at his house or in his car. In fact, anyone who'd recognized the value of the manuscript should have known that. It didn't make sense!

He slowed as he approached Barton Hills, an upscale community to the north of Ann Arbor. His house was located just on the outskirts, not quite close enough to claim status with the wealthy that made their home there, but sufficiently near to raise eyebrows. More than once, people had asked how he afforded such a house on a university salary. God was good to him. He didn't have the expenses of the average professor. No wife, no children who required private school tuition—none of the expenses that might be associated with mid-life. Through careful planning he'd made it through graduate school with very little debt to show for it. The net result was a surprising ability to pay for luxuries others considered out of reach, such as an Audi with leather seats and a smashed-in window, or a house near Barton Hills that some burglar had carelessly ransacked.

He grimaced as he pulled into his driveway. No matter how much financial stability he'd accrued, none of it gave him any real security. Only God could provide that, he knew, which made this more confusing. *Why had He allowed this to happen?* Jon had devoted his life to providing evidences for the faith. He viewed his work as something along the lines of an apologist. Surely the Lord could have offered him some protection from this sort of thing. He shook his head, knowing he was being unfair. A fragment of scripture trailed through his mind. *"God causes all things to work together for good, to those who love God, who are called according to His purpose."* Now, he just had to believe it.

His driveway lay open as he steered in, but yellow police tape cordoned off the front of the house, and a pair of cruisers with the Washtenaw County Sheriff's star emblazoned on their doors stood parked out front. He climbed out as a middle-aged woman in a plaid dress rushed forward to meet him.

"Oh, Dr. Munro! I feel so bad about what's happened!"

He guessed this was Vera DiMarco. "I'm sure everything will be fine, Mrs. DiMarco."

"It's 'Ms.' I hope it's alright," she said after a moment, "but I let the police in. I assumed you'd want them to start work right away."

"Thank you."

"Well, um," she wrung her hands. "Will you be needing a place to stay? I mean, it can be unnerving to have had your privacy violated. Almost like a rape!"

Jon tried not to grimace. "I'm sure I'll be fine. Thank you."

"Well," she said, retreating, "what are neighbors for?"

He watched her depart, and started up the front walk. A woman in a chocolate brown uniform with gold shoulder patches stepped forward to greet him.

"You Munro?"

He nodded and shook her hand.

"Detective Brown's inside. He'll have some questions for ya."

"Yeah, I'll need someone to look at my car. Someone broke into there, too."

"You don't say."

He nodded. "I drove with napkins to keep from messing up any prints…. I couldn't think of any other way to get here."

"How 'bout that? I'll have an officer take a look at it." She motioned over another deputy and spoke to him quickly. He nodded and headed for Jon's car.

She turned and walked with him toward the house. "Helluva way to get outta class, eh? Someone said you go to the university?"

"I teach."

"No kiddin'! Thought you looked kinda old for a student. I take computer classes there part-time. I ain't never seen you there. You full-time?"

"Yeah. In the Graduate School."

"So you're a professor, huh? And what time d'you leave for work?"

"Seven thirty."

"Early. Same time every day?"

"Except weekends."

She nodded and held the door for him. "Regularity. That's what they look for, you know?"

He stepped into the house and looked at her. "Who's that?"

She shrugged. "Whoever it was broke into your house, I expect. Nothing quite like predictability for a burglar." She closed the door behind him. "You got any enemies, Doc?"

"None that I know of."

"Anybody might have it in for ya? Disgruntled student? Former co-worker? Angry parent? Might not be someone you'd expect. Ex-lover, perhaps?"

Kaufman's email flashed into mind. He dismissed it almost immediately. "No, I'm sorry."

She looked at him a moment, as though she caught the hesitation. "Huh." She moved past him into the kitchen. "Yo, Detective!"

Jon followed, but saw the glass spilled across the kitchen floor, and paused. Against the cabinets lay a large cinder block in broken pieces. It had gouged a severe scar into one of his cabinet doors. The frame of his screen door had bent in from the impact. Jon stepped around the glass, staring at the mess and the shattered door. He swore quietly.

"Don't mind us," said a voice. He glanced back at a man dusting the front drawers of his cabinets. "We're just collecting forensic evidence. You mess up the crime scene and slow down our investigation, it'll be your own loss."

"Oh," he said, stepping backward. "Sorry."

"You Munro?"

"Yeah. I live here. This is my house."

"Yeah. No kidding. I'm Detective Brown." He rose and shook Jon's hand, then returned to his work. "We're gonna need to get a set of prints off you, if you don't mind."

"Why?"

"Need a reference set. Officer Hagel?" He rose again and held out the brush to the deputy who'd walked him in. "Would you mind taking over for me? I'd like to ask the good professor here some questions."

"Yes sir." She took the brush from him and started dusting the next drawer. Detective Brown came out of the kitchen and walked Jon back to the living room.

"Know anyone who'd want to break into your house, Dr. Munro?"

He shook his head.

"Anyone have it in for you? Maybe threaten you in some way?"

"No. Look, your—uh—coworker here already asked me these questions."

"Officer Hagel."

"Yeah. We weren't introduced."

"Uh huh. And what did you tell her?"

"Nothing. I don't know anyone who'd want to do this."

Brown nodded. "What do you do at the university?"

"I teach. Paleography. Textual criticism, that sort of thing."

"Yeah. I have no idea what that is."

"Ancient writing. I teach people how to read it."

"Huh. Pays well, I imagine. This is a nice house."

"I do alright. I budget carefully."

"I bet you do. Paleography. So you handle stuff that's in museums and such? I imagine some of that stuff's quite valuable."

"The words 'priceless' and 'irreplaceable' come to mind."

He nodded. "Ever take your work home with you?"

"You mean the actual documents? Never. I'm lucky enough to look at them, much less touch them. I could never take them out of the university."

"Keep anything valuable at home?"

"I don't know. TV or stereo, I guess." He pointed at the electronic appliances in the living room.

Brown glanced behind and nodded. "And yet, they're still here."

Jon furrowed his brow. "Did they take anything?"

Brown took a seat on the arm of the lounge chair. "That's what we'd like to know. Nothing appears to be missing: You've got a computer upstairs, a flat panel LCD TV downstairs, a quality stereo system, two framed coin collections in the hallway, and an expensive set of steak knives. None of it's missing. So either this was an act of sheer vandalism—"

"Or they were looking for something in particular."

Brown nodded. "You read my mind, Doctor. It leaves me to wonder: what were they looking for? I don't suppose you could tell me what that might be?"

Jon swallowed against the hollow pit forming in his stomach. His conscience tweaked him. "Am I under investigation here?" His voice sounded tiny in his ears. Intimidation. He hated the feeling.

"It sure would help us recover your property, Dr. Munro, if we knew what we were looking for."

"I've already told you—I don't know who would do this." His head swam. "I don't know what they'd be looking for. I don't know why this happened. And I don't appreciate being interrogated in my own home."

He stared hard at the detective, who returned his glare with a bemused expression. His anger abated, and the hollow in his stomach felt like it would grow and swallow him whole. He sat down on the couch and put his face in his hands, deflated. "I don't know what I can say that will make any of this make sense. I got into my office after class this morning, and someone had been in there."

"Someone broke into your office?"

"Well, no, they didn't break in—I don't know how they got in. All I know is that stuff was moved. I get out to my car, and someone's smashed in the driver's side window and moved the seats around. And now here. I don't know what they want. I don't feel terribly safe right now." His hands trembled. He clenched his fingers to make them stop. "Al…alright!" he finally said. "I think they were looking for Egerton." He blew out a long breath, relieved to get it off his chest.

"Who or what's an Egerton?"

"It's a manuscript. A possible fifth gospel."

"A gospel?"

"Yeah, you know. Story of Jesus? That's what they used to call them before it became a style of music."

"Yeah, I know what a gospel is. Why is this important?"

"It's old. Second century. It's on loan to us from the British Museum. I'm not really supposed to have it. It was just a favor, just a professional courtesy. Honestly, I didn't think it would lead to this."

"So this Egerton is missing?"

"No. No, it's completely untouched. Believe me, I'd know."

Detective Brown glanced pleadingly at Officer Hagel. She shrugged. "So they don't touch the…gospel, and they don't touch the steak knives. Or anything else. Maybe they're just trying to scare you?"

"Well, they're succeeding. But why?"

Brown scratched his ear. "I got nothing. We'll get those prints from you. Anything that don't match we'll run through AFIS. Might take a while. We can print your car, also, 'cept you'll probably need it. Other than that—"

"Other than that, what?"

"Other than that, we ain't got much to go on. You're not exactly the ideal victim, if you know what I mean. You're not involved in any known criminal activity. No known enemies. No reason for anyone to break into your house, your office, or your car unless they were looking for something in particular. Maybe this Egerton thing, but that's just a guess, isn't it?"

He nodded.

"We'll do what we can, but I don't think we're gonna find much."

Jon sat down on the couch and buried his head in his hands.

"Officer Hagel here will get you a copy of the police report for your insurance. I'm sure you'll want that. We learn anything, we'll let you know."

"Alright. Thank you, Detective."

Detective Brown nodded and headed for the door.

Jon turned and looked helplessly to Officer Hagel, who simply shrugged and resumed dusting the kitchen for fingerprints.

An hour later he'd secured the back door as best as he could with a sheet of plywood from the garage, and swept up the glass. After taking his prints, Officer Hagel told him they'd keep a car on tight patrol in the area, whatever that meant, and left. He looked around the barren kitchen, feeling lost.

Finally, he threw up his hands and drove back to the university.

The Lost Scrolls

CHAPTER
4

"Dr. Munro, I didn't expect to see you back!"

He nodded numbly to Leon and dropped into the leather armchair, wiped out.

"How bad is it?"

He ran his hands through his hair. "I don't know. They went through the sliding glass door in the kitchen. Glass was everywhere. It was quite a mess."

"How much did they get?"

"Nothing."

"Nothing?"

"Everything's right where I left it, 'cept the door, of course. That's another thing. Whoever broke into my car went right through the driver's side window. I tell you, I've about had it up to here with broken glass. I think my next car's gonna be a tank."

"Why would someone do that?"

He shrugged. "I don't know. I really don't. I've lived in that house for ten years. Ten years. And I'm not an idiot. I lock my doors at night. I don't keep money under the mattress. I don't understand why God let this happen. You make yourself small so no one will think to come after you, and for the most part, no one does. But all it takes is that one time." He looked at his hands, relieved they weren't shaking anymore. "Now

I'm thinking about buying a gun. At least getting a security system." He muttered, "I don't like thinking this way."

Leon said nothing for a moment, then, "Michaels wants to see you."

He glanced up. Dr. Anthony Michaels was the university's director of antiquities, his boss. If there was one thing Jon appreciated about his job, it was his boss's hands-off approach.

"You didn't mention Egerton, did you?"

Leon shook his head.

Jon frowned. He should probably come clean about it. Keeping secrets wasn't good. "Did he say what it was about?"

Leon shrugged and turned back to the term paper he was reviewing.

Jon scratched his ear and stood. "This day just keeps getting better."

Dr. Anthony Michaels was slightly further past middle age than he cared to admit. He worked out regularly to stay fit. After he began losing his hair in his thirties, he kept his head shaved. Age slowed down too many men who should've been in their prime. He would not be one of them.

In the refrigerator behind his desk sat a bottle of water and a carefully prepared lunch of feta cheese and spinach salad containing the precise caloric intake his doctor prescribed. No more, no less. He wouldn't open it until twelve o'clock, despite the hunger gnawing at his stomach, and drank a sip of water instead.

The line of text he attempted to read moved in and out of focus. He frowned and pushed the bifocals back up the bridge of his nose, pulling the words into clarity. The body was the servant of the mind. That it should betray him was unacceptable.

He stared at the line of text on his computer, not at all pleased with what he read, and took another sip of water. A drip clung precariously to the edge of his lip, and he sucked it in as he tapped out a reply. A knock on his door interrupted him. His fingers snapped to the ALT / TAB keys, and the screen switched to a benign report on the university's enrollment stats.

He turned away from his computer. "Come in!"

Jonathan walked through the door, closing it behind him. "You wanted to see me, Tony?"

"Come in, come in." Michaels plastered on a smile and waved Jonathan to a chair. He'd been dreading this conversation.

"Is this about the break-in?"

"I heard something like that happened. Did they get anything?"

"Not that I can tell."

"Do you know what they were looking for?"

"I…no."

"I see. Well, how are things going in your classes?"

Jonathan shrugged and sat down. "Well, fine, I expect. We've got term papers coming in. The usual sophomoric drivel." He picked at a piece of lint on his tie and shifted in his seat.

Michaels reminded his mouth to smile. "Yes, yes. Anything your graduate assistant can't handle?"

Jonathan frowned and looked up. "I suppose not. I still grade my own papers."

"Well, that's not what I meant. You shouldn't have any worries about your position here, of course."

Jonathan straightened. "The first thing that happens when you tell me not to worry about my job is I start worrying about my job. And frankly, I've got enough to worry about already. Is there something I should know?"

"No, no, of course not."

"Leon's not ready. And even if he were, I'd be surprised if he wanted to stay here."

Michaels managed to look hurt. "Jonathan, I—"

"Just hit me with it. It's been a bad enough day already. What's going on?"

"Well, actually, ah, I was wondering if you'd talked with Dr. Kaufman."

Jon cocked his head. "Stephen? No, no I haven't."

"Or perhaps his lovely sister?"

"We don't talk anymore. Not since graduation. What is this about?"

Michaels looked at his hands. "I had an idea he might try to contact you."

Jon glanced at his Blackberry, frowned, and put it away. His expression urged Michaels to continue.

"Dr. Kaufman has been in the employ of the university for about a year now. He's been performing some work for us in southeast Turkey."

"Wait a second. You hired Stephen Kaufman and didn't bother to tell me?"

"Dr. Kaufman is highly qualified, as you yourself are well aware—"

"I don't trust his qualifications—"

"—and whatever your personal quarrel with him, he is the best man for the job."

"I'm on the committee. I shouldn't have been left out of this."

"We did what we thought best."

Jon pushed his head back in the chair and stared at the ceiling, stunned. "You didn't think I could handle it. That I could be professional, put my differences aside and look at it objectively."

"That's hardly the point now."

"What is this? Some sort of game with you?"

"Jonathan, please. Dr. Kaufman went missing."

He stopped and stared at the director. "What do you mean, 'missing'?"

"Just what I said. He contacts us regularly. Every five days. Lets us know of his progress. Sends us his field reports, that sort of thing. Three weeks ago he sent us a startling claim—and then all contact stopped." He reached into his desk drawer, pulled out a sheet of paper, and handed it to Jon.

"I've made the find of the century," Jon read. He looked up. "What find?"

Michaels's voice grew serious. "The *Domo tou Bibliou*."

Jonathan's face froze, then cracked into a broad smile. "You gotta be kidding me."

"No."

"He told you that?"

"Yes."

"Did he also tell you he found the ten lost tribes of Israel? Or the continent of Atlantis?"

"Jon—"

"This is hyperbolic crap!" He stood and paced. "The *Domo* is a myth. It was dreamt up by some overzealous monk in the eleventh century to rally support for the Crusades. I'm all for faith, Tony, but this is ridiculous."

"As you, of all people, should know, the fact something has never been found does not mean it never existed."

"I can't believe you fell for this. What did he do next? Request more funding?"

"Well, that's hardly the point."

"It's precisely the point! Kaufman is a con man. He makes stuff up. He's probably sitting on a beach in the south of France sipping mai tais or whatever it is they drink over there."

"Actually, he's in a hospital in Ankara. He's not expected to make it."

"What?"

"Two days ago we learned he'd been stabbed in the street."

Jon looked like his heart would drop out of his chest onto the floor. "Isabel?"

Michaels collected his papers from the desktop and slipped them back into his drawer. "We haven't heard."

Jon swore. "I knew this would happen. Someday, I knew it would catch up to him. I tried to warn her."

"Yes, I'm sure you did your best."

He paced, then stopped. "Wait a second. How do you know he was stabbed? You said you hadn't heard from him."

Michaels smiled and leaned on his elbows. "We weren't unaware of Dr. Kaufman's, ah –questionable reputation. We had a man watching him."

"Who?"

"A local."

"Can you trust him?"

"Well, yes—"

"You can't, can you? How much are you into him for?"

Michaels hesitated. "A hundred thousand."

"A hundred thousand dollars? And you can't even verify the claim? How do you know your man in Turkey isn't getting paid by Kaufman on the side?"

Michaels sighed. "All these issues have been brought up already."

"Really."

"The board has asked that we send someone to independently verify the claim. We need someone who could certify whether what Dr. Kaufman has found is, in fact, the genuine article. If it is, it must be brought back to the university. If not, then we would need someone willing to testify to the Turkish authorities on our behalf."

"Well, who are you gonna get to do that?"

Michaels smiled thinly, and watched as understanding dawned in Jonathan's eyes.

"You're not serious."

"The board requested you personally."

"You want me to go to Turkey and clean up this mess. Unbelievable."

"All your expenses will be covered, of course."

"And if you had kept me in the loop like you should have, none of this would've happened."

"Please be a scientist. You're assuming the outcome before you've made a thorough investigation."

He threw up his hands. "Forgive me. I forgot you believe this. Tell me something: What story did he use to win you over to this cockamamie idea?"

Michaels cleaned his glasses. "That's precisely the point you've been missing. He didn't come to us. We went looking for him."

CHAPTER
5

Sean MacNeil opened his eyes. It was still dark, but a pale glow gathered on the horizon. Sunrise would soon fill the sky with vermilion hues. A moment later, a tiny beep sounded from the alarm on his wrist. He gently silenced it and lay there a moment, listening. Outside the window of the bare apartment, a pair of swallows chirped greetings to one another. Two floors down the sounds of an early morning television program filtered up through the floorboards. The resident there, Gilbert Smith, worked the night shift. He was single. He usually came home around four a.m., and would spend the next hour unwinding before turning off the TV and pulling the shades to his bedroom. From farther off came the incessant rush of traffic on the expressway outside Wellington.

The rest of the apartment was silent. Moving his head as little as possible, Sean glanced around, taking in the shadows leaning against undecorated walls, the single chair and table set just outside the kitchen, and the dark bureau squatting in the corner. He detected no unexpected movement, no furtive breathing in the closet, and no one waiting for him, this time.

Not that they would have waited for him to get up, anyway. He wouldn't have waited.

He pushed himself to his feet and picked his way to the bathroom where he splashed some water on his face, bringing his senses fully awake. With the money he'd stashed away in Zurich, he could easily have afforded a much nicer place, even a new identity to chase away the demons haunting his memories. But at thirty-five, he had no desire to drop out of the game just yet, and he had other people to consider, like his brother's family. Maybe in a few more years.

He filled the tea kettle and set it on the stove, then began a series of slow warm-up stretches across the bare, wooden floor. He started with his arms and worked his way down to his legs. Touched his nose to his knees, feeling the resistance of his muscles. After sixteen years, he wasn't as flexible as he used to be. The workouts would only delay the creep of time, not stop it altogether. He kicked his legs out into a wide straddle stretch and pushed himself down until he touched the floor. After a count of thirty he lay back and began his regimen of crunches, working each abdominal muscle group independently until his core throbbed with the sweet burn.

The last attempt on his life had been five years and seven months ago. A pair of MI6 agents had caught up with him outside Dubai and made a fatal attempt at arrest. They'd almost caught him, too. He left the two agents sitting across from each other in their own hotel room—each one wearing in his skull a slug from the other's gun.

Still, despite his cleverness at covering his tracks, they'd gotten close. Too close. He was more careful these days. The irony of it still annoyed him—that the British government would be so bent on catching a man who'd long ago abandoned Ireland's revolution for less noble pursuits.

What did it matter? The revolution was dead. Politicians betrayed Ireland for money long before he hung up his guns. Why should it matter if he took them back down for a little money of his own, now and then?

He turned off the tea kettle just before the whistle blew and poured himself a cup. High up on a shelf was an unopened bottle of Glenlivet—a gift from his sometimes regular employer. He kept it as a challenge to himself—a warning from the demon that had claimed his father's life. Drink would never rule him.

He took a sip of tea and set the cup down again, then brought his feet together into *Heisoku-dachi*, bowing to no one across the room. This morning's *kata* was *Bassai*, the Okinawan karate form that meant "to penetrate a fortress." The form taught perseverance as well as defense. He loved the feel of the movements as he brought his fists together, the left cupping the right over his groin at the beginning of the form. Always protect the obvious targets first.

By the time he finished the *kata* and returned to his starting position, he was sweating profusely, but not out of breath. The forms were all about control. Self-discipline. He lived for it.

After a shower and breakfast, he powered up the laptop and logged into the wireless network of the internet café next door. The café kept their link active all the time, freely letting anyone who chose to log onto the internet at will. He downloaded his email from a secure server stationed in North Korea. The site was expensive, but it protected his documents better than any firewall. The Echelon system would attempt to trace any communications sent to him or from him, if he logged into a country a bit more cooperative with the West. He cared not one whit who might benefit from hosting his domain, or what they might do with the money. The security was all that mattered.

In plain English, the email said, *Papa has a job for you.* He snorted. Beaufort liked to call himself that. He'd never met the man, but everything he'd learned about him confirmed his initial reaction. The man was a pompous windbag who got lucky in the stock market. If Sean ever did meet him, he wouldn't hesitate to terminate their relationship if he thought it advantageous. But Beaufort paid well. Extremely well. And these days that's all that mattered.

Beaufort had attached an encrypted file. Sean downloaded it to his flash drive and logged off the internet, pulling the router card from the computer and permanently severing any connection should anyone be attempting to record his keystrokes. Finally, he sent the computer into revert, resetting the hard drive to a previous configuration and eliminating any trace of his recent activity. Once this was finished he'd defrag the hard drive.

He took the flash drive over to a second computer, a desktop model with no internet connection. Plugging the drive into the USB port, he first scanned it for any viruses or Trojan programs, before opening the zip file and reading the message as he sipped his tea.

There were times when the protections he took felt excessive, but caution was a character trait learned the hard way—and not easily forgotten. He closed his eyes, remembering the face of his brother Daniel, just before the bomb exploded and scattered his body into a million unrecognizable fragments. The Brits had hacked into his carefully constructed system and taken Daniel out before he could deliver the package. It had been more than ten years since he left Belfast, but he would never forget.

And he'd never let it happen again.

Later, after working out the specifics of the plan and leaving coded messages on a second server, he picked up his cell phone. It was a disposable model. Untraceable. He dialed the unlisted number from memory. It rang twice before someone answered.

Sean didn't wait for the person to say "Hello," knowing there wouldn't be a greeting. Instead, he said, "Brian Laherty. Michael Doherty. William Higgs. Ankara market—two days."

He hung up, pulled the SIM card from the back of the phone, destroyed it, and tossed the remains of the phone into the trashcan. His contact would get in touch with the men directly. According to the instructions he'd left ahead of time, each would find his own way to Ankara. Two would come in first by plane to Belgrade, then by train via Istanbul, arriving separately. They could've been there in two hours if he'd asked it. But the third, William Higgs, would come by boat. For that reason alone, they'd delay.

He had his reasons for Higgs coming by boat. For one thing, the change would throw off any suspicion. But more importantly, Higgs would bring the box. He picked up a sheet of specifications printed from the PDF Beaufort had sent him. The box had been specially ordered. It measured a foot and a half long by a foot deep, and appeared to be nothing more than a small safe. But it was airtight, capable of sealing its contents in a vacuum. If needed, the box could be closed and dropped into the ocean. It even had a radio transceiver built in for precisely such a contingency. He supposed a hundred years or more could pass before its contents would be in danger.

It wouldn't be much of a problem getting the box into Turkey. Getting it out again was a different story. Ever since the Al Qaeda attacks on America, security around the globe had tightened significantly. Turkey was especially difficult, given both its Muslim sympathies and close ties to the West. The

Turks wanted to assure the West they belonged in NATO. The mujahidin saw a potential gateway to shipping arms to sleeper cells overseas.

He snorted. They'd have an easier time going through Dubai. He always did. Still, it would be a problem. What he intended to carry back to the States in that box was no bomb: it was far more explosive.

What really troubled him was the offhand comment Beaufort's dealer had made about the box when he asked for it. Something about how surprised the dealer was. It was the third such request in a week. There'd never been such a spike in demand before.

On the one hand, the spike might mean nothing at all. Simply a coincidence. But Sean had long ago stopped believing in coincidences. More than likely, there were more players in the field. He'd have to be careful. It was possible Beaufort hired more than one team—it was the sort of stupid move someone like "Papa" would dream up, never realizing how quickly men died that way. If that turned out to be the case, he would be sure to deliver the box to Beaufort personally, and then exact whatever just recompense was due.

He set the spec sheet to one side and finished his tea, now quite cold. He had a lot to do.

CHAPTER
6

"You went looking for Dr. Kaufman," Jon repeated. "I don't understand, Tony. Why would you do that?"

"You mean, why didn't we come to you?"

"Well, not precisely, but, now that you mention it…"

Michaels pressed his lips together. "We needed someone motivated."

"What's that supposed to mean?"

"Someone who could take our hunch and run with it. Someone with everything to gain and nothing to lose. You are a reputable scientist. Dr. Kaufman, on the other hand—that debacle in Southeast Asia destroyed whatever credibility he once had. But think of it. If he has found the *Domo tou Bibliou*, Dr. Kaufman's reputation would be restored. And we would have the greatest archaeological discovery of all time in our grasp. The funding for the university alone—the increase in student enrollment—your own department! We could hire both you and Leon at the same time. Give your assistant a reason to stick around."

"Unbelievable. It's all about the money with you, isn't it?"

"That money pays your salary. The problem with you academics is you believe your work occurs in a vacuum, untainted by real world concerns, like money for research."

"Don't patronize."

Michaels frowned. "Kindly refrain from the same. It's not about the money. The money is a tremendous side benefit, to be sure, but the quality of the find piqued our interest. I've no more use for going off on wild goose chases than I have for the state lottery. But this, my friend, was no mere gamble.

"About nine months ago, a construction crew in the town of Dokuz broke through the ceiling of an ancient church, buried for centuries in the sands. Within the ruins, they found an inscription that tells of the location of the *Domo tou Bibliou*."

"Wait—wait a minute. Turkey strictly forbids the export of antiquities. Anything more than two hundred years old automatically belongs to their museums. You can't buy it, sell it, export it—you can't even possess it. What are you getting the university into?"

"We're not talking about oriental carpets or old coins!" He slammed his hand on the desk, swallowed, and caught his breath. "This could well be the greatest archaeological discovery of the twenty-first century. The Turkish Ministry of Antiquities has publicly disavowed the existence of the *Domo tou Bibliou* many times. Do you know how we found out about the church in Dokuz? A foreign exchange student mailed us some pictures he took with his cell phone. We were fortunate this student took the photos at all—shortly after, the construction crew finished bulldozing the site. We had to reconstruct the inscription from pictures. All that history is lost. And you've seen the respect they've shown the churches in Cyprus. Looting and defacing the frescoes! You're a religious man, you should understand this! Their hands are not clean, Jonathan. They hide behind the law and use it for their own ends. We absolutely cannot allow the book to fall into their hands. It would be immoral to do so!

"Afterwards," his voice grew conciliatory, "when we've had our chance to confirm the finding—perform our own tests—if the government of Turkey wants the manuscript returned to them, we can do so. We will at least be negotiating from a position of strength, instead of begging for that which we have the right to see. After all, we found it! They were content to bury it again! Turn the evidence of its existence into a parking lot!"

"You're not even sure it's real."

"Then there should be absolutely no problem in your retrieving it."

"I haven't said I'm going."

Michaels came around the desk and sat on the edge of it. "I'm not asking you to dirty your hands. I'm only asking you to verify the claim. Investigate this for us. We haven't even decided that we will take possession—just that we'd like to." He gave a nervous laugh. "Find out what happened to Stephen, for God's sake. There are those who believe as we do: that we found it! That's why they attacked him. They will stop at nothing to obtain it. In the very least, you can find his sister, Isabel. I'm quite worried about her."

Jon bit his lip.

"Think about it. Can you really allow her to pay for what others have done?"

Jon shook his head. This was low even for Michaels, but he had a point. Isabel could be in real danger, and not just from the despoiled reputation of her brother. He glanced up as Michaels reached into his desk and pulled out an airline ticket and boarding passes.

"All you have to do is go. It's only four days."

Reluctantly, he took the ticket. Michaels smiled.

A loud rap on the door, and they both turned their heads. Michaels turned back to him. "I have another appointment. I look forward to hearing from you when you get back." He ushered Jon to the door and shook his hand.

Jon stared at the ticket as Michaels opened the door. He bumped into another man as he left the office and mumbled an apology. A moment later, the door was closed and he was on the outside. He glanced back. Something about the other man struck him as odd. He pursed his lips, frowning. It might have been the beard, or the dark complexion.

He shook his head. No, it was nothing. Michaels had him on edge. That was all. He glanced down at the ticket. O'Hare to Esenboğa International Airport. His flight left in three hours. He swore. There was barely enough time to pack! Shaking his head, he rushed back to his office. If he missed his flight, he could always point out to Michaels that he'd never actually agreed to go.

"You're going where?" Leon swiveled his chair to face him.

"Ankara. Turkey. All expenses paid." He flipped open his laptop and started logging into his email. He frowned when the computer refused to connect.

"Servers are down." Leon's voice was monotone.

"You're kidding."

"Routine maintenance or something like that. So I guess you deserve a vacation, huh?"

"It's not a vacation. It's a business trip."

"Uh-huh."

Jon glanced at his assistant, who wore a puzzled grin. "Really, it's a wild goose chase. They've got me chasing a mirage." He filled him in on the meeting.

"What about Egerton? What about your house?"

"I…I don't know. It might be good to get away from the house right now. I can drop the car in the shop and arrange for contractors to replace the back door while I'm gone. The police can do their job without my help. I'd rather not go back and have to deal with that by myself anyway. And as for Egerton…" he came over to stand by Leon's shoulder. Leon hadn't moved from his chair since Jon left for his meeting. "Just keep it in the safe. My contact is David Lewis. He'll be calling for it. Just explain the situation when he contacts you. But don't let anyone else know we have it."

"What about your research?"

"There's no time. I have to catch my flight."

Leon nodded and said, "You don't think there's anything to it, do you?"

"What? The book? No. That's what Stephen does. He thinks archeology is Indiana Jones. He travels around the world pursuing wild-goose-chase theories and cockamamie half-truths all in the name of selling books and sensationalist TV programs." He closed his laptop and grabbed his coat. "He's never dirtied his hands on a real dig in his life. Stephen is all about the excitement, not the science."

"Well, have a good trip anyway."

He nodded, his hand on the doorknob. "Right. I'll see you in a few days."

The Lost Scrolls

CHAPTER
7

White. Pure, blinding white. Stephen hurt, but it was a welcome relief to the black silence that threatened to engulf him.

For a long time Stephen had seen nothing but blackness. Heard nothing but silence. Felt nothing but—

A flash of light glinting off a cold knife.

Pain!

Was this hell? He hurt all over.

Then light, so bright he wanted to shut his eyes, but still preferable to the darkness. Slowly now, he became aware of noises, too. One was an intermittent tone with no source—nothing visible to justify it. Carlos Castañeda talked about a meaningless sound. Was this what the guru meant? He felt no enlightenment.

Other sounds crept in. Muffled voices too distant to discern, ghosts whispering to each other of fading memories and abandoned hopes.

And weeping.

Was there white light in hell? It was supposed to be a place of darkness and torment. Surely, there wouldn't be light there. Unless the light itself was a form of torment. It lacked definition. Offered no clarity. Illumined nothing.

A false hope.

Whatever was going on, it felt distinctly un-myth-like. If he was in hell…

Isabel. Why couldn't he remember her better? He could almost see her face—raven hair, dark eyes staring at him. She was barely there, saying something in her melodic voice. It was like looking at her through a shower curtain, hearing her from far away.

If only he could—

Darkness closed in again, and her face faded from view. Nothingness took him.

The next time he saw the white light, he also saw tiny black spots grouped in patterns. They might have been birds. Or bugs. Oh God, please don't let them be bugs! He stared at the spots. Would they move? Would they fall from the white light onto his body and begin crawling, biting, burrowing—?

The spots remained completely still. After a moment, he noticed the spots were contained in a large rectangle, bordered on all four sides by smooth lines of a color slightly less white than the rectangle. There were several rectangles, all arranged in perfectly geometric order right in front of him. He could've sworn he'd seen them before. The shapes begged for recognition.

He knew what this was. He knew! Why didn't he know?!

Then he saw her. Isabel's face was back, frowning down on him. Why was she frowning? She was sad. Had he done something to upset her? It wasn't fair. He'd worked so hard this last time to make it right, to be a better brother. Not fair!

Something cold touched his lips and trickled down his tongue. It was amazing, an achingly satisfying experience. This couldn't possibly be hell. No way could that experience be in the place of the dead.

It couldn't be heaven though, either, could it? If this were heaven, then why was he surrounded by darkness and bugs? He looked again at the rectangles. They might not be bugs at all.

"Stephen?"

His eyes flicked back to her face. It was her voice, plain as day. What was she doing here? Wherever this was? He looked again at the rectangles—and knew what they were.

Ceiling tiles.

A wave of relief washed over him, so intense it hurt. He wasn't dead. He wasn't in hell. He closed and opened his eyes, crying. Isabel. There was still time to make it right.

"Izzy," he whispered, swallowing convulsively. His throat hurt. His nose felt stuffed, hard to breathe.

"Shh," she said. She placed an ice chip on his lips, let him again taste the sweet wetness. "The doctors say you lost a lot of blood. You need to rest. Regain your strength."

"H-how long?" he rasped.

"Three days. We almost lost you."

Three? How could this have happened? Three days! Think! Why couldn't he think?! "Izzy."

"Just rest."

"No. Please." A sharp twinge of pain coursed through his abdomen. He grit his teeth, swallowing again. Something felt stuck in his throat. "Listen."

"Stephen—"

"You must find—Jonathan." He put his hand to his throat. Every word was fire. "Take him to the chapel." He felt the darkness closing in again. He fought for the light. She had to know. She had to understand. "He'll know…." He tottered at the ledge—slipped—fell into blackness.

"Stephen?"

Isabel watched him fade away again. She stared at the monitors, watching the heart rate drop. The green numbers pulsed, dropping lower...lower.

Oh God, please. Not like this.

They stopped falling.

She exhaled, surprised she'd been holding her breath. Her hands ached. She'd been gripping the rails of the bed, afraid to let go. Doctor Aybar said it could be like this. Stephen had lost nearly a liter of blood. They'd given him that much and more during the seven hours of surgery to repair the damage the knife had done to his insides. He was still at a high risk for infection.

She let go of the bed rail and kissed his forehead, then turned and left the room. Outside, she leaned against the wall to let the tears flow.

But they didn't come.

She looked up at the ceiling, a broken laugh escaping her throat. Typical. She wanted to cry. Needed to cry. She knew this. Her body refused to respond.

It wasn't fair. None of it was.

She loved her brother Stephen as well as anyone could. She'd certainly tried harder than anyone. She willed herself into believing he'd change, live up to his promises.

Except he didn't.

She shook her head, and went to look for a drink. In a very real way, this was all her fault. She nodded to the Catholic priest who smiled at her in the hall, and wondered what he'd say if she confessed this to him, what penance he'd offer to soothe her guilt.

She never should have sided with Stephen in the first place. Jonnie had loved her, too, in ways her brother could not. Jonnie offered the stability and security. But Stephen was her brother—the only family she had left. She hadn't believed Jonnie when he'd told her Stephen cheated on his final exams. He was simply acting out—trying to drive a wedge between them. It was so distasteful. Stephen expressed sadness that his roommate would stoop so low.

Only now she knew Jonnie was probably telling the truth, and that he'd only wanted to protect her. She hadn't believed him. Didn't want to. That was her sin.

She found the coffee pot and poured herself a cup. It was overcooked and bitter. Now Stephen wanted her to talk to Jonnie, to take him to the chapel he'd shown her only a week ago. She knew where the chapel was, or at least where Stephen said it was. What they would find if—when—she took him there was beyond her.

She sipped the coffee, making a face. Something nagged at the edge of her mind, and for a moment she wondered what it was. Then it dawned on her.

What was a Catholic priest doing in a hospital in Ankara? To her knowledge, there were only two Catholic churches in the entire city, with only a small number of adherents. She couldn't honestly remember when she'd last seen a priest. She frowned. What were the odds one would be wandering around a hospital?

Unless someone misread Stephen's file and called the priest by mistake. She dropped the coffee in the trash. The priest might have discovered the error by now, but it'd help if she were there to explain things. She rubbed her eyes and started back down the hall.

Philip stared down at the man in the bed. The archaeologist was not Catholic—or much of any religion according to his dossier. The irony was that he'd supposedly dedicated his life to proving the claims of the Bible. He'd been throughout the Middle East, claiming he'd located Noah's ark, or the remains of Sodom and Gomorrah, or King Solomon's mines. His latest attempt had been to search for the Ark of the Covenant in Southeast Asia—though what led him to that particular region Philip was at a loss to know.

Why did so many need evidence to justify their faith? Why not simply accept Scripture for what it was? He paused. And how was that so very different from what Cardinals Rauschad and Cellino were asking of him?

It wasn't, of course. The compromises he'd have to make—he'd already made—would not justify whatever benefit the Church would gain by claiming their precious treasure. But for the Indulgence granted him, he'd have refused the assignment. It would cost him his faith otherwise. Yet the Indulgence precluded any objections he might have made and left him with a simple choice: to obey...or not.

He picked up the chart at the foot of Stephen's bed and scanned his condition. They'd stabilized him two days ago, following a grueling course of surgery to repair the knife wound to his mesenteric artery and bowel. He wasn't on any particular medications at the moment, just simple intravenous fluids and painkillers. He frowned. The painkillers might make his job a little more difficult. He needed the archaeologist awake.

He stepped over to where the IV catheter looped over the bedrail into the man's arm and pulled a small vial and syringe from his cincture. He fit the syringe into the vial and withdrew several ccs of sodium pentothal, pressing out the air before inserting it into a port in the catheter. He glanced down at Stephen and hesitated.

This wasn't right. Not without asking him first. He left the syringe in the tube and leaned in close. "Dr. Kaufman?"

A quiet sigh rose from the bed. He tried again. "Dr. Kaufman? Wake up." He tapped his cheeks.

Groaning, Stephen opened his eyes. Philip smiled, and made the sign of the cross over him. "*En nomine Patri, et Fili, et Spiritu Sancti, Amen.*"

"Wh—who are you?" Stephen mumbled.

"I am Father Philip." He pulled out a second vial—this one of olive oil—and poured a dab onto his finger. He made the sign of the cross on Stephen's forehead. "Through this holy anointing, may the Lord in His love and mercy help you with the grace of the Holy Spirit." He followed up with Stephen's hands. "May the Lord who frees you from sin save you and raise you up."

Stephen furrowed his brow. Philip capped the oil and put it away. He took Stephen's hand. "It's time to confess."

"I—I'm not Catholic."

"Shh. Maybe a long time ago, huh? But here we are now, for you, at the end of all things. Unburden your soul to me."

"Uhh. Oh, Izzy."

"Yes, your sister."

"I was…I wasn't good to her."

"Mmm. You led her to many places."

"It was all lies. I knew it was. There were so many lies."

"And you led her here, yes?"

"Yes."

"Was this a lie?"

"No." He smiled.

"What was it, then? What did you find here?"

"Truth."

Philip smiled. "Tell me about the truth."

"It was—so beautiful. So amazing. Exactly where they said it would be."

Philip shifted closer. "And where is it?"

Stephen's smile faded. Confusion overtook him. "Who are you?"

"Oh, we've been over that." Philip reached down and pushed the depressor on the syringe. "I am Father Philip." He watched the liquid disappear into Stephen's vein. The effect was quick.

Stephen's eyes grew wide and his breaths labored. "What—? What have you done to me?"

"You were telling me about the *Domo tou Bibliou*. You must tell me where it is. We haven't much time."

"The—*Domo*?"

"Yes! Stephen, help us find it!"

He panted heavily, and shook his head. "No, I don't—no."

"Stephen, you must!"

An alarm sounded on the monitors. Stephen's heart was racing, the numbers climbing rapidly. He convulsed on the bed. Philip swore under his breath and watched as Stephen's eyes rolled back into his head.

"What are you doing?!"

"He's crashing! Get a doctor!" He glanced briefly behind at the striking woman who'd entered. Her face went ashen. She stepped back and screamed from the door.

"Help! We need a doctor!"

"Hold on, Stephen," Philip said. He pressed his lips in a tight smile. This wasn't supposed to happen this way. A moment later, doctors and nurses swarmed the room, shouting instructions to each other. Philip stepped back, his eye catching the syringe still attached to Stephen's catheter. He hadn't had time to remove it. And he'd left the vial on the bedside. It'd be impossible to retrieve now. He cupped his hands together as if praying, and quickly left the room.

Isabel stared at her brother, watching the doctors work on him. Doctor Aybar pulled a syringe from Stephen's catheter, frowning. He snatched a vial from the bedside and read the label. His face grew angry. He shouted instructions for medicine. Isabel didn't recognize it. He confronted her with the vial.

"Who gave him this?"

She stared at it, dumbfounded. "What is it?"

"Thiopental. It is used for anesthesia, medically induced coma, and in combination with Pancuronium Bromide, euthanasia. Who gave it to him?"

She shook her head. "S-somebody tried to kill him?" she said. She ran a hand through her hair. *God, this can't be happening!*

The doctor took a deep breath, dropping his hand. He glanced back at Stephen and shook his head. "If that were the case, he'd be dead already."

"What then?"

"There was a brief attempt in the seventies to use it as a truth serum. That has been discredited, of course, but sometimes…." He stepped close and whispered, "Whatever your brother was working on, dangerous people want to know about it. As soon as you can, you should take him from here. I don't want my hospital mixed up in this."

She clenched her teeth and nodded stiffly. "I want the police. I want someone to guard this room."

"I'll make a phone call. As soon as he's stable to move, we'll let you know."

She glared at him. "Believe me. You needn't ask twice."

CHAPTER
8

Jon pushed back against the airline seat and fidgeted. His knees pressed against the seat in front of him. Its occupant had reclined the chair almost into his lap and was now snoring loudly. He was tempted to reach over and pinch the man's nose.

Instead, he swore at himself for not looking over his ticket more carefully. His seat was far forward in the plane, just not far enough. What with all the university was paying Stephen for this wild-goose chase, he should've demanded first class. Not that he'd had time. He'd barely made the flight as it was. He turned and stared out the window. A massive expanse of clouds lay below them, obscuring his view of the earth. The cumulus topography was rutted and patchy, with wispy tendrils of mist rising almost to the tips of their wings. It had been that way for more than an hour now, and he wondered whether he'd be able to see anything on this flight at all. The whole point in taking the window seat was for the view. He'd have been more comfortable in the aisle, where he could at least stretch his legs. Instead, a ten year old sat there listening to his iPod, his feet barely touching the floor. The pulse of gangsta rap buzzed feebly from his headphones, like a mosquito with hiccups. It was beyond annoying. He'd offered to trade with the kid early into the flight, but the boy shook his head, "No thanks," and disappeared into his music.

Jon barely remembered the last time he was on a plane. It might've been his trip to Israel. He couldn't be sure. He won it through a Christian radio contest. He'd flown coach then, too, but the flight hadn't seemed as bad as this. Memory had a way of cleansing such experiences. Or maybe that time, he'd had a view.

A bump of turbulence jarred him from his self-pity, and he remembered he was angry. Angry at whomever it was who broke into his house and car. At Michaels for taking him away from the Egerton papyrus and putting him on the plane. At the university for hiring Stephen without talking to him first. At Stephen for being the cause of this whole mess. Mostly at Stephen.

The anger felt...powerful. He snorted. It was easy to confuse forgiveness and passivity, and maybe that's what he'd done all his life. Maybe that's why God was calling it out now, letting these circumstances jar him into action. It had been a long time since he remembered feeling anything resembling righteous indignation. The last time had been at Stephen, too, when he realized Stephen was cheating on his exams.

During their studies, Stephen was the one with the computer. The internet was a relatively new phenomenon, and most people didn't know how to take advantage of it. Then again, Stephen never had a problem taking advantage of anything. Jon had turned on Stephen's monitor, intending to type up a report, when he saw the test. He stared at it for a long time, not wanting to believe what he was seeing. When he confronted him about it, Stephen played it off and said he found it on a message board. All the questions that had been on the mid-term exam. He'd said he'd been studying.

It wasn't entirely his fault their professor was copying his tests from somewhere else. This fact alone was probably why Stephen got away with it. Professor Murphy could've been in a heap of trouble himself. Stephen was simply lucky enough to go to the same source.

That didn't change the fact it was cheating. At first, Jon was stunned his roommate would stoop to such a level. Then he began noticing other things. Like how Stephen always asked to borrow his notes. Or how willing he was to let Jon use Stephen's computer to type his reports and save his files on the hard drive. It was a very simple matter for Stephen to rephrase and make minor changes to Jon's reports before turning them in as his own.

But the worst thing was Isabel.

Jon shook his head, not really wanting to remember. He and Isabel had dated six months, but after he confronted Stephen, she grew inexplicably distant. She'd cancel their dates, find reasons they couldn't spend time together. At first he thought she was getting behind in her studies and wanted to concentrate. Then he wondered if she wasn't getting pressure from her brother.

It wasn't until Stephen himself talked to Jon that he realized what was going on. Stephen hadn't pressured her at all. She simply felt more love for her lying, cheating, scumbag of a brother than she'd ever feel for him. Jon felt like a fool. They were gone at the end of the semester. So much time had passed between then and now. He thought he'd forgiven them, but maybe he'd just been a doormat instead. *God help me,* he prayed, not really feeling that much better.

Hamid leaned back in the seat and closed his eyes. There wasn't much point in vigilance now. It wasn't as if the good professor was going anywhere. At first, his only concern was whether Dr. Munro would recognize him. But there'd been no indication Dr. Munro had any idea Hamid was following him. So far he was proceeding exactly as he thought he would. Dr. Munro was turning out to be a remarkably easy mark, despite his great intelligence.

Hamid smiled. It always amused him—this outsmarting of men who were supposed to be so learned and wise. His client believed this work worth an additional fifteen percent. Yet it was a simple operation, in principle. He merely had to relieve Dr. Munro of the key and proceed as planned. If what he'd witnessed so far was any indication—this would be the easiest money he'd ever made.

Even getting through airport security had not been a problem. The knife blades hidden within his prosthesis garnered no attention. The wand they'd used detected the metal, but no one was willing to have him remove his arm to check. Instead, they smiled sympathetically and waved him through.

He watched as the seat belt sign came on. It wouldn't be long now. Once they were on the ground, he'd wait for Dr. Munro to retrieve his luggage, and then he would strike. The plane banked to the right as the captain announced they would be landing. He turned and looked again at Dr. Munro, watching as the professor stared out the window. The ground must have been rushing toward them now. He was like someone who had never been on a plane before—a child, perhaps.

Easy money.

Maybe he'd find himself a prostitute for the evening. With the key in hand so quickly, he'd have ample time. He could even afford one of the nicer hotels in the city—like the Sheraton. It was all very simple, and it was coming together so easily.

If there was a God—he was smiling on him now. Perhaps he wasn't as lost as he'd believed.

The Esenboğa International Airport, northeast of Ankara, was an imposing, modern structure of polished marble, blue skylights filtering natural light, and an impressive indoor eating area on the main floor. Jon stared at the parallel rows of rounded trees and wondered if Dr. Seuss had inspired them. Beneath and between them were ten rows of white, square tables with orange, bright green, red, and mustard yellow plastic chairs. A series of ten lamp stands the size of streetlights lit each one. The lamp stands had twin halogen lanterns shining against a concave reflector that diffused their light back down to the floor. His rumbling stomach pulled him from his observation, and he looked for the escalator to conduct him to the floor below.

With no desire to convert his dollars into *liras*, he hoped one of the food joints would accept his credit card. He strode across the marbled floor, surprised at the sight of a Burger King. *Thank you, Jesus,* he prayed. At least in there, he knew what he'd find. Relieved that the girl at the counter spoke English, he ordered a Whopper with cheese, fries, and a Coke. And, yes, he would like a receipt. If Michaels were going to send him on this ridiculous quest, he could at least spring for the meals.

He took his food and turned around, catching sight of another man watching him. The man looked familiar, with dark curly hair, a beard, and a prosthetic arm. He wondered briefly, where he'd seen him before—then recognized him as one of the passengers on the plane. He raised his cup in greeting and sat down at one of the tables.

The man turned abruptly in another direction.

Hamid flushed with embarrassment. *Amateur!* If Munro were to see him in another circumstance, his suspicions might be aroused. He ground his teeth and turned to find some kahvesi at the café on the other side of the court. Munro may have been a child, but he was not stupid, and he, Hamid, had better remember that. He'd gotten careless.

Now things were complicated.

From a seat at a table high on the second floor, overlooking the food court, Sean MacNeil watched the befuddled Hamid slip away for his coffee. He smirked. The man was clearly an amateur. No formal training at all. He smoothed out his tie and opened his brief case. From within, he pulled out a manila folder and set it on the table in front of him. Inside was an eight-by-ten blow up of Hamid's face.

He fingered through the pages. At first glance he would've sworn there were dates and pages missing. But Hamid Al-Assini had only been in the assassination business for three years. Before that he'd found work as a petty thief. The dossier was complete after all.

Hamid was originally from Pakistan. Who his parents were was anyone's guess. He grew up in a Madrassah and trained for terror at an early age—probably destined to become a suicide bomber or some other such unfortunate fate, had his own carelessness not saved his life. True, he lost his hand, and they summarily threw him out of the Madrassah to fend for himself, but had he stayed he would be dead by now, along with whomever else he'd have managed to take out with him.

All that for the promise of seventy virgins? If only they realized just how difficult satisfying seventy virgins would be.

He hid his weapons in his prosthesis. A gun stored where the arm pushed into the cuff. Knives without handles inserted into the device, in place of the hand. Like Captain Hook. No doubt, Hamid thought the lack of fingerprints would protect his identity. Instead, a trail of handle-less knives marked every crime and murder he'd ever committed. Of these, there were plenty. Sean scanned the list. He may have been an amateur, but he was prolific and dangerous.

Sean put the dossier away and pulled out another—this one on Dr. Munro. There wasn't much to it. Dr. Munro was exactly who he seemed to be: a bookish professor on assignment to recover an artifact the university believed it owned. That removing it from Turkish soil, rather than turning it over to the proper authorities, would make him an international criminal either didn't bother him, or hadn't occurred to him at all. He wondered exactly how the professor intended to make off with the artifact—or if he'd even thought that far ahead.

There was the distinct possibility that he had. Dr. Munro was smart—not streetwise, but smart in his own way. If he were given time to assess and understand his situation, he'd likely foil them all. Sean needed to move quickly, before the professor had time to consider his options.

Sean checked his watch. His team wasn't due to arrive for at least four more hours. He looked down again into the food court and saw Dr. Munro leaving. Hamid was maneuvering to follow. He packed up his materials and headed for the escalator, pushing the Bluetooth headset into his ear and speed-dialed a local number. He was out of time. His local contact would have to provide support now.

The Lost Scrolls

CHAPTER
9

Philip ducked out of a side exit to the hospital and pulled free his clerical collar. He slipped on his tan jacket, and looked like any other tourist wandering the streets of Ankara. All people ever saw was the collar, never the man behind it.

The hairs on his neck stood on end. A tingle of warning tickled his spine. He stole a glance over his shoulder. Someone was following him. He ducked his head and thrust through the crowds.

In the reflection of a shop window, he caught sight of his pursuer. The man looked older, but quite large, with a full beard and broad nose. Not local authorities. Possibly a friend of the family or a coworker of Stephen's? Philip pressed his lips into a thin smile and reached inside his jacket for the 9mm Beretta he'd obtained yesterday. Regardless, the man wouldn't get much further.

Philip turned down a side street and into an alley, ducking quickly into a doorway. He consciously slowed his breathing, listening. Footsteps.

He pulled out the 9mm and waited. The man was near. He took a breath and stepped out of the doorway, raising the weapon.

"That's far enou—!"

A sharp blow to his chest knocked the wind out of him.

Something carried his right arm up and over his shoulder, yanking down hard toward the ground. His back bent, his legs slipping out beneath him. He had no choice but to roll backward or risk his head bashing against the pavement. He somersaulted away and came up in a fighting stance. The gun was no longer in his hand.

Instead, he stared at it, pointed at him in the hands of the bearded man. The man smiled and raised an eyebrow, then dropped the clip into his other hand and ejected the chambered round. He twirled the gun in his hand and offered it butt-first to Philip.

"Father Philip Bellamy, late of the St. Martin's parish in Baltimore, Maryland, and previously of the Central Intelligence Agency, United States of America."

"Who—who are you?"

"I am Brother Demetri of Mount Athos."

Philip blinked. A monk? He'd been disarmed by an Orthodox monk? Even for a man of Demetri's size, it was tough to swallow. He accepted the gun and held out his hand for the clip. Demetri held onto it.

"What do you want?"

"I want to know you won't try to shoot me if I hand you the bullets to that gun."

Philip smiled and pulled out a second clip. He slammed it into the grip and holstered the weapon. Demetri chuckled. He retrieved the bullet he'd ejected from the Beretta, reset it in the clip, and handed it over.

Philip shoved the clip into his pocket. "I don't believe disarming techniques are taught at the monasteries."

The monk nodded once.

"So either you're not a monk, or I've completely lost my touch."

Demetri smiled. "Do not come down upon yourself so harshly, my young friend. I, too, once served the Beast before I gave allegiance to Christ and foreswore my former masters."

Philip straightened. "And it isn't chance that has brought you down from the Mountain."

"We are here on common purpose, Little Brother. May I buy you a drink?"

Philip looked across the table at his new "friend". Demetri was nothing if not careful. He'd chosen a table toward the back of the outside café, from where he could not only view all the traffic going past and into the restaurant, but which was also close enough to a side street that he could disappear into the throng of pedestrians at the first sign of trouble. He'd sat Philip across the table, leaving his back uncomfortably exposed to the sidewalk. Philip contented himself by regularly glancing in the windows of the restaurant, which reflected the street clearly.

The man was a mystery. Philip had removed his priest's collar as soon as he left the hospital, looking now much like any other Westerner taking in the sights and cuisine of the city. But Demetri still wore his black cassock, refusing to blend in with the crowd around him. Everything he'd observed about the monk so far—from the way he'd disarmed Philip to his choice of cafés and seating—told him Demetri had a background in clandestine service. His age and time on the Mountain, which he'd freely shared, suggested he'd retired after the fall of the Soviet Empire. His name was undoubtedly Slavic, but Philip couldn't determine the country of origin. His choice of apparel was confusing, and it only added to Philip's determination to procure a dossier on him as soon as possible.

"So," Demetri sipped his kahvesi, "Rome has given you an Indulgence."

"How do you figure that?"

"Why else would a priest carry a nine millimeter Berretta?"

"Protection, of course."

"With two clips?"

Philip smiled.

"It must be comforting to have such permission. We of the Eastern Church do not escape so easily, I am afraid. The Eastern Churches are not subject to whims or will of a singular pontiff. And we have no doctrine which allows us to act with impunity."

"Let's cut to the chase."

"You Americans are so impatient."

"Whatever. What do you want?"

He motioned him to silence, staring ahead at the sidewalk. Philip studied the windows' reflection, trying to see what Demetri was looking at, but after a moment gave up and turned around. He didn't see anything on the sidewalk or across the street. He looked back to find the monk sipping his coffee like nothing was wrong.

Demetri set down his cup and said quietly, "I want Dr. Kaufman left alive and unharmed."

"And what are you accusing me of?"

"I think you know. Thiopental is not so easy to come by."

"Now wait just a—"

"Please, please! I know you purchased the drug recently. I have more contacts in this city than you can possibly imagine. Or have you forgotten that Byzantium was once the heart of my church?"

Philip grit his teeth, returning Demetri's stare. Finally, he said, "I have no desire to harm Dr. Kaufman."

"And yet you would resort to a dangerous truth serum to procure information from him."

"What business is it of yours?"

Demetri's face was hard. His eyes burrowed into Philip. "Dr. Kaufman. Alive and unharmed."

"Alright. Fine."

Demetri reached forward and took the other's hand. Philip pulled back, but the monk held fast. "I ask this for your benefit, Little Brother. You do not want that man's death on your conscience. No Papal Indulgence will cure such guilt. Believe me."

"I said alright!" The table shook as Philip pulled his hand free. Demetri smiled at a couple nearby who glanced their way, and returned to Philip.

"What do you want with him anyway?" Philip asked.

"The same thing as you, no doubt." He took another sip.

"And that is?"

"The scroll, of course."

"What scroll?"

Demetri smiled. "You make sport with me. You know very well of which scroll I speak."

Philip smirked. "And how do you intend to get it?"

"Simple. I shall ask him for it."

Philip laughed aloud. "And what makes you think he'll just tell you where it is?"

"Because, Little Brother, it belongs to us."

Philip sat back in his chair, surprised. Whatever skills the monk had acquired over the years were overmatched by his absurdity. If this were the effect of a monastery, Philip would be sure to avoid them in the future. "On what basis can you possibly make such a claim?"

"Several. Geography, for instance."

"You're kidding."

"As I said, Byzantium was once—"

"—the heart of your church, yes, and you lost it to the Muslims in 1453. Your claims mean nothing here. Turkey is a secular state. And if it weren't, it would be Muslim. As it is, the Roman Catholic Church has two active rites within the country."

"As do we. Do you believe your claims are greater?" Demetri chuckled. "Do not lecture me on what ground the Church has lost. You lost Europe to the Protestants. Germany to the Nazis. Your own Italy to the Fascists."

"And Russia fell to the Communists. Your point?"

Demetri sighed. "The *Domo tou Bibliou* was entrusted to the churches of Asia Minor. All these churches remained with the Eastern churches until they were lost to time. That which was entrusted to us should remain with us."

"Why? You haven't shown yourselves to be particularly trustworthy."

"This is pointless. You are too young to realize what I am offering. Too much you think about winning."

"At the moment, I haven't heard you offering me anything."

"Why do you think I brought you here? Hmm? To discuss theology? To debate controversies? Surely you cannot be that foolish."

Philip paused. Had he underestimated him? The monk had already demonstrated his ability, even if his methods seemed foolhardy. What would the monk do when Stephen refused him, assuming the doctor had survived?

"Alright. So what is your offer?"

"Very simply this. We work together. We are possessed of a common purpose. We have equal claim to the book. And our two churches have both expressed the mutual wish to heal the division that has existed between us for the past thousand years. We may allow our superiors to debate which church should possess the book. But what we agree on is this: it must come to one or the other of us." He paused for effect. "Or do you imagine that you and I alone have come to Byzantium, seeking her secrets, her lost treasures?"

Philip picked up his coffee, long left untouched. "What do you know?"

"Are we in agreement?"

"I, too, am a man under orders. I have to consult my superiors. I must tell them something. Given the lengths to which they've already gone to secure my assistance…well, you can imagine their suggested course of action if I give them nothing more than an Orthodox monk with a penchant for aikido who has requested we work together."

Demetri nodded. "There are others here seeking the *Domo tou Bibliou*. An hour ago a plane landed. On it is a professor from a university in America who will claim the scroll. And I've learned a private collector has expressed his interest as well. You must understand. Private collectors and non-believing universities must never possess the scroll. The book is sacred. It must be treated with the reverence which only our church will give it."

Our church. What a crock. Pope John Paul II and the Patriarch Teoctist may have called for healing of the Great Schism, but that didn't mean he and Demetri shared the same goals. On the other hand, the monk had resources Philip could use. Once they took possession of the scroll, then he could decide what to do with him.

"Alright," he said. "What do you propose we do now?"

The Lost Scrolls

CHAPTER
10

Isabel paced the floor, chewing her fingernail. The polished linoleum tiles reflected the stark glow of the fluorescent lights in the ceiling, marking a cold and uncertain path down unknown corridors. Dr. Aybar had said they'd stabilized Stephen, but his condition remained critical. It was little relief. Despite everything that had happened in their lives together— despite all the loss and insanity and craziness and adventure— nothing had prepared her for this. She paused at the hallway's end, afraid if she turned to the right or the left, she might not find her way back again.

Someone had tried to kill her brother. Twice.

She'd known there were problems almost from the beginning. The very fact the university had hired him when every reputable institution held him at arm's length was a mystery. Then there were the envelopes of cash she'd seen him stuff into his coat pocket. Where he'd gotten the money, she still didn't know. Only that he'd grown quite angry when she confronted him about it. His explanation, "It's a payment for business associates of the university," did little to quell her fears. It was bribe money. Plain and simple. They had to pay off certain officials so they'd provide them with permits or… look the other way. It was a normal cost of doing business in some parts of the world. She'd seen it before. Why he hadn't simply said so confused her. She reasoned he wanted her to think he was going straight, and somehow paying out bribes would tarnish that effort. Still, she thought he ought to admit it when she pressed him about it.

She had accompanied him on the dig, marveling at the millennia-old frescos in the exterior chamber he'd uncovered. They told the story of the Gospels in exquisite detail, from Jesus' miracle at the wedding in Cana to the ascension into heaven. The tiles were chipped and faded with time, and in some places, missing entirely. But it was altogether an amazing find. If the Turkish authorities approved restoration work, it would take years—but the tourist dollars would more than compensate the expense, of this she was sure.

Stephen spent almost no time cataloging what he'd found. He let her take pictures with the digital camera, and while she was photographing the walls, he busied himself in the back of the chapel, unearthing a crypt. She wandered into the interior chamber and asked him who it was.

"Dear, why don't you just photograph those enchanting frescoes? There's nothing to see here," he murmured.

She traced a hand over the crypt. He stopped his work when she touched the tomb. "Who do you suppose it is?" she asked.

"It's no one."

"But surely—!"

"I said it's no one!"

She leaped back, stung by his tone. He waited until she left the room, then resumed digging.

When they returned to the house, he kept checking the windows, leaving the shades drawn. She didn't know what to make of it then. Still didn't. She only knew that someone was after him, trying to hurt him, and only one thing made sense.

Stephen had found something. Something he didn't want her to see, or to know anything about. Either he was trying to deceive her, or he was trying to protect her. She shook her head. This was different, and not just because her brother was lying in a hospital bed, stabbed and drugged.

He'd kept her in the dark before. He'd lied to her more times than she could count. But always there was a cover story, something to soothe her in the dark. There were reassurances. Promises. Explanations.

Now there was only darkness.

Just a simple request. Find Jonnie. Take him to the chapel.

She turned from the corridor and retraced her steps to Stephen's room.

Leon rubbed his eyes and felt a sudden pain beside his nose. He jerked his hand away and realized he'd nearly poked out his eye with his pencil. That was close. He set the pencil down on the desk and looked around for a mirror. His face stung, and he wondered if he'd punctured the skin. He rubbed the spot, looking for blood on his finger.

Leave it to Dr. Munro to have no mirror in his office. The man genuinely did not care what he looked like, or what others thought of him. He was the typical absent-minded professor: his mind so intent on the forest, he'd lose track of the trees. Countless times Leon had seen him rush into a classroom with his hair unkempt and his tie askew, looking so much like a mad scientist that other graduate assistants had taken to calling Leon "Igor." He took it in stride. It would have been worse if Munro had taught biology. But then, Leon wouldn't have been his graduate assistant.

The telephone interrupted his reverie. He rubbed his face again as he picked up the receiver.

"Yes?"

A woman spoke in a heavily accented and richly exotic voice, and Leon quickly forgot about his close encounter with the pencil. "Yes, I am sorry. I'm calling for Jonnie – I mean, Dr. Munro."

"Uh, yeah. This is Dr. Munro's office. Leon speaking."

"Who?"

"Leon. I'm his graduate assistant."

"I see. May I speak with Jonnie, please?"

"I'm sorry. He's not here at the moment."

"When will he return?"

"Oh, I don't expect him back for several days. He's on assignment right now."

"Assignment?"

"Yeah. Is there something I can help you with?" There was silence on the other end, and he wondered if she'd hung up. "Miss?"

"Please. I am sorry. Is there a way to reach him?"

Leon scratched his nose. "Umm... I don't think I can give out his cell number over the phone..." *But you can have mine.*

"Cell phone?"

"Why don't I take down your number, give it to him, and have him call you?"

Another silence. Then, "Alright. Do you have a pen?"

"Yeah, hang on a second." He picked up a scrap of paper and set it on the draftsman's table, then looked frantically for a pen. He stopped when he realized the pencil was still on the desk where he'd set it moments ago.

She gave him the phone number and hung up. Leon set the receiver down, a bit reluctantly. She hadn't left her name. But God! What a sexy voice. He pictured Catherine Zeta-Jones.

Only, why would someone like that be calling Dr. Munro?

No matter. He checked his watch. Dr. Munro's plane should have arrived twenty minutes ago. He didn't suppose he was out of baggage claims yet, and probably wouldn't want to be disturbed until he got to his hotel anyway.

Besides, Leon was still in the middle of this transcription. No doubt Jon would be surprised—maybe angry—but a transcription was what he wanted, and for all that Jon had done, it was the least Leon could do.

He lifted the pencil and returned his attention to Egerton.

The phone rang.

Leon furrowed his brow. It could be the sexy lady again. He should at least get her name. *Who knows? Maybe she has a thing for graduate assistants.* He picked up the receiver.

"Dr. Munro's office."

"Yes, this is Detective Jim Brown of the Washtenaw County Sheriff's office. I need to speak to Dr. Munro."

"Oh. Umm. Regarding?"

"Regarding none of your business, son. Put Dr. Munro on the phone, please."

"Uh, I can't."

"And why's that?"

"Well, he's not here. He's been sent on assignment."

"On assignment?"

"Yeah. For the university."

"I see. Where'd they ship him off to?"

"Uh, well, I'm not sure I can say—"

"Son, don't make me come down there and arrest you for hindering a criminal investigation."

"Uh, Tur—Turkey."

"Good boy. Turkey. As in the country?"

"Yeah."

"Not turkeys in the country."

"No. No, the—"

"The country of Turkey. Very good, son. Well, you tell him I called. Would you do that?"

"Yes sir."

"Are you writing this down?"

Leon remembered his pencil. "Yes sir."

"Good." The detective left his number and hung up. Leon set down the phone for a second time and stared at the messages. He bit his lip and picked up the phone.

Detective Jim Brown kept his hand on the receiver in its cradle. In his other hand, he held a file folder with a large, eight-by-ten photograph in it. Finally, he relaxed and leaned back in his chair. He stirred the swizzle stick in his coffee, and lifted the beverage to his lips for a prolonged sip. At no time did he take his eyes off the photo. The man in the picture was Middle Eastern. According to the file, he was originally from Pakistan. Known in some places as "The Rat," his real name was Hamid Al-Assin, and he was wanted for questioning in more than a dozen unsolved murders.

The investigation produced only a partial print, but it was enough to declare a match and deliver this file folder and picture to Detective Brown's desk. So what was an international criminal doing in the house of a humble university of Michigan professor in rural Washtenaw County?

And why was that same professor now on a plane to Turkey, the last known whereabouts of The Rat?

Brown leaned back in his chair and set down his coffee.

Turkey was outside his jurisdiction, but he knew people who'd be very interested in anyone linked to Al-Assini.

"Hagel, c'mere a second!" he called out.

A moment later, the officer appeared at his desk. "I need you to work your computer magic for me. See if you can find a phone number for the Turkish version of our Department of Homeland Security, alright? Oh, and do you have handy the number for Judge Moore?"

"It's on speed dial, sir."

He looked disapprovingly at her. She picked up the phone and pressed the number. He rolled his eyes as she left. In a moment, a clerk answered the phone. "Hello, this is Detective Jim Brown of the Washtenaw County Sheriff's Office," he said. "I need to speak to Judge Moore about a wiretap. Patriot Act stuff."

When the clerk put him on hold, he muttered in his best Ricky Ricardo, "Dr. Munro, you've got some 'splainin' to do."

The Lost Scrolls

CHAPTER
11

From the airport Jon took a cab straight to his hotel. All along the way, the city unfolded before him. Ankara was a bold metropolis emerging into the twenty-first century. Other cities of modern Europe had evolved gradually, gently preserving the old while cultivating the new, or had been blasted into the twentieth century by the ravages of World War II. But Ankara's growth was more an explosion of neon commercialism and Western capitalism which all but obliterated the past and left antiquated structures scattered like so much historical debris. Ancient mosques of crumbling stone competed with golden arches and glowing ads on animated billboards, while numerous cars hurried past, oblivious to the cultural Cuisinart for which they were both consequence and cause.

At first Jon gripped the seat and door handle through startling turns and sudden stops, until he forced himself to relax and trust the driver to handle the traffic without his help. He turned and stared out the window as the panorama of gaudy businesses flew by. Globed streetlights hung like ripe, white fruit over broad sidewalks, and colorful signs above bright store windows enticed him with exotic deals. He felt dyslexic trying to read their offers. The letters were familiar, but the words they formed were indecipherable. As a paleographer, he was literate in ancient Hebrew, both classical and Koine Greek, Latin,

Aramaic, and Arabic. Modern Turkish was not something he'd ever considered studying.

The roller coaster cab halted at the Houston Hotel, a beautiful edifice of steel and glass rising nine stories above wide tree-lined streets. He extricated himself from the backseat and thanked the cabbie—mostly for letting him arrive in one piece—as the man wordlessly retrieved his luggage.

Inside, the hotel greeted him with a polished display of granite countertops and teak wood trim. Padded lounge chairs huddled beneath illuminated wall hangings, and frilly trees grew from large pots in the corners. A balcony curved around the second floor landing, beneath which the front desk beckoned.

A few guests glanced up when he came in, muttering to each other in odd dialects and glancing his way. Once again, he felt the panicky tendrils of culture shock wrapping around his gut. He blew out a relieved sigh when the front desk clerk spoke English.

"Yes, Dr. Munro." The clerk smiled cheerfully. "Welcome to Ankara. How was your flight?"

He'd glanced behind himself as she spoke. Evidently, the guests had decided he was no one of consequence and returned their newspapers. He turned around. "It was fine. I don't suppose you have a room reserved for me?"

"But of course. You are in room 709. Here is your key."

"Again, thank you."

"The porter will take your bags up, and you have a message waiting for you."

"Okay. You wouldn't happen to know who called?"

She shook her head. He smiled and thanked her, then followed the porter with his suitcase to the elevators. At the seventh floor, the porter showed him into a large room, and left with tip in hand. Jon put his billfold away and looked around.

The room was spacious, with dark green carpet and cream walls. A pair of auburn lounge chairs huddled in one corner of the room, next to a set of table and chairs before the draped wall of glass that looked out over the street below. On the other side of the room, a second table stood before a dark hutch and a cabinet with a large television sitting atop it. A queen-sized bed with a large, wooden headboard stretched across the wall. He poked his head in the bathroom, surprised by the stately green tile, granite sinks, and polished porcelain tub and toilet. There was no denying it: he was impressed. Why had Michaels agreed to spend so much on him? Was it sheer gratitude for his going on this little adventure? Pulling out his Blackberry, he plugged it into the charger. He set his suitcase in the corner, wondering how long Michaels expected him to be here, and whether or not he could extend his stay.

On the bedside table, the message button flashed red on the phone. Jon lifted the receiver and punched in the code. Leon's voice greeted him with news of two phone calls he'd received back in the States. The first was from Detective Brown asking Jon's whereabouts. He probably just wanted to deliver an update. It'd be nice to know if there were any leads. Jon would have to look into it when he returned.

The second caller hadn't left her name, but Leon said she had a very sexy voice. The number she'd left had come from an exchange in Ankara.

It had to have been Izzy. Jon disconnected the message recording and started dialing the number. Then stopped.

Lord, what do I say to her?

He set the receiver down. In all his haste, he hadn't taken time to think this through, let alone pray. Isabel Kaufman had been out of his life for so many years now. Any lingering feelings were nostalgic only. He wasn't the same man she'd left. Finding God had changed that. He wondered if she'd even recognize him.

There was nothing for it. Stephen was in Gazi Hospital, according to Michaels. Doubtless, Isabel would still be there. He picked up the phone again and asked the front desk to call him a cab. Then he washed his face and went back downstairs.

As he stepped into the cab, he chanced a glance over his shoulder and frowned. A man standing near the hotel lobby looked disturbingly familiar, but the man turned and walked away in the opposite direction.

Must be culture shock. All the Turks were starting to look alike to him. He put it out of his mind.

Lieutenant Kahil Çapanoğlu set down the phone and scowled. The message from the county detective in America was succinct enough—but still confusing.

What was a known assassin on the terrorist watch list doing in the house of a simple language professor in Michigan? And why was that same professor now in Ankara?

He stared at the fluorescent lamp above his steel desk, watching the periodic flicker in the tubes behind their plastic screen. Beneath the lamp's glow, the third floor offices of the Turkish Gendarmerie in Ankara were cold. They were also surprisingly quiet, but not silent. Busy officers hunched over computer terminals and sipped coffee to keep warm. Some perused files of wanted criminals or spoke in hushed voices over their phones. Most of the desks were battleship gray with matching steel file cabinets. Sunlight flowed into the room, but the opaque-glass block prevented anyone from seeing into the room from the outside. It had the added effect of removing all warmth from the sunlight and contributing to the overall chill of the room.

Kahil made a notation on the file Detective Brown had faxed over to him. There were two possibilities, both troubling. Either the professor was working with The Rat, or he was his target. Neither possibility was a good one.

He picked up the photograph of Jonathan Munro retrieved from the University of Michigan's website and studied it. It showed the professor in a smiling pose, meant to accentuate his teaching credentials with something the Americans called "likeability." He snorted. The man seemed harmless enough, but looks could be deceiving.

Working with Interpol's anti-terrorist unit had taught him that. Kahil's thinning brown hair, carefully trimmed mustache, and average build made him look every part the docile businessman of the city. He had a soft-spoken manner to complete the illusion, and it served him well in the various surveillance activities to which he'd first been assigned ten years ago.

The anti-terrorist unit was the closest he could come to striking back at those who'd killed his brother, though after a few months he'd grown enamored of the work itself, and no longer thought of his new role in terms of revenge. He spent most of his days at a computer, tracking criminals through known associates and last-known locations, and surmising through these relationships what they might do or where they might turn up next.

On rare occasions, one of them landed on his doorstep. Like now. He picked up his files and walked into Captain Tabak's office. Captain Tabak was a graying man with brown eyes whose midlife paunch belied the firmly muscled body he retained from his youth. He glanced up when Kahil walked in.

"What is it, Lieutenant?"

"Captain, I've received a communiqué from America." He handed Tabak the picture of Hamid. "The Rat has left his paw print in the house of an American professor, Doctor Jonathan Munro." He handed him the second photograph.

Tabak smirked. "And I assume you are about to tell me why this is not simply America's problem?"

"The print was lifted after the American's house was broken into. This morning. A little later the American boarded a flight." He handed him the flight manifest.

The captain raised his eyebrows. "Here?"

"His plane landed at Esenboğa not two hours ago."

"Do you know where he is now?"

"We have learned he is staying at the Houston Hotel. He told Customs he was visiting a friend in the hospital."

The captain nodded, then said, "Wasn't an American stabbed two weeks ago in Baljat?"

"And The Rat left his calling card at the scene. A handleless knife."

The captain leaned back. "Inform the general directorate of security the American is no longer a police matter. In light of these developments, the Gendarmerie Command will be taking over the investigation, as should have happened when Al-Assini's calling card was found on the scene."

"Do you think they tried to keep that from us?"

Tabak sighed. "Interagency rivalry. We lose so much time on these provincial disputes. Find out which hospital the American is in. Alert hospital security, but be sure they allow this Munro to enter the building. For that matter, he may already be there. But do not allow him to leave. Take some men with you and bring him in for questioning."

"And the Rat?"

"Inform the directorate to keep watch. He's bound to come out of his hole any time now." He rose from his desk. "Perhaps we can use this Munro. Cheese to bait the trap."

Kahil saluted smartly and turned to go. The captain said to him, "And Lieutenant?"

"Yes, Captain?"

"Good work."

The Lost Scrolls

CHAPTER
12

Jon entered the building and gave his eyes a moment to adjust. The lobby of Gazi Hospital was designed for function, not comfort. Pale walls and a white ceiling supported by square columns gave the room a cavernous feel, with the last light of the sun glowing dully through the glass windows in front.

"Jonnie? What are you doing here?"

The greeting seemed to come from everywhere at once, and he turned very nearly in a full circle before he recognized who'd spoken his name.

"Hello, Izzy."

She came forward and wrapped her arms around him in a tight embrace. He realized with a sinking feeling that, by coming here directly instead of calling ahead, he'd only hastened the inevitable, and he still had no idea what to say.

"You haven't changed a bit, Izzy."

"You look good, too."

He smiled. "Meaning I'm fatter and have less hair."

"I did not say that."

"You don't have to. It's true. How's Stephen doing?"

Her face clouded, and she whispered hoarsely. "You heard? Oh, Jonnie, they're trying to *kill* him!" Her voice seemed to echo from the walls.

He glanced around. "Who is?"

"I-I don't know. He was stabbed in the street. They left him to die."

He searched for an answer. "Was it a random attack? A gang? A mugging?"

"It was deliberate. They're after him."

"That doesn't make any sense."

She pulled away and glared. "Just this morning a Catholic priest was in his room."

"Stephen's Catholic?"

"No. But the priest tried to poison him."

"Poison."

She nodded.

"So your brother has been stabbed and poisoned, and yet still he survives. That's a hell of a life expectancy."

"Please don't make jokes."

"I'm not. It just strikes me as somewhat incredible odds he's survived two recent attempts on his life. Given the man's a known pathological liar, it makes me wonder whether or not the whole thing's—well, you know—a set up."

As soon as he'd said it, he wished he hadn't. Isabel's eyes flared in brief indignation, then hardened into stony resolve.

"Unbelievable. You are still jealous. After all these years." She waved her hand and muttered at the sky.

He shook his head. "No. I'm sorry, I shouldn't have said that."

She went on as though she hadn't heard him. "My brother lies dying in a hospital bed, and all you can think of is yourself."

He chose his next words carefully. "You're only angry with me because you've thought it yourself. Don't tell me you haven't."

"Always the skeptic. Your problem is you have no faith in people."

"I'm a scientist. Your problem is you have too much."

She put her hands on her hips and stared at him coldly. Behind them, the elevator doors chimed open and shut. "Why are you here?" she said. "Why did you come to Ankara?"

"On assignment. Michaels sent me. He was concerned for Stephen. And, naturally, he means to protect the university's investment."

"Is that all this is to you? Money?"

"No. I flew two thousand miles so I could gloat." He bit his lip. "The university paid for my flight because they were concerned about the money. I came…I came because Stephen was once my friend, and despite everything, I still care what happens to him. And to you."

"Oh. And to me?"

"Sure. You're an old friend, Izzy. Why wouldn't I care?"

"Well, you need not concern yourself with me. I'm not the one who's—" Her voice broke. He reached out for her, but she pushed him away, angrily reasserting control. "I'm not the one who's dying." Her resolve crumbled, and the grief rushed to the surface. She turned away from him.

Jon watched her, wishing he could console her, knowing he'd already obliterated that chance. He'd left her bereft of the friendship she now needed the most.

"I'm sorry. I didn't know it was this bad. Please forgive me."

She kept her eyes off him. He watched helplessly as she struggled to regain her composure.

"Maybe I should see him, now."

At last, she nodded and took his arm, letting him escort her to the elevators. As the elevator doors slid shut, his eye caught something in the lobby, something that should not have been there.

That face. That same face he'd seen at the hotel as he was leaving. And once before, too. At the airport.

The same man who'd been on the plane.

Hamid whirled and stalked across the hospital lobby. He'd been made. Munro had seen him. The unmistakable look of recognition in his eyes.

Maybe now was a good time for one of those American swear words he'd been learning so much of recently. He pulled out his cell phone and speed-dialed a number.

"It's me," he said without waiting for a greeting. "I'm at the hospital. Munro has seen me."

"What does he know?"

"He doesn't know anything. But he'll start asking questions if I show my face again."

"That's your problem. I couldn't care less. I want to know what he knows about the book. Find out. Use any means necessary."

"And afterward?"

"Use your discretion."

He hung up and headed for a steel door marked "Stairs." Once inside, he leaned against the corner of the door and pulled a Glock 23 from a side holster beneath his coat. He pushed the grip into the lifeless fingers of his prosthesis and took a small cylinder from inside his pocket. He screwed the silencer onto the end of the semi-automatic pistol, then transferred the gun back to his left hand, tucking it inside his jacket.

He took a deep breath and started up the stairs.

Lieutenant Kahil made the first phone call to inform the general directorate of security that he would be taking over the investigation into the stabbing of the American. Would they kindly turn all files and materials over to him? He listened to the director bluster for five minutes before telling him he also needed a contingent of men to go with him to the hospital.

The director launched into a tirade—mostly in Turkish, some in Arabic, with a few choice English swear words thrown in for good measure—about taking this up with the Ministry of the Interior. After a few more minutes of this, Kahil finally intimated the directorate would prefer blood in the streets to catching the assassin. The director's voice lost its shrill tone and dropped into a low growl.

"Be careful, Lieutenant."

At least he had the director's attention now. "Forgive me, director. I am only trying to bring the man in. He has information about an international terrorist and an assassin. He could be very dangerous."

"And you don't believe my men can bring him in."

Kahil pinched the bridge of his nose. This wasn't getting anywhere. He wanted to reach through the phone and throttle the director. Instead, he said, "Respectfully, director, I believe your police are very good at guarding the city and securing the welfare of our citizenry. It is a job for which your men have been specially trained. But going after an international terrorist is a job for which I have been specially trained. Your men may certainly receive credit for the arrest, even of The Rat, if it comes to that. But they must be under my direct control."

"Then why not take your own men?"

"You know as well as I we have too few. Most of our men are in the East dealing with the Kurds. We have no time to recall them to assist. I am confident your men under my supervision will be up to the task."

There was a long moment of silence, and he began to wonder if he'd been cut off. "Director?"

The director sighed. "Very well. You have your men."

"Thank you for your cooperation, Director." He almost slammed the phone down, but caught himself just in time. Captain Tabak was right. This was nothing more than provincial interagency rivalry.

Still, he hadn't done much to ingratiate himself to the man, either. He sighed. Politics was never his forte. He picked up the phone again and dialed the hospital.

CHAPTER
13

Jon dismissed the presence of the man from the plane as the elevator climbed its way to the seventh floor. It was likely the man himself had come to Ankara to visit a sick relative. That they'd both been on the same flight heading for the same hospital was mere coincidence. And a pity. They might have shared a cab.

He turned to Isabel, who'd regained her composure.

"Do you mind if I ask you a question?" he said.

She glanced at him and shrugged.

"I'm not implying anything, but what was Stephen doing? I mean, why did he wind up in a hospital?"

She spoke quietly. "Why are you asking me this?"

"I'm just trying to understand. Michaels said a student with the university found something, and they asked Stephen to look into it."

"You mean the church."

"Yes."

"Stephen took me there. Once. A few weeks ago. He was… distracted, rude even. So unlike him. Something happened. He found something, maybe…I don't know. He stopped talking to me. Started looking over his shoulder. I think he knew someone was after him for what he knew or found." She focused on him. "Didn't he tell you?"

He shook his head. "I haven't heard from you or Stephen since you both left." He tried to smile. Something nibbled at the back of his thoughts, a nagging suspicion he was forgetting something. Again.

"That was a long time ago. You could have called."

"So could you."

"Or written."

"And what would I have said?"

The question hung in the air, and they fell to silence until the elevator doors opened and they stepped onto the floor. Pale light from fluorescent tubes glowed dully from the ceiling, and the beige walls seemed to drop away into a drab blur as they walked ahead. On their right was the nurses' station, and just beyond that, a door with a single guard who leaned casually against the wall. He straightened up when he saw Isabel.

"Good afternoon, Naþit. This is my friend, Dr. Munro."

Naþit nodded curtly and opened the door for them both. Inside, Dr. Aybar greeted them brusquely and bent over the supine form on the bed. Isabel led Jon to stand on the far side of the room, out of the doctor's way. After a moment, Dr. Aybar straightened and came to her.

"How is he?" she whispered.

Aybar shook his head. "He's septic. We're giving him a course of antibiotics to fight the infection. There isn't much more we can do for him right now."

"Will he make it?" Jon asked.

"*Inshallah*. But I won't give you false hope. If he makes it through the night, I would give him even odds. He needs his rest."

"We won't be long," said Isabel.

"Don't be. I have rounds. I'll come back to check on him afterwards."

"Thank you, Doctor."

He nodded and left the room. Isabel went over to the side of the bed and looked at her brother. Jon came up on the other side. *Dear God,* he thought. *What happened to you, Stephen?* What lay on the bed looked nothing like his former friend. Gone was the robust complexion of youth with sandy locks and a healthy tan. In its place lay a man with skin that was pale, almost white, and sunken around the bones of his face. His hair had become a salt and pepper mop, and two day's growth of silver stubble masked his jaw line. Ugly purple and reddish spots covered his cheeks and chest, what Jon could see of it. If he hadn't known it was Stephen, he might never have recognized him.

"Stephen?" Isabel said, taking his hand. It looked old in hers. Out of place. Jon swallowed, not knowing what to say.

After a moment Stephen opened his eyes. He looked up at her and tried to smile, but coughed instead. She took a tissue and dabbed at his lips.

"Where did you go?" he said, his voice barely a whisper.

"Nowhere. I've been right here."

He blinked and managed to smile.

"I brought someone to see you."

Stephen turned his head, slowly, as though he were moving a great weight. He caught Jon's eye and looked him up and down, to the point where Jon wanted to look away.

"Jon."

"Hello, Stephen."

Stephen opened and closed his eyes. He started breathing harder. "No. Why are you here?"

Jon glanced at Isabel, then back down. Stephen wasn't making sense, but he was obviously upset about something. "Stephen, Dr. Michaels sent me."

"Michaels?"

"He heard what happened. He was worried. I think mostly for his, rather the university's investment, but you know Michaels."

"Why?"

Jon furrowed his brow.

"Why are you working for Michaels?"

"He's the director of antiquities, head of the department. Of course I work for him." Stephen was shaking his head. Jon's confusion deepened. "I thought you worked for him."

"No. Not anymore."

"What happened?"

"Please, Jon. You can't let them have it."

Naþit smiled when the nurse called him over. He'd been glancing her way ever since taking his post outside the American's room. Terrible thing, what happened to the American, but good for Naþit. He'd seen her once or twice before during his six months on the hospital security staff. Always she smiled in his direction, though he'd not yet had the nerve to speak to her or ask her name.

All he knew was she had beautiful dark hair, deep eyes, and a body meant to be covered by more than her nurse's uniform. No other man should be allowed to see such perfection except him, Naþit, her future husband.

His brother, Omer, had the nerve to ask if she were truly Turk, and not Dönme, or Armenian, or, Allah forbid, a Kurd. As if such distinctions should matter. That Allah deigned to grace her with such beauty was proof enough of his divine approval. What did Omer know of women, anyway?

He pulled away from his post and walked the few steps

to where she beckoned him, wondering what she wanted, if she knew how he felt. He could read her nametag from where it was pinned just above her left pocket. Açelya. What a beautiful name.

"Are you Naþit?" Her voice was like music.

"Yes."

"You have a phone call." She held out the phone to him.

"Yes."

She furrowed her brow. What a delightful expression. "Naþit?"

"Yes? Oh, sorry!" He flushed and took the phone from her. *Congratulations, Açelya*, he thought. *Your future husband is an idiot.*

"Hello?"

"Officer Naþit? I am Lieutenant Çapanoğlu of the Gendarmerie. You are guarding the American?"

"Yes sir."

"Another American will be coming to see him. I want you to let him in the room."

"Yes sir. He's there now."

"Now?"

"Yes, sir. The American's sister brought him up not ten minutes ago."

"I want you to listen to me very carefully, Naþit. The man is wanted for questioning. The police are on their way. Do whatever you can to keep him in that room. But be careful. He could be dangerous."

"Dangerous?" he said. Açelya glanced at him, and he straightened up smartly. "I will do my best, sir."

"Thank you, Naþit. We are coming now."

"Yes, sir," he said, and realized he was speaking to a dial tone. He handed the phone back to Açlya, feeling rather proud to have such an important assignment. "That was the police. They said the man in that room is dangerous. But do not worry. I will keep you safe."

Açelya smiled at him. It was the last thing he saw. A silenced bullet tore through his brain, and he dropped to the ground. Açelya opened her mouth to scream before a second bullet whispered through her skull, and she fell back into her chair.

Hamid ducked into the corridor and ran to the guard's body. He glanced around the nurses' station before dragging Naþit's corpse to the other side of the counter. He could do nothing about the blood at this point. Blood on a hospital floor was not unheard of, and without the body, it would raise more questions than alarm. It was a chance he had to take.

"I don't understand, Stephen. Can't have what?"

Stephen labored to breathe. His heart rate increased.

"Jonnie," Isabel warned. Her eyes were full of doubt and fear. He nodded.

"Maybe now's not a good time. We can talk later."

Stephen grabbed his sleeve. "No! No time. Did you—did you bring the key?"

"Stephen, please relax," she said.

"Did you bring it?"

Jon tried to pry his sleeve loose. He shook his head, bewildered. "What key?"

He started laughing, shaking his head. "They'll never find it. Don't worry about the *Domo*. I hid it with style. Izzy, take him to—" He gasped. The line on the heart monitor went flat. An electronic alarm screamed. He fell back into the bed, his eyes open, staring at the ceiling.

"Stephen!" Isabel punched the call button pinned on the sheets. "Help! We need a doctor!"

Jon didn't think. He pulled the pillow away and tilted Stephen's head back. Two quick breaths into his lungs. He straightened and started chest compressions. "One, two, three, four, five!" Two more breaths. Five more compressions.

The heart monitor stayed flat. The monotone alarm wailed through the room. Jon continued CPR. Isabel dashed to the door. Where was that doctor?

She screamed. Jon whipped around, still counting. Isabel was backing slowly into the room, away from a man holding a vicious looking gun pointed at her face. Jon stared. It was the man from the airport and the hotel…and the hospital lobby.

The man glanced at Stephen on the hospital bed, then at Jon, whose compressions had faltered at seeing the gun. "He is dead. Turn off the alarm, please."

"There's still a chance," Jon said.

The man turned the gun toward him. Jon backed up. A slight cough from the gun, and Stephen's body jerked in the bed. Isabel stifled a cry, her hand on her mouth. Jon turned and stared wide-eyed. A round hole in the center of Stephen's forehead leaked a trickle of blood down his face.

"I think not," the man said. "The alarm, if you please."

The Lost Scrolls

CHAPTER
14

Sean looked out the window of the van at the hospital looming fourteen stories before him. In one of those rooms lay the man at the center of this mission. He frowned. It had been almost an hour and a half since he'd left the airport, and they still weren't inside.

Abruptly, he turned to the men seated in darkness behind him. "Are you bloody ready yet?"

"*Allahu akbar!*" was the reply. That, and the sound of a round being chambered.

Terrific, he thought. *I ask for professionals and they give me the bloody mujahadeen.* "Alright, listen up! We go in quietly. Keep your weapons ready, but for God's sake, keep them out of sight. We've got a hospital, yeah? A lot of sick people. Our target is on the seventh floor, room 709. We go in fast. We take the stairs to the seventh floor. We get the professor. We get out fast. No one gets hurt. Any questions?"

The glow of a cigarette winked in the shadows. A man in the back raised his hand. Sean looked toward him, trying to make out his face. *Bloody hell, they all look alike to me.* "Speak up, yeah?"

"Why do we not use the elevators? You said 'use the stairs.'"

"Yes, why do we not use the elevators?" echoed another.

"I am just saying it is a lot of climbing."

He rolled his eyes. *Unbelievable. They want to use the bloody lift! How were these Kurds managing to wage any kind of war for independence? It's bloody ridiculous!* "Right," he sighed, "it's about control. The lifts have security systems. Look, cameras in them. Building security can shut them down between floors if they wanted to. We control the stairs. And then there's the problem of access. The lifts are in the center of the building. Stairs are on the outside. The fewer people what see us, the better, yeah?"

"I am just saying it is a lot of climbing."

Sean sucked his lip. "Yeah, are you saying you're not up for it?"

"That is not what I am saying."

"'Cus they told me you were the best."

"*Allahu akbar!*" said a third.

"We are the best, and that is not what I am saying. You are putting words into my mouth."

"I'm about to put my bloody fist in your mouth!"

Cla-clack! Two more rounds were chambered. He held up his hands placatingly. He took a breath. "Whoa, now. Let's calm down a wee bit. At the end of the day, we all want to get paid, yeah?" He let the subtle threat sink in. "Gentlemen, this is my operation. We do things the way I say we do them. That is what I hired you for. That is what I am paying you for." In the darkness, he looked at each of them in what he hoped was approximately eye level and said, "Are we clear on that?"

There was the briefest hesitation, then nods and grunts of assent.

"Right." He nodded toward the doors. "Off we go now."

The side door of the van slid open, and they piled out onto the pavement. Sean stepped out last, closing the door behind him. The four men were dressed in casual clothes, as ordered, with dark ski masks tucked into their back pockets. He looked them over, wondering if they'd had the insight to buy or at least borrow some clothes for the operation, or if they were wearing something others would recognize. Either way, it wasn't his problem.

He stepped ahead of them and strode the remaining yards to the hospital, tucking his 9mm Beretta into the back of his pants and pulling his coat over the top of it. He glanced briefly behind to be sure his hirelings were doing the same.

They entered through the side door on the south side of the building. There was only one person there, an orderly Sean greeted heartily with, "D'you mind if I ask you a wee question?" before dropping him with a soft finger strike to a pressure point. The Kurds paused behind him, clearly impressed. Once inside, he led them to the stairs. They glanced at him as they entered, but said nothing.

It was just as well. He followed them up.

Kahil pulled up in front of the hospital and stepped out of his car. Three other cruisers parked behind him, and six officers climbed out. One of them, a sergeant, introduced himself.

"Sergeant Bahar." He offered his hand. Kahil took it.

"Lieutenant Çapanoğlu. Have you been briefed?"

"Briefly, sir."

Kahil smiled. "The man we are looking for is Dr. Jonathan Munro." He handed the six men pictures of Jon. "He is tied to a known terrorist, an assassin known as The Rat, also known as Hamid Al-Assini, a Pakistani. The Rat is wanted for more than twenty murders in fourteen countries." Now he passed out copies of Hamid's photograph. "Including," he added, "the attempted murder of the American attacked two weeks ago in Baljat, Dr. Stephen Kaufman.

"Dr. Kaufman is here in this hospital, room 709. Munro has come to see him and is in the room as we speak."

"Then why are we standing around here?" asked one of the officers. Kahil glanced at him. The officer was young and passionate.

"We do not believe Munro himself is an operative," Kahil said, "or that Dr. Kaufman is in any immediate danger from him. A guard at Dr. Kaufman's room will delay his presence there, if necessary. He is only wanted for questioning. In fact, Munro might not know Al-Assini is a terrorist.

"But we know The Rat paid him a visit yesterday, in the United States. He burglarized Munro's house. The American police positively identified his fingerprints. Now Munro is here, and The Rat may have followed him." He paused. "It's possible Munro himself is in danger. Be on your guard."

They nodded in agreement. He led them to the door.

"Oh, my God! You shot him!"

The man with the gun shrugged. "He was already dead. The alarm, please. Now. I will not ask again."

Jon turned to the monitor. Now all the lines were flat. He looked for a button to silence the alarm and finally settled on the plug in the wall. The monitor switched to battery mode and continued chirping. A moment later, he found the switch that shut it down. The monitor flicked off and the wail dwindled to silence. He turned back to the assailant. How could this man be so calm?

"What…what do you want?"

"The same thing as you, no doubt."

"I don't know what you're talking about."

"Then I will ask the questions. The scroll. Where is it?"

"What scroll?"

The man smiled. "I wasn't speaking to you, sir. I was speaking to Ms. Kaufman, sister of the very recently deceased Dr. Stephen Kaufman, world famous archaeologist and finder of rare artifacts."

Jon looked at her. "Isabel?"

Sean waited at the top of the stairs. He peered through the doorway, not seeing anyone. He frowned. Something told him this wasn't right. There should be nurses or doctors milling about. He checked his watch. It could be near shift change or break time. Still….

He glanced down the landing as the men rounded the final step and climbed up toward him. He held his hand out, palm down, motioning them to be quiet.

One whispered to his comrades. "I told you it would be too much climbing."

"Shh!" Sean pulled out his gun. Silently, the others did the same.

"I don't have it!" Isabel cried.

The man shook his head. "Already one man has died for this secret. Shall I make it two?" He pointed the gun at Jon. Jon went pale.

"Izzy?"

"I don't have it," she held out her hand toward the assassin, "but I know where to get it. Jon, we need the key."

Jon gulped. "What key?"

"The one Stephen sent you."

"I haven't received anything from Stephen!"

"Jonnie!"

"He's pointing a gun at me! You think I won't give him whatever he wants? I don't have it!" Inwardly, he prayed, *Jesus, help me!*

"That is unfortunate." The man raised his gun.

"Wait a minute! Just wait. Let me think. When did he send it?"

"Two days ago."

"Well, it probably hasn't arrived yet."

"Jonnie, don't play games!"

The assassin lowered the gun and leaned against the wall. "I believe you."

Thank you, Jesus! Jon blinked. "Wait a minute. I saw you. You were on the plane. You were... you were in the U.S. You're the one who broke into my car. My house. My office!"

He nodded. "No key."

"Stephen wouldn't have my home address," he said to Isabel. He glanced at Stephen's body on the hospital bed and turned away just as quickly. "He must've sent it to the university." He thought for a moment. "Uh—maybe it hasn't arrived yet. My assistant picks up the mail."

"Then I suggest you call him." He nodded toward Jon's hip. Jon glanced down at his Blackberry.

A small, black object bounced into the room. Their heads turned to follow it. The assailant's eyes grew wide, and he dove for the ground.

Jon and Isabel stared at it.

The room exploded.

CHAPTER
15

Sean had seen the man toss the percussion grenade as he peered at the room. He had no time to protest. His men had found the bodies of the guard and the nurse barely hidden behind the bloodstained counter just a moment before. The directional blood spatter on the nurses' station and the distinct, cordite-like odor told him what had happened.

The grenade was a reasonable action, given the presence of at least one weapon within the room.

Reasonable, hell! It was bloody stupid, that's what it was! He looked at the man. "Is that your idea of quiet?"

The man grinned and shrugged. Sean motioned. Rush the room.

They stumbled forward, firing their weapons. "*Allahu akbar!*"

Hamid forced himself over. He still held his gun. Two men rushed into the room, weapons at the ready, their eyes searching. He reacted more on instinct than anything else. His gun coughed four times, two shots in each man. They fell to the ground. His ears rang from the explosion. Bullets tore into the room, shattering the windows. Almost everything had been knocked down or blown over, but there was no shrapnel, no burning.

Percussion grenade. They were lucky they hadn't ruptured the oxygen lines in the walls. The whole floor might have gone up.

He fired two more shots through the doorway, not aiming at anything in particular. Curses and return rounds answered him. Pushing himself to his feet, he vaulted over the hospital bed, stumbling on the corpse of the late Dr. Kaufman, and tumbling to the other side in a tangle of arms and legs. He pushed the body off himself and fired again, then glanced at the unmoving forms of Isabel and Jon.

Were they dead? If so, his only link to the scroll was lost. He wiped his eyes and shot again through the doorway.

Kahil led his men into the lobby of the hospital, nodding toward the security desk as they entered. He brought the arrest warrant to them with a brief explanation and directed two of his men to stay at either end near the entrances to keep watch.

Every phone line at the front desk flashed on, and the security guard went pale. Glass fragments showered the sidewalk outside. Kahil glanced at Bahar. They broke for the stairs.

Jon lay face down on the floor. Agony seared his face and sides. His ears rang. Except for the pain, he wouldn't have been certain he was alive. He opened his eyes, unsure where he was. The floor stared up at him, glittering in the light. A moment later, he realized tiny glass fragments surrounded him. Whatever had happened had shattered the cabinets in the room.

He groaned and tried to move, but succeeded only in turning over onto his side. He glanced across the room, his throat constricting in panic. Isabel lay crumpled to the ground behind the door, her hair splayed around her head like she was sleeping. She didn't move.

Oh, God. Was she dead?

He had to know. He tried to call to her, but couldn't hear his voice.

The bed beside him shook. He looked up at it. Stephen was gone. But where? What happened to the man with the gun?

Kahil and his men reached the seventh floor. He glanced quickly through the window in the door. The sound of gunfire echoed through the door into the stairwell. There were men behind the nurses' station taking aim at a room across the hall. He counted three of them. From the way they ducked, it looked as though someone was firing at them from inside the room.

He said to Bahar, "Take the stairwell on the other side." The sergeant nodded and raced back down the steps with two of the men. Kahil opened the door, crept outside, and crouched in one of the doorways. A gasp from inside the room brought him up short. He looked at the patients in their beds, staring at him wide-eyed. He put his finger to his lips. "Stay in your rooms. Get behind your beds if you can."

He motioned for the two police officers to take up positions on either side of the hall. With each providing cover, they crept from room to room closer to the firefight.

Hamid ducked behind the bed and checked his clip. He was out. He set the gun down and felt around for another clip in his pocket. Nothing. Two more shots rang into the room.

Now what? He peered around the corner of the bed. He didn't see the gunmen, but he soon would if he didn't do something quick. His eye caught something dark on the floor. It was the gun of one of the dead men. Just out of reach. He could dive for it. Or…

He slipped his prosthesis off and held it at the ready. Dropping to the ground, he flung the arm out, the plastic hand landing on the weapon. He willed the fingers to close around it as he dragged it towards himself.

Voices outside. They were coming.

He dropped the arm and picked up the gun. A figure appeared in the doorway. He shot. The man collapsed to the ground.

Jon watched in disbelief as a prosthetic hand reached out from nowhere and grabbed one of the guns from the floor, dragging it back behind the bed. A moment later, a man leaped into the room, only to fall to the ground from a very loud gunshot. So that's where the assassin hid. He looked over the gunman's body at Isabel. She moved her arm.

Relief flooded through him. Thank God, she was alive.

She was also perilously close to the doorway. He pushed himself up and crawled forward. Bullets lanced the wall above her.

He stopped. How could he get to her?

Kahil watched as Bahar pushed open the door at the far side and stepped into the hall. Bahar pressed his back to the wall and waved the other two policemen onto the floor. He nodded once at Kahil, who rose from his crouch.

"Police! Freeze!"

Kahil shot a glance down the hall. The order came from the young man he'd met earlier, the one so eager to get into the fray. He stood open and exposed. Fool!

One of the gunmen behind the nurses' station squeezed off a round. Kahil fired, dropping the gunman with a shot to the back of his head. Too late. The cop was dead.

Bits of plaster and tile shattered from the ceiling above Kahil's head. They were firing back at him. He ducked into the room. Something round and small bounded down the hallway.

"Grenade!"

His chest tightened as one of his men dove for the grenade, smothering it. The explosion killed the man instantly.

Sean watched as one of the Kurds tossed a grenade at the policemen. The cop jumped on it, absorbing the blast with his body. Bloody hell! He stared at the two Kurds, unnerved by the wild ferocity in their eyes. He knew that look. He'd seen it on his brother Daniel in Belfast, just before he died.

The operation was over. He had to get out of here. Police and Gendarmerie would swarm the hospital any minute now. He glanced at the third aisle that T-junctioned at the nurses' station, surprised no one had thought to come that way. He put his weapon into the back of his pants and retreated down the hall, hoping for an exit.

A second explosion shook the building. Jon covered his head as more debris rained down on him. Then silence. He moved toward Isabel, but froze when the assassin came around the bed. The assassin didn't look at him. He just walked to the door and peeked into the hallway.

Jon leaped for Isabel. She stared at him wide-eyed, shaking. He helped her to her feet, tugging when she resisted him, and pulled her away from the door, over to the window.

More gunfire erupted in the hall. Jon glanced back. The assassin ducked back into the room and fired through the door.

Jon peered out the window. The roof of the lower building lay a tantalizing twelve feet below them.

"Come on," he whispered. "We can make it!"

"No, no, no, no!"

He lifted her into an embrace and started pulling her out the window. "Climb on my back."

"No! Jonnie!"

She twisted onto his back. His legs went out the window, finding no purchase on the stone below. He started lowering himself down. His arms burned. His fingers started slipping.

"Izzy," he breathed, "climb down."

"Jonnie!"

"I can't hold us." He pushed his arm back onto the window. A cry behind him, and the weight on his back vanished. "Izzy!" He twisted to see her sprawled on the roof of the building. He lost his grip.

And hit the rooftop below.

Pain shot up his legs. He collapsed and rolled onto his back, gritting his teeth. He stared up at the window of the hospital room. Isabel's face appeared above his, her eyes filled with concern.

"I'm alright," he said. "You?"

She nodded.

"Let's get out of here."

The Lost Scrolls

CHAPTER
16

Hamid ducked his head back into the hospital room. Two men at the nurses' station took turns firing at the policemen on either side of the hall. There was no way out for him.

He'd emptied his clip in the last exchange of gunfire. He dropped the gun and picked up the second weapon, peering again at the nurses' station. If he came out now, they'd kill him. If he waited, the cops would take out the gunmen, but they'd arrest him for sure.

He was trapped, unless he had a hostage…

He looked around the room, and saw no one. He slipped behind the heavy privacy drapes around the hospital beds. No one was there. He glanced at the window. The glass was shattered from the gunfire.

Surely not! This was the seventh floor. He stepped to the window and looked down. The roof of the lower building lay only twelve feet below him. He shook his head.

Hamid glanced back at the door and made his decision. If they could do it, so could he. He dropped the gun where he'd found it and picked up his own, putting it back into its holster. Let the cops think these other two were to blame. He'd stay out of it. He retrieved his prosthesis and climbed onto the window ledge.

The sun had set, and the wind blew cool into his face, buffeting his body with heavy gusts. On the street below, dozens of police cars and fire engines converged on the hospital, their blue and red lights flickered against the building. He took a deep breath.

And jumped.

In less than a second he rolled on the roof of the lower building, hot fire shooting through his legs. He picked himself up and stumbled forward, moving far more slowly than he wished. Each step was agony, like tiny knives shooting up his calves and knees. He clenched his teeth and tried to get his bearings.

On the far side of the building, a tree reached the top of the roof. He saw no other way down. Shouts and gunfire pierced the growing darkness above him. The battle was not going well for anyone. A large crowd had gathered near the circular fountain below, pointing and staring at the room he'd just left. He wondered if any had seen him leap from the window. Did they have any idea what part he'd played in the conflict? Someone might be waiting for him when he got down. On the other hand, they might have been waiting for the professor and the archaeologist's sister, too. Catching up to them might not be as problematic as he feared. Either way, the tree was his best hope now. He shook his head and made a run for it.

At the far edge of the roof he stopped, frustration building in his chest. The tree stood well over seven feet away. Several of the top branches were freshly broken. They'd definitely come this way and jumped. It was a bold move, even with two hands. He must reconsider the capacities of this Dr. Munro. The man showed himself to be more of a challenge than Hamid gave him credit for.

No matter. He took a few paces back, then ran full speed and leaped from the ledge, a yell escaping his throat even as he crashed headlong into the pine. The tree pitched forward and swung back. His hand fought for purchase in its branches.

For a moment, he thought he was going to fall. At the last second, his fingers closed about a firm branch, the heavy tar gripping him almost as greedily as he clung to it. He gasped, and with a throaty groan pulled himself onto the trunk.

He hung there and panted for almost a minute before he came to himself and started the arduous climb down.

For this alone, I promise you, Hamid, he thought. *When we catch them, there will be blood.*

Sean took the steps two at a time. At the fifth floor, he left the stairwell, rushed down the corridor to the other set of stairs, and kept running. Two more floors and he changed stairs again, putting as much horizontal distance as vertical between himself and the firefight. By the time this was over, the police would be calling it a terrorist attack by the separatist Kurds. He had little doubt the Kurds would die in the gun battle, willingly or not. But even if they were captured, they wouldn't be believed no matter what story they told. The Turkish authorities would reject anything that might throw suspicion from the most obvious motive. This was one reason why he'd chosen the Kurds in the first place. That and they were more ready than most to stage an assault on a Turkish hospital.

When he reached the bottom floor, hospital security anxiously escorted patients and visitors from the building. Sean was whisked toward the front door as a whole contingent of police in full riot gear converged on the stairs.

Blaze of glory, he thought. *Just like Daniel. Oh, to die for a cause.* He thrust his way through the open front door into the night air. Police with lighted batons were directing the flow of foot traffic. Several medical personnel asked questions of each person, assessing their condition—whether they were hurt, traumatized, or among the hundreds evacuated who were sick. Ambulances from the other hospitals in Ankara lined the sidewalk, whisking patients away to facilities with less violence tonight. Across the street several news crews focused their cameras on the building and the front entrance. He turned his face away, pretending interest in the flashes of light and pops of automatic weapons fire shattering the night seven stories above him.

"Are you alright, sir?"

A hand touched his shoulder. Reflexively he grabbed it, prepared to snap the wrist, and drop the offender. He stopped himself just in time. An EMT stood there, concern etched across his face, his eyes just beginning to register confusion at Sean's reaction. Anyone with training would've recognized his defense, would've started asking questions. Thank God it wasn't a cop.

"I'm fine," he said, patting the man's hand. "I just need to get out of here."

There was no lie in that. The EMT nodded and looked ahead to the next refugee, and Sean hastened his pace away from the building. Once on the sidewalk, he navigated through the crowd to where he'd parked the van in shadows across the street. There was a slim chance they'd identified the vehicle, but it was unlikely. The security cameras on the side entrances only had a visual range of about ten meters, or so he'd estimated from their angle. He'd parked well over fifteen meters away. Still, better safe than sorry. He entered through the passenger's door, away from the camera's view.

He fired up the van and crept away, deliberately driving slowly to not attract attention. He was just another driver gawking at the scene, not involved in any conceivable way. As soon as possible, he steered into Mevlana Boulevard in front of the hospital and disappeared.

Several blocks away, he parked and yanked a rag from the glove box. Beginning with his fingerprints on the steering wheel and door handles, he thoroughly wiped every surface inside the vehicle. Ten minutes later, he grabbed a screwdriver and popped the vehicle identification number from under the windshield. The harder the van was to trace, the more time he had to disappear.

Naturally, the VIN's removal would immediately prompt them to pull it from the engine block and list the van as probably stolen. But it would hamper the investigation nonetheless, and that bought him time.

Satisfied he'd done all he could, he wiped his keys, locked them in the van, and walked away, pulling out his smartphone as he did so.

Brian Laherty was due to arrive first, though it was possible Michael and even William were in town by now. There'd been a minor hiccup getting the box he'd ordered. Something to do with the other boxes on order. He wondered if they'd been able to track down the other interested parties. What were the odds he'd just eliminated some of the competition already?

SM: More people came to dinner than expected. RU ready?

He pressed send and waited. He'd love to simply phone it in, but there was always the chance one of them wasn't able to speak freely, and the texting was encrypted, whereas the phones were not.

A moment later, a reply flashed onto his screen.

BL: All is ready. Extra plates 4 2.

He smiled and typed a reply.

SM: Met 1 already. Can't make it.

BL: Heard. 2 more coming.

He frowned. *SM: Who?*

BL: Father Philip Bellamy and Brother Demetri Antonescu.

He stopped and stared at the message. He was tempted to place the call anyway, if only to ask, "Are you sure?" He didn't have to, though. Brian wouldn't have said it unless the intel was good.

He didn't know the first name, but the second yearned for recognition. He pressed his palm against his forehead. Who was this guy? Why did he sound so bloody familiar?

SM: Haven't met PB. Unsure about DA.

BL: DA is a Major pain.

Major? Major Demetri Antonescu? Understanding dawned.

"Oh, bloody hell," he said aloud. Major Demetri Antonescu. Former agent of the Romanian secret police. And now a brother. Brian must mean a monk. So that's what happened to him. The old soldier got religion after Ceauşescu got the firing squad. Who could blame him? He was at just as much risk himself as his boss had been. All these years hiding out in a monastery. Only to show up now? It still didn't make sense.

Regardless, Antonescu was no one to tangle with willingly. He was as cunning as they came. And if he caught wind of them on the hunt, Sean had little doubt who'd come out on top. They'd have to take steps to avoid him.

This priest on the other hand....

SM: *Send info on PB. We'll prep for dinner at 8 pm. Let the caterers know.*

BL: *Done. See attached file.*

Sean downloaded the attachment and started reading as he crossed the street. The padre's hotel wasn't far. He could be there in fifteen minutes if he hustled.

CHAPTER
17

"No, Jonnie!"

He stopped and stared. Isabel pulled back from him, moving away from the police.

"We can't go to them."

He glanced at the flashing lights of the police and emergency vehicles assembling on the far sidewalk. He and Izzy could receive medical attention there. They needed to tell the authorities what had happened. About the assassin who killed Stephen.

If nothing else they could put this all behind and go home. This trip was already more than he'd anticipated. Getting shot at had never occurred to him.

His hands shook. "We have to tell them what happened."

"No." She was pleading with him. Was this shock? Was she unable to accept what had happened? Stephen's death? He could barely accept it himself.

"Please," she insisted. "You don't know what he found. He trusted you! You can't let them have it." Her voice broke and the tears flowed.

He came over and put his hands on her cheeks, holding her gaze to his own. "Isabel."

"You can't, Jonnie. You just can't!"

He pulled her head into his chest, letting her wring out her grief on his shoulder. This was obviously too much for her. For him. But what else could he do? He shook his head, pleading silently with the heavens. He needed to think!

"Alright," he said. "Let's go back to the hotel. We can clean ourselves up and sort this out there."

Isabel sniffled.

"Come on. We'll catch a cab and get out of here."

Clinging to him, she turned and walked with him away from the lights.

Philip slid the key through the lock in his hotel room door and stepped inside. He'd spent the rest of the afternoon and early part of the evening with Demetri discussing their options for retrieving the scroll. The man's insistence on submitting everything to God in prayer was nobly spiritual and damnably infuriating. What was worse, he and Philip wound up arguing for the better part of an hour over what manner of prayer was appropriate. Demetri's experience with the Orthodox rites had done little to prepare him for what he termed Philip's "casual and irreverent" practices.

Finally, he convinced the monk to let him return so he could contact his superiors about Demetri's offer. He shook his head. If it weren't for the former agent's obvious operational skills, he'd seriously think about dropping the monk altogether. Preferably in a river somewhere.

He flipped on the light switch—and reached for his gun.

"Don't." The stranger sitting in Philip's lounge chair aimed a Beretta at his chest.

Philip closed his mouth against the invective forming on his lips. Twice in one day, he'd been bested. The Church really should rethink their strategy of sending him on this mission. He'd been out of the game far too long.

He bit his lip and said, "Good evening. To what do I owe the pleasure?"

The man in the chair smiled. He looked English. "First things first."

Okay, thought Philip, *not English. Irish. Maybe Scottish.*

"Would you like a drink?" He approached the minibar and opened it.

"Two fingers, please."

"Of what? Scotch?"

"No. Two fingers on your weapon. Pull it out and toss it on the bed, yeah?"

Philip smiled and complied.

"That's a good lad," the man said.

"Don't quite know why I carry it. Hasn't done me a bit of good all day."

"Then I assume you've met our friend, Demetri."

"Partner of yours?" Philip poured himself a generous helping of whiskey. He reached for the ice.

"Competition."

"Ah." He took a quick shot of liquid fire, letting it burn his throat and warm his belly on the way down. "Would you like some?" he said, picking up a second glass.

"No thanks. Never touch the stuff."

"Forgive me. I mistook you for an Irishman."

"Not in a long time. But thanks for the insult to me kith and kin just the same. 'Twill make it easier when I put a bullet through your head."

Philip almost laughed. "Wow. You do take your work seriously."

The man in the chair didn't smile. "When as much money as I am about to be paid is on the line, you bet your bloody arse I do."

The priest swallowed the last of his Scotch. "Okay." He took a seat in a chair across from the bed. His weapon lay about two feet away from him, though he doubted he could reach it in time unless this man made a mistake. It was unlikely. "You've made your point. Now what exactly do I have to do to keep you from killing me?"

"I'm relieved we can discuss terms. Killing a priest would weigh heavy on my conscience. There are two things I'll be wanting from you. Number two: go home. Pack your things. Leave the country. Go back to wherever it was you came from."

"Okay. And number one?"

"Tell me everything that Dr. Stephen Kaufman told you."

Philip smiled. "You'd be better off getting that from him."

"And surely I would. But seeing as he's dead, it's a mite hard."

Philip put his head on his hands, wishing now he could pray. Brother Demetri may have been right after all. "How'd he die?"

"I can't rightly say. But given the amount of gunfire in his room tonight, I'm making it's a fair conclusion. What do you think?"

Philip hesitated. There was gunfire at the hospital? Was Demetri backing out on his promise? Finally, he said, "Well, I don't think I'll be able to help you any further."

"And why might that be?"

"His last words were spoken to me in confession. I am a priest. I'm sure you can appreciate how sacred that trust is."

"A sacred trust, is it?" The man opened a drawer in the end table and pulled out a familiar vial of liquid. "Is this what you call a sacred trust? Thiopental?" He put his hand in the drawer again and pulled out a second item. A syringe. "I'm thinking, Father, you've got your own confession to make."

At that moment, the hotel room door burst open. Three men piled into the room. Philip cried out and leaped for his gun. His fingers closed around the grip even as a heavy weight fell upon his back and arm, pinning him to the bed.

The last thoughts to pass through his conscious mind were how right Brother Demetri had been, and to wonder whether the old monk was praying for him. Then all went black.

Lieutenant Kahil stepped into the hospital room where Dr. Stephen Kaufman had been recuperating until recently. He glanced at the bullet holes peppering the walls and doorway, and frowned.

All the glass in the room lay shattered on the floor or somewhere out the window—fragmented reminders of the grenade the terrorists had tossed into the room. In the front of the room, closest to the door, three bodies lay face up in a crimson puddle. All had been shot at close range. He turned one over and found more glass fragments beneath his body. So they'd come in after the grenade had been tossed. Might even have been the ones to toss it. So who shot them?

On the other side of the bed, he found Kaufman, a similar wound to his head. Ballistics would confirm whether the same gun had shot them all.

Shell casings littered the floor. He picked up some of them. They were from two different caliber weapons. The first were .38s, matching the two guns on the floor. The second were .40s. He closed his fist around them. Things were starting to make sense.

"Lieutenant Çapanoğlu?" Kahil turned to see Captain Tabak waiting, his frame filling the doorway. Tabak didn't smile. "A word, if you please."

"Sir." He straightened and followed his captain out into the hall.

Tabak faced him, scowling. "Lieutenant, it is my understanding you were sent here to bring in an American professor for questioning."

"Yes, sir."

"And you were to bring him in peacefully, yes?"

"Yes."

"Then tell me why ten men are dead?"

"Sir—"

He grabbed Kahil's shirt and pulled him close. "The director is breathing down my neck. He wants my head on a platter, and I can only imagine what he has in mind for you. One of the men was a decorated police officer. There isn't enough left of him for his wife and children to bury."

Kahil sighed. "Officer Aziz sacrificed his life to save mine and that of his fellow officers and the patients in this hospital. One of the terrorists threw a grenade at us. He jumped on it."

Tabak drew in a deep breath and released him. "How did this happen?"

"Sir, if I may be permitted to finish my investigation, I will make a full and complete report of these events."

"You will make your report to me right now. I cannot begin to impress upon you how delicate this situation is for us. Kurdish terrorists here in Ankara? And we show up with one Gendarmerie and six city police?"

"Captain…." Kahil chose his next words carefully. "I consider it fortunate we were here. We came to question a suspect in an unrelated investigation, and walked into a terrorist operation as it was unfolding. The officers of the Ankara police performed valiantly in their duties, and together we thwarted a major terrorist operation before they could do any real damage. It was God's will that we were here at all."

Tabak's shoulders deflated. "That will do, Kahil. I will pass this on to the director. It should ease his tension somewhat. Well said."

"Thank you, Captain. I've had a good teacher."

Tabak ignored the compliment and said, "Now truthfully, are these events related?"

"Absolutely. This gun battle occurred in Dr. Kaufman's room. It appears that at least two groups were involved. One group, these terrorists." He handed Tabak the .38 shell casing. "The second group was in that room, and apparently well armed." He handed him the .40 caliber casing. Tabak weighed it in his hand, comparing it with the other shell. Kahil continued. "The Kurds attempted to stun the group in the room with a percussion grenade, but did not succeed. The resultant gun battle killed three of their men they sent into the room. I believe they were attempting to retake the room when we interrupted, allowing the group still inside to escape."

Tabak pursed his lips. "Alright. So who was in this second group?"

"According to the guard, Naþit, who must have been shot only moments after I spoke with him, the last person to enter that room was none other than our American professor."

"So," said Tabak, "it seems he is in league with The Rat. And now is at large in our city."

"Perhaps," said Kahil. "I've asked for some men to go to his hotel room and be sure he doesn't get away this time."

Tabak clapped a hand on his shoulder. "Very well. I'll make sure they are sent. Good work."

"Thank you, Captain."

CHAPTER
18

Hamid stepped outside the building and onto the sidewalk. He looked up at the Houston Hotel rising before him, counting the floors. Dr. Munro's room was on the seventh floor. He'd spied out the layout of the rooms on the lower floors. He knew where to look.

A polite bribe at the front desk might have given him the same information, but he was short on cash and had no wish to forewarn his quarry. For all he knew, Munro had already paid someone to watch for him. It's what he'd have done.

He crept around the left of the building, counting rooms. There. The shades were drawn in the window, but slivers of light bled through to the evening sky. They were in. He backed up to the wall and sank into a crouch against it. Pulling out a cigarette, he looked toward the street, then up at the room. From here, he had a perfect view of the front entrance of the hotel and of the room. If they tried to leave, he would see the lights go out. If the police showed up, he could disappear before anyone saw him.

If they decided to stay in the room.... He smiled darkly. He wouldn't put it past the Americans. Her brother was barely dead two hours, but anything was possible—Ms. Kaufman had a striking figure. He lit his cigarette and took a drag. What a way to pass the time: imagining what he would do to her if he were in Dr. Munro's shoes. There was always the distinct possibility he could change her way of thinking—given the right amount of time to persuade her.

As a boy at the Madrassah, he'd seen the imam take a young bride from one of the locals who owed him money. The girl was defiant and rebellious, with dark eyes and raven hair flashing under her veil. She had spat in the imam's face. For such an insult, the man would have cheerfully killed anyone else, but he had something else in mind for this one. He would break her, as a man breaks a horse, taming its wild spirit so it could be ridden without fear. All the students watched for months as he disciplined her with beatings, afterward speaking gently to her, winning her confidence with gifts, and finally becoming in her eyes the object of her affection—and ultimately—desire.

On the other hand, Ms. Isabel Kaufman was no mere girl. She was a woman—an American, even. That she was experienced in the ways of the world went without saying. But the religious constraints of the imam did not bind Hamid. He could employ other such measures as needed to win her affection.

He chuckled to himself and puffed on his cigarette. Breaking her spirit would be a difficult task, one he'd relish, given the chance. He wondered how difficult it would be to engineer such a chance. And why not? He had plenty of time to kill.

Jon sat in the chair by the desk, his elbows propped on his knees, his chin in his hands. He stared off into space—seeing only the gun in that assassin's hand, hearing the mild cough from the silencer, the hole appearing in Stephen's forehead.

Then the explosion.

He covered his eyes with his palms, pressing the images from his mind. On the corner of the desk stood a glass of bourbon from the liquor cabinet. He'd already lifted it to his lips twice now without taking a drink. Something was preventing him from downing the liquid.

He needed to think. He knew that. Alcohol would only cloud his judgment, slow down his faculties. There was too much data. Disconnected variables spun through his mind. His thoughts were a pinball machine with too many silver marbles pinging through a blur of exploding lights and deafening crashes.

One silver marble was in the shower right now.

He turned and looked up when the shower ended. Isabel had been in there for almost an hour now. He doubted it was long enough to wash away the stain of memory. He'd taken the clothes she'd worn from the bed where she'd let them fall, checked the sizes, and then rung the concierge to send up some fresh garments from one of the local shops. It wasn't much, but what else could he do?

He'd already scrubbed as much of the pine tar and dirt as he could from his hands and face and changed himself. He wanted to shower as well, but there were other considerations.

And he didn't want to risk Isabel leaving him alone in the hotel room, going off God knows where.

The door to the bathroom opened. He kept his eyes turned assiduously forward, feeling a strong temptation to look. "I got you some new clothes," he said, tapping the table. "I hope that's okay." His voice sounded flat and dull.

"It's more than okay." Isabel spoke in quiet tones, as though she were far away. "It's very kind."

She bent down and kissed his forehead. "Thank you. For the clothes. For saving me. For trying to save Stephen."

Her face contorted as grief tore her façade. Jon watched her, feeling helpless. He picked up the Scotch and downed it. Thinking hurt. He might be better off with a good night's sleep. Tomorrow he could go home.

He straightened and headed for the bathroom. At the sink, he looked in the mirror, surprised by the scratches covering his face. He hadn't seen them before. A particularly ugly one tore across his cheek. He didn't remember getting it.

Turning on the sink, he filled his hands with water and splashed his face, letting the shock of cold wash through him. A bath would be nice.

"Jonnie?"

"Think there's any hot water left?"

"Jonnie, what are we going to do?"

"I didn't mean that as an accusation. I just thought a bath would be—nice. What did you say?"

She came into the room, dressed in her new clothes. "I said, 'what are we going to do?'"

"Do? I thought I might take a bath. Maybe get some dinner. Get some sleep. I'm sure I can get them to change my flight. Go on stand-by if I have to."

"Flight? You're leaving?"

"Yeah. What else am I supposed to do?"

"I…I need your help."

Help? "You should call the police."

"I can't do that."

"What do you want *me* to do?"

"Help me!"

His control evaporated. "What am I supposed to do? What help do you want from me? Do you know, since I met you again, I've been held at gunpoint? I've been *shot* at. Blown up! I—I jumped out of a building for you!"

"I know." Her calm tone infuriated him.

"Let me tell you something, lady, I am not here to impress you. I may be just some boring professor to you, but I happen to like my life. And I plan to live a little longer, which means not being shot at anymore. So what else do you think you need from me tonight?"

"You're angry."

"Yes! Yes I am! That's—thank you! That's exactly what I am! I am angry! My God!"

"And you think it's my fault?"

"Well, whose fault is it?" He put his hands on the counter, leaned over the sink, and spoke to her reflection. "I didn't come out here for this. I'm not like—like Stephen. I'm just me. Do you understand that? And I very much want to keep me alive."

"Is that all that matters to you?"

"What else is there?"

She said nothing, but stroked his cheek. Her touch lanced his pain. He pulled away. "No! Just stay away from me." She retreated into the corner, watching him. He put his hand to his eyes down, and the words started tumbling out.

"I thought I was going to die," he whispered. "I thought you were going to die. I can't believe he just shot him like that. I've never been so scared."

"Jonnie, he's still out there."

"I know."

"You said he broke into your house?"

He nodded.

"He won't stop."

"We have to go to the police."

"We can't."

He leaned back and looked at her. "Why not?"

"Jonnie, please. Did Stephen tell you nothing?"

"We never spoke until—" his eyes grew wide. "The email!"

CHAPTER
19

Hamid crushed out his third cigarette and frowned. His back hurt and his legs cramped, falling asleep on the pavement. About five minutes ago, he'd spotted a rat scurrying toward the dumpsters near the back. And to top it all off, a light, misting rain had begun to fall.

The thought of waiting outside the hotel all night lost its appeal. To his right, a police cruiser crept by. He stiffened and shrank back against the fence, holding his position until the cruiser passed. He let out his breath. Walking around in the open was equally unattractive.

Something scraped and scurried beside the wooden crate on his left. Without looking, he knew the rat had returned from its foray in the dumpster. He slipped his hand onto the knife he wore by his ankle, feeling the blade come free of its sheath, and turned his head slowly. The bedraggled creature stood on its hind legs and sniffed the air. He flipped the knife in his left hand, holding the tip between his fingers. With a quick flick, the blade spun through the air, impaling the creature where it stood.

Rats. He shuddered. He wasn't that hungry, not anymore. He hadn't been since the two years after he'd left the Madrassah. After the explosion, when he had no place to turn, the rats of Islamabad fed him when no one else would. When the imam turned him out, and his father refused to let him come home, not even Allah cared what happened to him.

None of it was his fault. The explosion that cost him his hand was an accident, nothing more. But it meant he was good now for only one thing, and since he refused to strap on a vest and become a *shaheed*, a martyr, he wasn't even good enough for that.

After two years of living on the rats, he decided there was no God, and therefore no morality but what he chose for himself. He became a thief until the age of seventeen. They'd only caught him once, and removed what remained of his right hand. Then a second accident turned his fortunes once more— only this time decidedly better.

The man wasn't supposed to come home that early. Hamid ought to have had plenty of time to plunder his belongings and make his escape. But the lights came on and the man walked in, and what else could he do? What other choice did he have?

At first, he'd stayed far out of public view, so certain the police would descend upon him and drag him away. He watched the man's house for two weeks after he'd killed him. Gradually, he realized they were not looking for him. The man was dead, and no one cared. He never even learned his name.

There was no God, and there was no justice. But there was money to be made. Learning to kill was in some ways even easier than learning to steal, and in less than a year, he'd left the rats behind. He had money in the bank, and false papers that allowed him to travel anywhere.

Someday, he'd promised himself, someday he'd return to the madrassah and show the imam just how useful a one-handed assassin could be. But for now, living well was its own revenge.

This didn't explain why he was spending the night in the alleyway, getting soaked in the rain. He shook free the water clinging to his hair and looked again at the window.

The lights were out.

He started, then rose to his feet, checking the street once more. Either they'd gone to sleep, or they were on the move again. He retrieved his knife, wiping the blood on his trousers, and stole up to the entrance, looking both ways before slipping around the corner. At least he was moving again.

Jon cursed himself for letting his phone's battery die. It was still charging, but the service around here was spotty as it was. The only solution was to look for an internet café.

He glanced behind as they entered the café. The concierge from the hotel told him it was one of two internet cafés within walking distance. The café carried itself as an upscale establishment, offering Starbuck's coffee, sandwiches, and free computer access in a dimly lit room of muted earth tones and glowing neon lights. The other café was near the American embassy. He'd wanted to go there, but Isabel insisted they avoid any place remotely official.

The restaurant wasn't overly crowded, and as they pushed their way to the back, he overheard some Western businessmen discussing the assault on the hospital that evening. He went pale and hustled past, cursing himself for not bringing his laptop. He honestly hadn't thought he'd need it. The hotel had dial-up internet, but it was of little use with no computer available. Even the computers in the business center had been occupied. He had little patience for dial-up as it was.

Toward the back of the restaurant, they found an available PC running Windows 98. It wasn't what he'd hoped for, but it would do. He logged on and found his unread mail on the university's server.

"Here it is." Isabel crowded next to him.

He smiled weakly at her and read, "Jonathan, I'm so sorry to bring you in on this, but I have no time and no one else I can trust. You've always told the truth, and I know you're an honest man. I need an honest man to help me now. I have found the *Domo tou Bibliou*. I realize you will be skeptical. In fact, I am counting on it.

"I wish to bring the scroll to you, to let you validate it. I will accept your honest judgment in this matter, I assure you.

"Nevertheless, circumstances beyond my control have prevented me from fulfilling this desire until now. Jonathan, the *Domo tou Bibliou* is real. As such, you can imagine the interest this find has generated—and I fear my life is in danger. If you do not hear from me in two days, know that I am probably dead. Take the key I am sending you to Isabel. She will lead you to the crypt. I have left you instructions there. I realize this is elaborate, but I beg your indulgence. I plead for it. Together we must ensure this treasure does not fall into the wrong hands. Your friend, Stephen.

"P.S, please forgive me for what I had to do. I hope you'll understand. Stephen."

Isabel tapped his arm excitedly. She faced him, her eyes pleading. "Do you see? He really found it. This thing. That's why he wants me to take you to it. He knew you would not believe him—but you would believe when you saw it."

Jon shook his head and leaned away from her. He logged off and led her over to the table where he'd ordered food. He had to explain this carefully. "Izzy, even if Stephen found what he believes is the *Domo tou Bibliou*, there's still no way to prove it."

"I don't understand you. I've been there! I've been inside it!"

He raised a cautionary hand. "You've been somewhere. There are a great many churches buried in the sands of this land. But to say the church you found is, in fact, the *Domo tou Bibliou*—even if the scroll were there—how could you prove it is what it's claimed to be?"

"What scroll?"

He furrowed his brow. "The scroll! The one the legend is all about. Don't you know the legend?"

"The *Domo* is a place."

"Yes. It's Greek. It means, 'home of the book.' The scroll is what it's all about, Izzy, not the church it's in."

"What is this scroll?"

"Assuming it exists—and I'm not saying either way—the scroll is a list of books. A canon of New Testament literature. Some say the Apostle Paul talked about it in his last letter, Second Timothy. He tells Timothy to bring him the scrolls he left with Carpus in Troas, and 'especially the parchments.' Supposedly, Paul collected the books he regarded as inspired, and recorded their names on this scroll. Later, his followers hid the books to protect them during the various persecutions, and they buried the scroll with a priest in a church."

"I don't understand. You said it was a canon. We have the New Testament."

"We have the canon the Church assembled at the Council of Carthage, five hundred years later. But more importantly, we don't have the autographs, the original manuscripts of the New Testament."

"I never gave much thought to the Bible. Stephen saw it as a curious antiquity, but that is all. Finding these books would be valuable, no? I mean, it would tell us whether or not the New Testament is reliable."

"You catch on quick. Finding the autographs—being able to date them and compare them to the copies—would prove beyond a doubt the accuracy of the New Testament. But it isn't necessary, Izzy."

"I don't understand. Isn't there a lot of doubt about the New Testament?"

He smiled, warming up to this. This was precisely the sort of thing at which he excelled. He loved to regale his Sunday school class with this sort of evidence. "Actually, the New Testament is the best collection of ancient manuscripts in existence. The rest of ancient literature pales in comparison."

"Surely not."

He smiled and stretched. "Ever read Plato?"

"Maybe once. In college."

"Plato wrote his Tetralogies somewhere in the mid fourth to fifth century B.C. The earliest copy we have dates to A.D. 900. That's about a twelve hundred year difference. We have seven of these ancient manuscripts. How about Aristotle?"

She shook her head.

"He wrote around the fourth century also. There are around fifty extant copies of Aristotle, dating to A.D. 1100. Fourteen hundred years later. Sophocles wrote in the fifth century B.C. We have almost two hundred surviving manuscripts, dating about fourteen hundred years later. But towering above them all is Homer. Six hundred and forty three copies. He wrote around 900 B.C. We have fragments dating back to 400 B.C. Only five hundred years between the writing and our earliest copy. That's quite extraordinary, actually. The rest of ancient literature rests on a handful of copies or fragments removed some thousand years or so from their date of authorship. So how well do you think the New Testament has fared?"

"I don't know."

"Take a guess."

"I wouldn't know where to begin. Maybe a thousand?"

"A thousand. Okay. The New Testament was written in the first century. How old do you think our copies are?"

"A few hundred years, perhaps. Maybe fifth or sixth century."

"Fair enough. A little better than Homer, yes?"

She nodded.

"Are you ready for this? At last count, there are somewhere over twenty-four thousand fragments or *whole* manuscripts still in existence today. The earliest of these dates between A.D. 125 and 150."

Isabel blinked, her mouth slightly open. "Twenty-four thousand?"

"Twenty four thousand. Possibly within twenty-five years of the New Testament. Old enough to have been hand-copied from the original."

She shook her head. "There should be no doubt."

"No, there shouldn't. There's more, though. The book of Acts mentions Gamaliel. He was one of Saint Paul's teachers. He is believed to have authored a sophisticated parody of Matthew's Gospel."

"Okay."

"The scholars of the Jesus Seminar insist Matthew compiled his book around A.D. 85 or 90. They don't believe he actually wrote it. This is how they account for the development of such a high Christology in the book. You see, all this is based on the presupposition that the divinity of Christ is an invention of His religious followers—not something Christ Himself claimed. But then comes Gamaliel with his parody. Now, Gamaliel died around A.D. 70."

"If he wrote a parody, then Matthew cannot be as new as they claim."

"Precisely. Also, the fact Gamaliel wrote a parody demands that Matthew had extensive circulation. He was well known. Otherwise, no one would have gotten the joke. It must have been written earlier. And the closer we get to A.D. 33, the more accurate the Gospels must be. They are what they say they are, Isabel. They are eyewitness accounts. You must either believe them or call them liars. In which case, you must then account for their willingness to die for their claims."

She was silent, a frown etching a line into her forehead. Jon sipped his coffee. Then he said, "There's just one thing that doesn't make sense."

"What?"

"Why Michaels would be so interested in the *Domo tou Bibliou*. He was a member of the Jesus Seminar himself. Even wrote a paper supporting it. If the autographs were found, it would shatter his life's work."

"Or confirm it."

"It's possible. But highly unlikely. The books are just too well documented."

"There's another reason."

"Hmm?"

"The money."

"Michaels? I don't think so. He has too much integrity."

"Money erodes integrity rather quickly, Jonnie."

"Not everyone is like Stephen."

"But why wouldn't you sell it? Surely, a scroll like this would be worth a fortune. Stephen was trying to protect it, Jonnie. That's why he was killed. That's why you must help me."

"Izzy...."

"Men have given their lives to guard this scroll. My brother is no different than they. To honor his memory, you must help me."

"Izzy," he said, "I have no wish to honor his memory."

She looked away, not letting him see her face. Finally, she turned back. "Then do it for me."

"Better yet," said a man coming up behind them, "do it for me."

Isabel stifled a cry, and Jon stared as the assassin from the hospital sat down next to them, pressing his gun into Isabel's side.

CHAPTER
20

"Oh my God!" Izzy cried.

The man shook his head, hissing. "Shh! Keep your voice down."

"Wha-what do you want?" Jon stammered.

"I'll have what you're having. It looks good. Maybe a sandwich as well. It's been a long night."

Jon stared incredulously. The man smiled. "When the waitress comes, place the order. Draw no attention to yourself."

Izzy's face was ashen. Her eyes were wide with fright. Jon glanced furtively around, feeling a cold knot tighten in his stomach. His fingers trembled, and he clenched them to make them stop.

"You should try the decaf." The assassin nodded toward him.

"Who are you?"

"Apologies. I forget we have not been properly introduced. I am Hamid Al-Assini."

"You killed my brother, you murderous bas—" Isabel began to cry.

"He was already dead," Hamid said, "Shh. Here she comes. Place the order."

The waitress came to their table. "May I help you?" She stared curiously at Isabel, who was crying uncontrollably.

Hamid nodded once to Jon, who said, "We'd like a-another cup of coffee, f-for my friend, here. A-and a sandwich."

She wrote on her notepad. "What kind?"

He looked at her blankly. "Huh?"

"Roast beef, please," said Hamid. "With provolone cheese, mayonnaise, a tomato, and a side of horseradish."

"Is she okay?"

"Oh, she just got some bad news. Her brother died tonight. Very tragic."

"Oh, you poor dear. I am sorry for you."

"Yes. We'd like that to go, please."

"Right away, sir."

As soon as she left, Hamid lost his smile. "Now. You will do exactly as I say, or I kill her right here."

Jon swallowed. "You don't want to do that."

"I don't?"

"No. She's the only one who knows where it is."

"I see. Then perhaps I shall kill you."

"I'm the only one who knows *what* it is."

"Ah. Then you leave me no choice. I won't kill either one of you."

Both Isabel and Jon gasped with relief. Jon hadn't realized he was holding his breath.

"However, if you don't take me to it this night, I shall have no more use for either of you. And again, you will leave me no choice. Oh, thank you," he said as the waitress brought his food. "Let's go," he said when she left.

There was an Audi A3 parked a block down the street. Hamid forced them inside one at a time, himself climbing into the backseat while keeping the gun trained on at least one of them at all times, leaving them no chance to escape.

Once inside he asked for his coffee and sandwich. "And turn the rear view mirror down."

"I won't be able to see."

"Use your side mirrors. Do not look back at me."

Jon glanced once in the mirror before turning it down. He cast an eye at Isabel, who returned his worry. "You can't eat and hold the gun at the same time, can you?"

"You'd be amazed what I can do. Pull into the street and start moving."

"Where are we going?"

"Perhaps Ms. Kaufman would be kind enough to give us directions. What kind of coffee is this?"

"Hazelnut."

"You Americans. Always changing the nature of things, calling it progress." He opened the window and tossed the cup out, leaving it to splash upon the pavement. "Directions, please!"

"S-south! Take the road to Konya. Ankara-Aksaray Yolu."

Jon nodded, assuming the words meant something. He wished he'd studied Turkish.

"Konya?" said Hamid. He leaned back and muttered something untranslatable.

"What's Konya?" said Jon.

"It's a city. Just a little more than a hundred sixty kilometers from here. About a two hour drive. Go the speed limit. I do not wish to be stopped."

Jon nodded and followed the signs to the thoroughfare. Within minutes, they were heading out of Ankara. The lights of the city dwindled to a pale, amber glow behind them, and soon the only light remaining came from the occasional truck passing them on the four-lane highway.

After several long minutes passed in silence, Isabel whispered, "Jonnie? I'm sorry."

"It's not your fault, Izzy. But for what it's worth, I am, too."

They said nothing else on the long drive south.

As they approached a large lake called Tuz Gölü, Isabel instructed him to turn south. After another thirty-seven kilometers, they turned left onto a narrow road winding up into the hills. Now there was no traffic to speak of, but a pale light began to gather on the horizon ahead of them.

"How much further?" said Hamid.

"Not far," she said, "I think."

"You think?" He poked his head into the front seat, grazing her hair with the muzzle of his gun.

"Stop that." Jon glared at him.

"What? This?" Hamid pressed the gun against her. Isabel flinched. Hamid smiled. "You see, it is important the woman think clearly."

"Well, how's she supposed to do that with a gun to her head? Just put it away, and leave her alone!"

"Fear has a way of quieting distractions. Clearing the mind." His voice took on a professorial quality. "It works like this." He shifted to Jon's side and pressed the gun against his head. Jon shrank beneath it. "You see?" Hamid whispered. "Now I suggest you stop giving orders, and shut up and drive." He drifted into the shadows of the back seat. Jon swallowed hard.

"There!" Isabel said. "Turn right up this road. The dig is not far."

Jon turned right.

"You see?" said Hamid, the paternal tone in his voice again. "Works every time."

After a few hundred meters, the Audi crested a ridge. Below them, still shrouded in darkness, yawned a large pit, looking very much like a gravel quarry. Jon parked the car and climbed out, joined moments later by Isabel and Hamid. Hamid handed him a flashlight from the Audi's trunk. Jon took it from him, glancing down at it a moment before realizing he'd missed the chance to disarm him while he'd been at the trunk. He cursed himself for not paying more attention.

Hamid motioned them forward. At the edge of the pit stood an aluminum ladder descending some fifteen feet to the ground below. Isabel went down first, followed a moment later by Jon, and then the assassin, once they were a comfortable distance away. Jon watched him descend, startled by how quickly he came down. He wondered if he could make it up again just as swiftly.

At the base of the pit stood a large stone structure with clearly visible doors and windows, now standing exposed to the air. The roof of the building curved upward in a smooth dome, and judging from the depth of the pit, would have appeared as a smooth mound from the ground. A breach in the roof showed where thieves in ages past had broken through, looting for treasure. No doubt, this was where the archaeological team first entered the church, determining where to dig from the layout inside. Only the front of the structure had been excavated. A large column, called a stylos, rose up in the courtyard. Nearby, another area had been dug up, revealing a keyhole-shaped baptistery. Overall, the building was about ten meters wide and about half again as long. The front entrance stood hidden in dark shadows.

Jon turned on the flashlight and reached for Isabel. Together they ducked through the doorway.

Sean lay with his team on a sandy hillock about two hundred meters from the site. He took the night vision binoculars from Michael and aimed them toward the chapel. Even with the night vision, the images were hard to see. Pale green shapes moved further into the darker green rock and disappeared.

"They're in," he said. Mike nodded and rose to his feet. He raced down the hill, a trail of dust roiling in the air behind him.

"Look at that dust. That kid's the frickin' Lone Ranger," muttered Brian.

Sean gave him a confused look.

"Obscure sub-reference. Cloud of dust, sound of hooves? Sorry, too much time in America."

Sean rolled his eyes and turned back to the hill. William said, "He starts yelling 'Hi-ho Silver,' I'll shoot him myself."

"It'd be your last move," growled Sean. "Mikey's me brother's son."

"Was it you that trained him, then?"

"Aye."

"Didja not teach him about dust trails?"

"Dust can't be helped. Mikey's as good as they come."

"Yeah? See if you say that when they come out and see his trail."

"They won't. Look, he's already there." Sean ignored the fact that neither William nor Brian had the advantage of his binoculars. He watched as Michael slid beneath the rear bumper, attaching the magnetic tracking device to the Audi's frame, then rolled free and scampered away. He loped the long way around the chapel and returned to their position just as the sun rose.

"You raised up too much dust," William groused.

He raised an eyebrow. "Aye? An' imagine the landslide if we'd rolled your fat arse down the hill. Why are we tracking them?" he asked Sean.

"The scroll's been moved, otherwise we'd have it now, wouldn't we? They're the only ones what know where it is. We follow them. They lead us right to it."

* *   *

"Incredible," Jon breathed. He panned the light across the ceiling, walls, and floor. The floor was a tile mosaic detailing the return of Christ on the clouds. A large sword extended from his mouth. Angels surrounded him, with all the disciples below watching and kneeling in worship. Princes, kings, and commoners recoiled in fear.

Hamid coughed and spat on the floor.

"Stephen was very—protective—of the next room," Izzy said. "The crypt is in there."

Inside they found a stone sarcophagus built onto the floor. The lid lay ajar across the top of it. Jon stepped around to the front. He pulled on the lid, then looked to Hamid. "You want to give me a hand with this?"

Hamid turned to Isabel. "You heard him."

Isabel pressed her lips together and stepped over to the crypt. Jon smiled apologetically. Together they pried open the lid. It moved ponderously, then slid off the side and fell to the floor with a crash, breaking into pieces.

Isabel looked inside the crypt, and screamed.

CHAPTER
21

"What is it?" Hamid demanded.

"There's a dead body in here." Jon stared at the corpse.

Hamid frowned. "It's a coffin. There should be a body."

Jon reached in and lifted up the hand so Hamid could see. "Wearing a watch?"

Hamid came closer. "Someone else has been here."

Isabel moved her hands away from her mouth. "It's the priest," she said, "the one who poisoned Stephen."

Jon stared at the priest, the ashen-gray complexion leaving no doubt about his demise. His eyes were wide, with tiny pinpricks of blood coloring the white. Purplish bruises stained his neck. Jon reached in and closed his eyes. "Well, he didn't climb in there himself, did he?"

"Who else knew?" Hamid pointed the gun at Isabel. "Who else?"

"No one!"

"You lie!"

"Stephen knew," said Jon. Hamid glanced at him. "The priest must have got it from him."

"But who killed the priest?" Isabel asked.

"Who attacked us in the hospital?"

Hamid withdrew his gun, turned around, and screamed an obscenity at the walls. The epithet rang in the chamber. After a moment, he turned back. "Pull him out."

"What?"

"You heard me. Pull him out! I want to see what's in the coffin."

"Whoever put him in here has already been through it."

"Do as I say!" He thrust the gun toward Jon.

Jon sighed. He pulled the man up into a sitting position, staring wide-eyed at the skeleton on which the priest lay. The second body wore the tattered remnants of a monk's garb, and must have been the remains of the saint for whom this chapel had been built. He hefted the priest up and slung him over his shoulder. Isabel went to him and helped him lower the body. Even so, there was a liquid smack as the head struck the floor. Jon grimaced.

Behind them came a loud crack. They straightened to see Hamid smashing the chest cavity of the skeleton.

"What are you doing?"

"Looking for it!"

Jon glanced at Isabel, then approached the assassin. "Do you even know what you're looking for?"

Reluctantly, Hamid retreated from the crypt. Jon shone the flashlight into the coffin, checking the folds of the robe, around the head and feet, and finally the chest cavity Hamid had opened. He'd doubted he'd find it there, if only because the monk's internal organs would have been intact when he was buried, and the resultant decomposition would have destroyed anything as fragile as parchment or vellum. He was about to give up, when he thought of something. Turning to the broken fragments of the lid, he picked up a large one and flipped it over.

Letters had been carefully carved into the undersurface of the lid. "This is it," he said. "Give me a hand."

Isabel came over and knelt beside him. "Oh my God. It was here all along."

"Something was." He began reassembling the fragments, holding the flashlight against his shoulder. It slipped out. Frustrated, he held it up to Hamid. "Hold this."

"I think not."

He swore at him. "You want us to help you? Then put down the gun and hold the flashlight!"

Hamid chewed his lip, then slipped the gun into his belt and took hold of the light. Jon turned back to the stone puzzle. After a few moments, he read, *"Hagios Simon tae Galitae. Kai idou erxomai taqu. Makarion hah throne toun logoun taen profaeteian tou bibliou toutou."*

"What's it mean?"

"Saint Simon of Galatia. And behold, I am coming quickly. Blessed is he who keeps the words of the prophecy of this book."

"So where's the book?"

"It's from Revelation. It's about the return of Christ."

Hamid snorted.

"Wait a second." Jon turned and hurried back to the front entrance. Hamid and Isabel followed. Jon was pacing around the floor mosaic. "It's the *parousia,*" he explained. "The return of Christ. The keepers of the scroll would have known how valuable it was. They would have hidden it, so that only the initiated could find it."

He stared at the mosaic, muttering. "The words of the prophecy. The words of the prophecy…the words of God…. 'The word of God is living and active, sharper than any double-edged sword.'"

He bent forward and studied the sword protruding from Jesus' mouth. Coming around to the top of the mosaic, he lined up his eye with the angle of the sword, following the line until it intersected the wall of the chapel. A column stood there, rising almost halfway up. It hugged the wall, but clearly was not part of the building's support structure.

Jon walked to the column and crouched before it. The floor beneath the column showed a thin line tracing the curve of the column's base, as though it had recently been moved and not lined up again properly. He took hold of the column and pulled on it. It didn't budge. He wrapped both hands around it and tried again, pulling back and straining. Finally, his hands slipped and he fell backward onto his seat. "No good," he panted. "We need something to pry it with."

"There's a shovel in the courtyard," Isabel offered. She glanced at Hamid, who nodded his assent. Within moments, she'd returned.

Jon propped the shovel between the column and the wall behind it and pulled against the handle. Stone grated on stone. The column shifted, pivoting on an unseen axis away from the wall, revealing a round hole beneath it.

Jon dropped the shovel and bent over the hole, thrusting his hand inside. His arm disappeared up to his elbow. "Wait a second. I think I've—got it!"

Lifting it out with his fingers, he withdrew a short, carefully wrapped piece of ancient vellum, about two and a half inches wide. One side of the vellum was chipped and jagged. The other was smooth and even.

Setting it on the floor, where a beam of morning sunlight peered through the crack in the dome's ceiling, Jon gently unrolled the scroll.

Revealing a Post-It note.

He picked it off, and read it aloud. "Forgive me. They were getting too close."

"That's Stephen's handwriting."

"Forgive him for what?" He looked again at the scroll, reading the line of text across the page, until the smooth line of the scroll's edge neatly sliced the letters in two.

It started as a whisper, and rapidly grew louder. "No. No, no, no, no! Oh my God, no!"

"What is it?" Hamid demanded.

"Stephen, how could you?"

"What?"

"I-I could kill him! How could you? How could you do this?!"

"What?!"

He held up the scroll. "It's been cut! Look at the edge here. See how smooth it is? He cut it with a knife! O-or a pair of scissors!"

"They were getting close," she said. Isabel bent forward and picked up the Post-It note from Stephen. She held it close to her chest and closed her eyes.

"What is that?" Hamid pointed at the scroll. "Give it to me!" Jon handed it over. Hamid studied it a moment before thrusting it at Jon. "Read it."

Jon took it back, bringing the severed scroll back into the light. "It's Greek. Written in minuscules—small letters. It's quite common. Some scrolls are inscribed with uncials, which are all capital letters—"

"Read it!"

"*Edoxae kamoy grafai kai katalego hay gramma.* It seemed good to me to write and to list the Scriptures received." He looked helplessly at Hamid. "It's cut off. Without the rest of it, we can't read it."

"Jonnie!"

Hamid and Jon looked down at Isabel, who was holding the Post-it note from Stephen. She read, "I trust you can put things together."

"Put things together?" He glanced between the two of them. "He thought we'd have the rest of it."

Hamid pressed his lips together and held the gun at Isabel. "You said you knew where to get the scroll. You said we needed the key. Dr. Munro, I believe it's time for you to make that phone call I asked you to make."

CHAPTER
22

Jon stared at the gun, then at Hamid. "Phone call?"

"To your associate. The one who picks up your mail. Obviously, he hid the rest of the scroll. The key will show us where."

He clenched his fists. *Sticking that gun in my face is getting really old. There probably isn't even reception out here.* He glanced at Isabel and pulled out his Blackberry. "I'll try." He checked for bars, wishing he didn't see the two that flashed on the screen. "You realize right now it's about nine-thirty last night. He might not be there."

Hamid remained expressionless. Jon dialed the number.

"Hello?" said the voice on the other end.

"Leon?"

"Dr. Munro! How are you?"

"I'm fine, Leon." He resisted the temptation to say, *Someone's pointing a gun at me, but other than that...*

"Did you find it? The *Domo*? Dr. Michaels told me about it. He wants to speak with you. He's standing here now."

"Yeah, hang on a second. Did a package arrive for me?"

"Like a FedEx?"

"Exactly."

"It's here now. You want me to open it?"

"No, don't do that. I need you to forward it to me. I'm staying at the Houston Hotel in Ankara."

"Okay."

"Do it right away."

"Dr. Munro, are you in some kind of trouble?"

He paused, hoping it looked like he was listening. "Why?"

"'Cus there's been a lot of people asking about you. Cops, I mean. Feds, you know?"

"Uh huh. Go on."

"That Detective Brown was here this morning. He said the fingerprints in your house and car came back to someone on the terrorist watch list! Hamid Al-Assini. They call him 'The Rat.'"

"You don't say."

"Anyway it sounds pretty serious. Oh, hang on. Dr. Michaels wants to talk to you."

"Yeah, okay." He stared at 'The Rat.' Hamid was growing obviously impatient.

A moment later Michaels was on the phone. "Jonathan?"

"Tony."

"Jonathan, I'm sorry we put you through all this. I heard about Stephen. Terrible news."

"Yes."

"I think you should come back."

"That's rather difficult right now."

"Just give the scroll to this Hamid fellow so you and Isabel can come home."

Jon frowned. Something wasn't right.

"Hang up the phone," said Hamid.

"I gotta go. I'll see you soon."

"Jonathan? Are you in trouble?"

"Just tell Leon to have Jim Brown send me the package if he can't do it himself, okay?"

"Jim Brown? The detective?"

"Okay. Thanks. Bye!"

He hung up, cutting off Michaels in mid-sentence. "That's it," he said. "We have to go back to Ankara. It'll take a day or two."

"Let us hope it doesn't take too long. I am not a patient man."

Behind Hamid, Isabel picked up the shovel.

Jon shrugged. "We can only do what we can. It's nine thirty or so now. There might be a midnight pick up—"

Isabel swung the shovel and hit her mark with a resounding "Clang!" Hamid fell forward, his unconscious body landing with a thud at Jon's feet. Isabel raised the shovel to swing again, but Jon snatched it from her hand.

"What took you so long?" he said.

"I didn't think of it till now."

"Didn't think of it?" He bent down and retrieved the scroll, shoving it into his coat pocket. He grabbed Isabel's elbow and thrust her toward the door. "Why do you think I asked for the shovel?"

"To move the column."

"You kidding? That thing moves like butter. Let's go."

* *   *

"Here they come," Michael said, glancing over his shoulder. Brian and William rolled onto their stomachs and peered down the hill. The sun was higher now, casting mandarin rays over the hills, but the ledge they hid behind was bathed in blue shadows.

"Check the signal," said Sean.

Michael glanced at the receiver, watching the red dot pulse on the map. "Strong."

"Right. Wait till they're out of sight. Then we go."

"Why don't we take them now?"

"No can do," Sean shook his head. "Our employer tells me there's a piece of the puzzle we don't have yet, and they're going to get it for us. We wait till then."

"What about The Rat?" said William.

"Do you see him yet?"

"No."

"Then you probably won't. What d'you think the shovel was for? Burying Father Philip?"

William smirked. "Thought that guy was a professional."

Sean grinned and took the receiver from Michael. "There's 'professionals,'" he said, "and then there's 'professional,' yeah?"

Below them, they heard a car start. Sean glanced down the hill in time to see the Audi peel out, leaving clouds of dust rising into the morning sky. "And there they go," said Michael.

"Right. We'd best be off then."

From a ridge just a little further away, Demetri watched the mercenaries scramble toward their vehicle. He frowned. It was all bad business. This mercenary team was good. Too good. He'd tried to warn the young priest, but he wouldn't listen. The man was foolish and headstrong—not unlike himself in earlier days. Too quickly he abandoned his calling, lured by the false promise of that silly piece of paper, that Papal Indulgence. He paid for his sins in a terrible way, and now he would stand before his Master to be judged, indulgence or no. There was nothing left but to pray the *Little Ektenia* for his soul, that he might be forgiven and find repose in the bosom of Christ.

He stepped down to his car, an old taxi he'd purchased from a used car dealership near Baljat. The scientist and the woman would need his prayers as well. Did they have any idea what they were mixed up in? Or the forces which opposed them? The mercenary team was the least of their worries. Soon, God would sweep away all those who stood in Demetri's path, and he would deliver the scrolls to their rightful place in the Church, where they would not be forgotten.

He drove to the entrance of the chapel and parked his car. Men were fools to think they could oppose Christ. He learned it in Romania, watching the priests lead the people to throw off the bonds of the antichrist puppet. Once God decided to act, none could stand against Him. All a man could do was submit to the Lord in humility, and serve as the Lord commanded. As he approached the ladder, a hand reached up, carrying a gun. He reached down and wrenched the gun from the man and pulled him up to the surface.

Hamid stared up at this strange, older man in the black cassock and beard. The man was huge. He'd lifted him from the ladder without effort. The man shoved the gun into the folds of his cassock and turned to Hamid. "'Tis a long way to walk through this inhospitable land. With that knock on your head you'll die of thirst before anyone finds you."

Hamid snorted. "Why do you care?"

"The love of Christ compels me, my unbelieving friend. Like you, I once followed the way of the gun." He moved past him and started down the ladder. "Then someone showed me a kindness. Now, I return the favor."

Hamid's eyes darted to where Jon and Isabel had driven off, and then back at the priest descending the ladder. "Where are you going?"

"To pray for his soul. Wait for me by the car. I'll only be a moment."

Hamid watched the priest disappear into the church. He looked at the taxi, wondering if he could hotwire it. They couldn't have gotten more than a few miles ahead. He tried the door. Locked. He banged his fist on the window and kicked a spray of dirt into the air. Finally, he sank down beside the passenger's door to wait. His head hurt like hell.

CHAPTER
23

"I was once like you. I lived by the gun. Lived for myself. I found it empty and cold and hard as steel. 'Tis no way for a man to be."

Hamid wished the man would shut the hell up. His head was still pounding, but he no longer believed it due to the shovel that had graced the back of his skull. He glanced at the monk and smiled scornfully. Ever since he'd stepped into the monk's car, Brother Demetri, as he'd introduced himself, prattled on incessantly about faith and judgment, and the emptiness of life without God. So much was better now that he lived on the Mountain, where there was no money nor women nor weapons. Hamid was beginning to wonder whether he'd have been better off walking.

Except if he had, he'd be dead, and the question of God's existence would no longer be a matter of faith. Brother Demetri had been right about that, at least. He gently touched the thick pad of gauze Demetri had taped over his wound. Fortunately, the man had a first aid kit in his trunk. The monk insisted on bandaging his injury before letting him in the car, despite his protesting. He forced himself to relax and accept the monk's generosity. Inside, he smoldered. He ought to have foreseen it. He'd been too focused on the prize in hand. He'd been careless… and paid for it dearly. Nearly with his life. Abandonment in the wilderness was a death sentence, especially with his head wound. And for that, he would repay Kaufman's sister with joy. Just as soon as he rid himself of this monk.

"If you don't mind my asking," he said, interrupting Demetri's speech on faith, "what is your interest in the scroll?" Demetri was silent for a long moment. "If you don't wish to answer...." He shrugged.

"No, my friend. Please understand. I was merely thinking how I could best answer you. I do not think you would believe me otherwise." He took a breath. "I might ask you the same question."

"My interest is simple," Hamid smiled. "Money."

"I thought as much."

"There is a buyer in America who is paying me handsomely to acquire it. I do not apologize for it. I am not a man given to causes beyond my own survival. I was once." He pulled free his mangled arm and showed it to the monk. "It did this to me. And then I was of no more use to God. So God is of no use to me. I intend only now to earn enough money to afford a pleasant life, then retire. Someplace warm, where I may enjoy the few comforts of this world in peace."

Demetri laughed.

"What? Why do you laugh at me?"

The monk shook his head. "What you want to attain through money, I have already acquired—by giving it all away. You should come with me to the Mountain!" He slapped Hamid's knee, gripping it. Hamid looked sideways at the monk's hand. What sort of mountain was this where there were no women?

Demetri continued, his eyes lost in rapt wonder. "There the breeze blows warm from the Aegean across the fields. I have no more cares but for my tomato plants and my prayers.

Look," he handed Hamid his prayer beads. At the end of them, next to the cross, dangled a handcuff key. How convenient, Hamid mused.

"What's this?"

"The key reminds me of my freedom. Through Christ, I live without fear, without hate. Such peace."

Hamid returned the beads. "Then why did you leave?"

"I go where my Lord commands. The autographs are a sacred trust. They are not meant for private collectors or museums. They must be kept safe. On the Mountain, we will preserve them for future generations. And all the nations shall come to the Mountain of God to hear His words. God wills it, you see."

"God wills it!" Hamid sneered. "That's what they said to me when I lost my hand, when they wanted me to strap on a vest of explosives and blow myself up. God wills it."

"That's different."

"No! It is the same. Gods are only useful for compelling men to sacrifice what they would otherwise preserve. You may keep your God, my friend. I'll find my own way to happiness." He turned to the window and stared at the passing scenery.

Demetri's voice was quiet. "I hope you learn this before it is too late, my friend."

Hamid didn't turn around. "Learn what?"

"There is no other way to happiness."

"Jonnie? Jonnie!"

He woke and blinked his eyes. Broad daylight streamed through the windshield, reflecting maliciously from the Audi's hood into his face. He covered his eyes and sat up. "What time is it?"

"About quarter to eight. I'm sorry to wake you."

"No, it's alright. Just the jet lag. Thanks for driving."

"Better than going off the road."

"How long was I out?"

"About ten minutes. You were snoring."

"I don't snore."

"How would you know?"

"Good point." He stared out the window at the unfamiliar setting. "Where are we?"

"Back in Ankara. What do you want to do?"

"Go back to sleep!" He snorted. "Sorry. We have to go back to the hotel and wait for the package, this key Stephen talks about." He pulled the scroll from his jacket pocket and examined it in the light. "I can't believe he cut it."

"He was only doing what he thought was best."

"By destroying a priceless artifact?" He grimaced. "Sorry, that came out wrong. I get cranky when I'm tired."

She nodded and said nothing.

He unfurled a leaf of the scroll, staring at the faded lettering, tracing the line of the script without touching the precious vellum. The acids in his sweat would erode the ink, dissolve the fragment into so much useless dust. It had already suffered enough violence for its secrets.

They all had.

"I owe you an apology," he muttered. "You and Stephen."

"What?"

"I didn't believe you. I didn't believe him."

"And now?"

"Well, we still have to acquire the rest of it. Put it together. Transcribe it. Translate it. We'll need to examine the shape of the letters, assess the language and grammar. And, of course, test the age of the vellum, the ink, the rate of decay, and so forth. Then we'll know for sure." He put the fragment back.

"Incredible." She propped her head on her hand, leaning against the door frame. Her lips were set in a familiar pout.

"What?"

"You still don't believe."

"Wait a second. Belief isn't the same thing as proof, Isabel. Belief is fine for faith, but this is a matter of science. For that, you need proof. Stephen asked me to prove this. That's what I intend to do."

She shook her head and said nothing.

He couldn't let it go. "For the record, I believe I was wrong—before. I believe you. I believe Stephen. I believe he was telling the truth. I just have to prove it."

Her eyes softened. After a few moments, she said, "I wish things had been different between you two."

"Different how?"

She opened and closed her mouth, then said, "I think he missed your friendship. You were like a rock to him. An anchor. You kept him grounded."

He stared at her a moment, then shook his head, chuckling. "I, uh, I don't know what to say to that."

"What is there to say? It's the truth."

"Wow. Maybe he should've thought of that before."

"Before what?"

"You know."

"Before he took me away from you?"

He shifted in his seat. "Yeah."

She laughed. "Jonnie. You are so arrogant."

He shook his head. "Izzy, you made your choice. I know that. You chose him."

"Yes, I did."

"Yes, you did. That's fine."

"And I'd do it again."

"Whatever. That's ancient history. But I'm not going to pretend it didn't hurt. Yeah, it broke our friendship. What do you want? That's college."

She tapped the steering wheel. "Why didn't you ever write?"

He snorted. "And say what?"

"Hey. How are you? What's new?"

He laughed. "Are you serious? What is this? The 'Why can't we just be friends' speech?" His voice softened. "Isabel Kaufman, you broke my heart. You were the first girl I loved."

"No way."

"Come to think of it—the only girl. God, that's pathetic."

"No, no it isn't. All these years you were pining away for me. Unrequited love. It's romantic."

"Romance sucks."

"And you wonder why you never married. I ruined you for other women."

"And you call me arrogant."

"Say it's not true."

He smiled and said nothing, looking out the window.

"You can't, can you?"

"I don't know. I never really thought about it afterwards. I tried not to think about it. Eventually, I didn't have to try anymore. That's the way it goes, you know?" He yawned and leaned against the door frame. Isabel smiled, but then her eyes grew distant and watery.

She sniffled. "I miss him."

He stifled another yawn and tried to be interested.

"He could drive me out of my skull sometimes. All those years assisting him. I was actually ready to leave him, before the end. Before the university hired him. Now he's gone."

He nodded and said nothing further. Within ten minutes, they parked the Audi and went inside the hotel. Once inside the room, Jon asked her to order room service. "Put it on the bill. Michaels owes me that much." He collapsed onto the bed.

A few minutes later, there was a knock at the door. "That was fast," she remarked, opening the door.

Isabel wilted. The men standing there were not room service.

The Lost Scrolls

CHAPTER
24

Sean swore quietly. So very little of this operation was going right. But now this! He stared out the windshield at the Houston Hotel, watching as the police led a very distraught couple out in handcuffs and loaded them into a police van. A crowd started gathering on the sidewalk, but it evaporated as the van sped away.

"Now what?" growled William.

"Go search the room. And watch out for cops. Here," Sean pressed a tracking chip in his hands. "Take this with you."

William nodded and stuck the chip in his pocket. "And if we find anything?"

He rolled his eyes. "What do you think? You bring it back!"

"Come on, William," said Brian, climbing out of the vehicle. "Sean's getting testy."

Sean swore and said little else. He watched as the two men crossed the street and entered the hotel.

"And what happens if they don't find nothing?" Michael twisted in his seat to face Sean. "What will you do then?"

Sean stared after the men. "We'll burn that bridge when we come to it."

Michael nodded and sank back into his seat. After a moment of chewing his lip he said, "Sean?"

"What?"

"Oughtn't we cross the bridge first, and then burn it?"

Sean glared at him. "Shut up!"

Lieutenant Çapanoğlu stared through the one-way glass at the man sitting at a steel table in the interrogation room. In an adjacent room, a woman sat at a similar table. Both of them had been in the separate rooms for a solid hour. The man rested his head on the desk. He appeared to be asleep.

Kahil clenched his teeth and stifled a yawn. He hadn't slept since the assault on the hospital last night. He'd spent the night tracking down leads from the bodies of the Kurdish rebels. They weren't currently associated with any known terrorist organizations. He found a reference to at least one of the rebels in a two-year-old deposition, suggesting the man had turned mercenary.

But if that were the case, who had hired them? And why?

And then there was the matter of The Rat. Since the hospital, there'd been absolutely no leads on him whatsoever. Until now.

He turned when someone else came in the room, then returned to the window. Sergeant Bahar stood by his elbow, his lips pressed in a tight line. The sergeant had been incredible. His response during the incident warranted a commendation, and Kahil would be sure he received it. Afterwards, his assistance in the clean up and investigation to follow had been invaluable. He wondered why the sergeant hadn't risen higher in the ranks. He'd been there long enough.

"Sleeping beauty," Bahar muttered. "You want to wake him? Or start with the woman?"

Kahil regarded the man a moment longer. "Let's wake him up."

Slam!

A gun! Izzy!

Jon's eyes flashed open. He stared around, uncomprehending. The dull slate room did little to comfort him, but neither did it reveal where the gunshot came from. He looked up at the two police officers who stood before him, one younger, one older. The older one had his hand on a phone book, which he'd just dropped onto the table.

Jon swallowed.

The younger man's uniform was a dark green, while the older wore navy blue. Jon surmised they must represent different branches of law enforcement. The younger man spoke first. "I am Lieutenant Çapanoğlu of the Turkish Gendarmerie. This is Sergeant Bahar of Ankara Police. And you are Doctor Jonathan Munro, professor of paleography at the University of Michigan, USA."

"Where's Izzy?"

"Your companion is quite safe. You will see her as soon as we are finished." He opened a file folder and pulled out an eight-by-ten photo, sliding it across the table. "Have you seen this man?"

Jon stared down at the fuzzy image of Hamid. He nodded vigorously. "Yes. Well, not before today. But yes." Bahar and Çapanoğlu exchanged glances. Jon continued. "That's Hamid Al-Assini. They call him 'The Rat,' right? He more than lives up to his name. Guy like that needs to be locked away for a long time. He came to the hospital last night. I was visiting a friend—a fellow scientist. Dr. Stephen Kaufman. This man," he tapped the photo, "shot Dr. Kaufman. And then, then all hell broke loose. Izzy—Dr. Kaufman's sister—we got out through the window onto the roof and ran for our lives. Later—I don't know how—but he found us and kidnapped us. He threatened to shoot us if we didn't take him to an archaeological dig my friend had been working on—before he was stabbed. God, that sounds crazy!" He licked his lips and watched for a response. There was none. "Anyway, we—umm—Izzy hit him with a shovel at the dig and we got away."

Lieutenant Çapanoğlu leaned back and folded his hands across his chest. "That's a rather incredible story."

"You don't believe me."

"Why should we not believe you? Aren't you telling us the truth?"

"Yeah. That's what happened."

"And where is this dig you spoke of?"

"Konya. North of Konya. North and east. I could probably show you on a map."

The lieutenant whispered to Bahar, who nodded and left quickly. "We will check it out," he said. "With luck this 'Rat' will still be there."

Jon frowned. "He might be dead. I mean, I don't think she meant to kill him. But she hit him pretty hard. After what he did to Stephen, who could blame her?" He licked his lips. "Is Izzy going to be in trouble?"

The lieutenant smiled and said, "Tell me why you didn't come to the police."

"He had a gun on us."

"Before he kidnapped you. After you escaped the hospital. Why didn't you come to us?"

Jon thought a moment. Why hadn't they gone to the police? He wanted to, but Izzy insisted they couldn't do that. "You can't let them have it," she'd said. "Not in this country."

His next thought sickened him. What if Izzy hadn't told him everything? What if the cops were in on it? Worse, what if Izzy were in on it? What, after all, did he know about her—except that for twelve years she'd stuck by a known liar and con artist? What tricks of Stephen's trade had she acquired in that time?

And who could he trust now?

"We didn't think of it," he shrugged. "We were scared. I mean, don't take this wrong, but I'm in a foreign country here, and I don't know how things work. And you always hear about Turkish prisons...." He started laughing, but stopped when Kahil refused to smile. "Oh boy," he muttered.

"In most western countries, it is generally considered prudent to go to the police when you have been involved in a terrorist action. Unless, of course, you are the terrorist."

Jon laughed nervously. Was he sweating? "I'm not a terrorist. I'm just a guy in the wrong place at the wrong time. Should I be talking to my embassy?"

"Why are you here in Turkey, Dr. Munro?" Kahil kept his eyes on his folder, as if uninterested in Jon's response.

"I told you. I was visiting a colleague."

"Dr. Kaufman. And what is his line of work?"

"Archeology."

"And what was he working on?"

"The dig I mentioned. He found an ancient church. Hamid was searching it for artifacts."

"Can you tell me why Dr. Kaufman had been injected with Thiopental?" He looked up and met his eyes, handing Jon a hospital report listing the incident. Jon was relieved to look at something besides the lieutenant's eyes. He studied the report.

"I don't know anything about that. Izzy mentioned something about it. She said the priest had poisoned him."

"Priest?"

"Yeah. The one we found at the dig. He was dead."

"You found a dead priest at the dig?"

He nodded.

"And you didn't think to report this, either?"

Jon shifted in his seat. "We just got back. It's been a crazy couple of days."

The lieutenant tapped the folder on his desk, staring at Jon as though he were looking through him, reading his soul, weighing what he found.

Jon clenched and unclenched his fists. "I really would like to talk to my embassy."

Lieutenant Kahil cocked his head. "You aren't being charged with anything, Dr. Munro. You are, however, a material witness to a series of homicides and an attempt by terrorists to blow up a hospital. I am not sure your embassy will be interested in helping you."

"Except I didn't do anything!"

The lieutenant smiled, a thin line between his lips. "I think, Dr. Munro, it would be best for all concerned if you were to simply go home. I am recommending your entrance visa be revoked."

"And what about Izzy?"

"She will be permitted to claim the body of her brother. Then you both must leave the country. For your own safety, if for nothing else."

After a half hour, the hulking forms of Brian and William returned to the car. Sean watched the front door of the hotel and surrounding street for any sign they were being followed. Once inside, Brian leaned his head into the front seat.

"Nothing," he said. "Whatever they found, they took it with them."

"In which case the Turkish police are now in possession." He swore and slammed his palm against the steering wheel.

"What now?" said Michael.

Sean said nothing and shifted the car in gear. He'd figure something out. He had to.

CHAPTER
25

Jon didn't return to his hotel until later that afternoon. He met with numb disinterest the cold stares of the hotel staff. Evidently, they were not keen on serving an associate of Kurdish terrorists, nor happy he was back in their hotel. He offered no explanation, no defense. He didn't care. He'd barely slept in thirty hours. He was past tired. All he wanted was to crash out on the bed for about ten hours or so before his flight the next morning.

Isabel was under police escort. They would drive her to the hospital to claim Stephen's body, then to her house to retrieve her personal belongings. She'd paid her rent through the end of the year, but it didn't matter. There would be no refund. He'd meet up with her at the airport.

He drew the blinds in the room, hung the Do Not Disturb sign on his doorknob, and crawled beneath the covers of the bed he hadn't slept in once since arriving in Turkey. As he closed his eyes and waited for sleep to come, he couldn't escape the nagging impression he'd missed something. What was it?

His body was exhausted, and though he struggled to catch his train of thought, his mind skipped the track and plunged headlong into dreams. Ideas and images collided with each other—jumbled, twisted and disordered—falling into the abyss of unconsciousness. One of those images was a severed scroll tumbling loose and eluding his grasp. The scroll became Isabel, cut off from him by Stephen's knife, disappearing in the blackness.

Somewhere in his sleep, a gunshot punched him awake. Somnolence shattered. He cried out and flinched. His eyes went wide, furtive. Swallowing, he panned the room, searching for the source of the sound. His heart hammered against his chest.

Shadows ensconced the room in shades of slate and gray. Beyond the heavy window curtains, golden rays of sunlight peeked longingly, like a forgotten child urging a reluctant parent to come out and play. He sat up in bed. It must've been a dream. His brain was foggy. His eyes burned with grit. He rubbed them clear.

He glanced at the clock. Six. Morning or evening? He felt like he'd either slept too little or too much.

He found the remote and turned on the TV, relieved when the onscreen clock read 6:02 am. Well, at least he'd adjusted to the new time zone. Now that he was leaving. He turned off the TV, ordered coffee from room service, and on second thought added some breakfast to the order.

He dressed and opened the windows, and had just begun packing his clothes when someone knocked on the door. His pulse quickened. Slipping to the side of the door he called out, "Who is it?"

"Room service."

He hazarded a glance. Through the peephole, he saw a clean-cut member of the wait staff standing behind a steel cart laden with breakfast and coffee. He swallowed hard and opened the door.

"Good morning," the waiter said, wheeling the cart into the room. "Your breakfast and coffee. Also, the front desk asked me to remind you that check out time is at eleven."

Jon smirked at their not-so-subtle way of saying, *"Go away."*

"My flight leaves at ten. I'll be gone before then."

"Very good, sir. And they wanted me to bring this up to you." He handed Jon a white, red, and blue package tightly sealed with packing tape. Jon thanked him and pressed a couple of folded bills into his hand. He had no idea how much it was. The waiter returned his thanks and left.

Jon closed the door behind him and turned over the package. It was addressed to him. The return address was from the university.

Leon. The key.

The other half of the scroll! What happened to it? He dropped the package and dashed through the hotel room, checking his pockets, turning out his suitcase and pawing through the clothes. He pulled open drawers and checked under furniture. For a horrid moment, he culled through the trash, relieved that none of it had been collected yet.

After twenty minutes, he sank onto the edge of the bed and picked up a slice of cold, dry toast. Maybe if he ate, fed his brain, he could search systematically. While he crammed the toast into his mouth, his eyes flitted around the room trying to see what he may have missed.

The rest of the meal was as cold as the toast. The coffee, mercifully, was slightly better than warm. He drank it in large swallows. After pouring his second cup, he opened the package.

There was no note inside, but a brass key slipped free and fell into his open palm. He held it up, examining it. Stenciling on one side said Esenboğa International Airport, Locker 227. The other side said what he presumed to be the same thing in Turkish. Well, that was convenient. He was heading to the airport anyway. Had he received the key in time, he would have used it already, and the intact scroll would now be in his possession.

Or The Rat's.

So what happened to the rest of the scroll? The last time he remembered having it was in the car. Could it have fallen out of his pocket? He went pale at the horror of a two-thousand-year-old vellum scroll tumbling to the sidewalk and lying in the dust and the elements.

In which case, all he had left was whatever was in the locker at the airport.

He swallowed the last of the coffee. There was nothing for it now. He'd go and find what he could. Perhaps Michaels would be satisfied with that. Half a scroll was better than none.

He picked up his suitcase and was about to leave when the phone rang. It could be Izzy. He reached for the receiver.

"Hello?"

"Good morning, Dr. Munro. I trust you slept well?"

His heart sank. "Who is this?"

"Your old friend. I have another friend with me who would like to speak to you."

There was a momentary rustling, then Isabel's voice came through. "Jonnie!"

"Izzy!"

"She can't talk right now. But if you wish to see her alive again, you will meet me in an hour at Sevilla's in the Ankara Tower. You will, of course, bring the key."

"Hamid! Don't hurt her!"

"And why not? I still owe her a knock on the head at least." There was a sound of a loud smack over the phone, and Isabel crying.

"You son of a—if you ever want to see the scroll again, you'll leave her alone!"

Hamid chuckled. "Ankara Tower. One hour."

Jon checked his watch. He was supposed to be boarding a flight home by then. There was no time.

There was less choice. "Alright," he said. "Ankara Tower. One hour."

"It goes without saying, Dr. Munro, you will not call the police. But in case you do, I'll know if you have. The open terrace at Sevilla's provides a commanding view, and it is a very long fall."

"Alright, I hear you!"

"One hour."

Jon hung up.

Oh God, what was he going to do now?

Demetri set down the parabolic mic and frowned. This was unexpected. No one should have been hurt, least of all this archaeologist's young sister.

He stared at the high-rise complex from the flat he'd broken into across the street. Inside a fourth floor apartment, The Rat had made his den. Demetri had followed him after agreeing to drop him off on the streets of Ankara, knowing Hamid might lead him to this Dr. Munro, who was in possession of the scroll. Hamid had been decidedly tight-lipped about the whole deal, leaving Demetri with little other choice.

He equally hoped Hamid would *not* lead him to the scroll. He prayed Hamid would have been touched by his kindness and repent his life of violent greed.

It never was much more than a frail hope.

But even then, he did not expect the violence with which Hamid dispatched the woman's police escort, dropping the four men with rapid shots to their heads and leaving Isabel no time to even register what was happening, let alone scream.

Fool! he berated himself. *What did you expect to happen? Show kindness to a snake, it does not cease to be a snake!* He shook his head.

The old Demetri, Major Antonescu, would never have allowed this to happen. He wouldn't have picked up the man left in the decaying chapel. If he bothered at all, he'd have simply shot him as just one more obstacle to be removed. But Major Antonescu was gone, replaced forever by the kinder, gentler Brother Demetri, who would show compassion to even a snake.

Just because he had changed did not mean the rest of the world had. He should have known Hamid would try something like this. *Were the old you in this man's position, would you have done any differently?*

"It doesn't matter," he growled. "What's done is done. What matters now is what to do next."

Should he take steps to rescue the woman? Or wait and see, let circumstances play out as they would? Regardless, he'd eventually have to deal with this Hamid. And for that....

He picked up the Glock 23 he'd taken from the assassin and held it out in front, sighting expertly down the barrel at his target—a round nail head on the opposite wall of this vacant apartment. The nail head rode steady above the sites, balanced perfectly above the center site as if they were one piece. Then the nail head wavered and fell, the illusion shattered as his hand began to tremble. He dropped his arm, letting the gun fall to the table.

It was no good. His days with the gun were over. The haunted memories of so many lives taken would not let him go back to what he was. Funny. Such thoughts would normally comfort him, reminding him he was indeed a changed man.

Instead, he felt only fear.

CHAPTER
26

Hamid pulled out a knife and fit it onto his prosthetic cuff. He turned around, facing the woman tied to the chair. Her dark hair hung unkempt before her face. One or two strands lay trapped beneath the hastily applied tape across her mouth. He'd tied her feet together and drawn her hands behind her back, pushing her chest out. She regarded him with a mixture of fear and hatred. Her expression only intensified when she saw the knife.

"You know," he said, fingering the knife's edge, "I still owe you for hitting me with that shovel."

Her eyebrows arched, her face twisting away. He walked forward, played the edge of the knife along her cheek, side of her neck. He let it fall further, tracing the curves of her torso.

Hamid smiled at her whimpering. "There are many things I could do to you. I want you to think about it." He leaned in close and whispered in her ear. "Fantasize about it." He walked behind her, dropping to a crouch and placing his arms around her shoulders, the knife in front of her face. "I want you to dream about how it would feel to have me touch you with this. And when your lover caresses you, you will remember me."

He brought the knife down between her wrists and sliced cleanly through her bonds. Isabel tore her hands free, but stopped when he caught her arms between his. He bent his mouth forward, his lips grazing her neck. She cringed. He withdrew and walked in front of her, his back turned.

"There isn't time," he said, removing the knife and reattaching his prosthesis.

She pulled the tape away from her mouth and wrists, and finally her legs, and looked up, startled that he'd been watching her. She stared back at him, uncertainty joining the fear and hatred etched on her face.

"Now," he said, "be a good girl, hmm? Or we come back here and finish what we've started."

Jon stumbled out of the elevator and to the front desk counter. His bags tumbled to the floor next to him. He straightened and faced the front desk clerk.

"Checking out, sir?"

"Yes, please."

"And did you enjoy your stay in Ankara?"

He stared at her, unsure how to answer. The question was ridiculous, but appropriate for someone who didn't know what his stay had been like. He mumbled, "It's been interesting," and handed her the room key and credit card, waiting while she processed the transaction. A moment later, he signed the receipt and picked up his bags.

Hamid's car sat across the street where they'd left it the day before. Jon didn't think the assassin would mind him using it now. Frankly, he didn't care. He pushed through the front door and onto the sidewalk.

He didn't see the two men follow him out until they were right behind him. A large van screeched to a stop in front of the hotel. He jumped at the sound. The side door slid open, and the man inside aimed a gun at him. Jon barely had time to open his mouth before the two men picked him up by both arms and thrust him inside. A second later, they tossed in his luggage and slammed the door. The van sped away from the curb.

Jon sat up against the back door of the van, staring at the grim faces of his captors. One of them, a blond man with arctic eyes and a day's growth of beard, spoke first.

"So, you are Doctor Jonathan Munro."

"Who are you? What do you want?"

"I think you already know what we want. A man of your intelligence has surely drawn a conclusion by now, yeah?"

Unbelievable. Would this never end? "You want the scroll."

The blonde laughed an epithet and looked at his friends. "The man's a genius, yeah?"

"And what if I don't give it to you?"

One of his friends laughed. "Genius, huh?"

The blonde feigned hurt. "Och! Don't you be proving me wrong now, Jonnie boy! I highly suggest you cooperate."

Jon licked his lips. "Cooperation, huh? That's a two-way street, isn't it?"

The man with the gun grunted. "The man's got bollocks, eh, Sean?"

Sean cuffed his shoulder. "Don't be using my name, you stupid fool! I'll shoot you myself." He sighed and looked at Jon. "A two-way street is it? What did you have in mind?"

Demetri checked his watch and waited for the elevator doors to open. After leaving the vacant apartment, he'd driven straight to the Ankara Tower and taken the elevator to the restaurant at the top. The Atakule was a 125-meter communications and observation tower in the Çankaya district. It resembled an enormous microphone, from the slender rise of the shaft to the oversized globe of the observation deck and restaurants. The lower café, called "The UFO," was a slender disk of windows around a broad concourse extending evenly into space. Directly above the café sat an open terrace around "The Sevilla" restaurant, and further above was the round tower's roof, housing "The Dome" restaurant.

Inside, Sevilla's red carpet curved away in either direction around the interior of the restaurant. A single row of tables sat against the outer wall, with seating for four around most. The tables were decorated with red linens to match the carpeting, dinner and salad plates, and had simple flower vases for the centerpieces. As he searched for a suitable place from which to watch the elevators, Demetri felt a dull hum vibrate through his feet, barely at the level of consciousness. He looked out the windows and realized he was in motion. He snorted. The restaurant rotated, providing its customers with a spectacular, panoramic view of the city.

He found a table partially hidden by ferns, with an indirect view toward the elevators, and insisted the maitre d' seat him there, even though he was one person. He said he was expecting company. It wasn't entirely untrue. Demetri ordered a cup of tea with lemon just to rid himself of the man, and checked his watch again. Seven fifty. The exchange between Munro and Hamid was to take place at eight o'clock sharp. Unless Hamid was already in the restaurant, which he doubted, he'd see him arrive.

He took a sip of tea, feeling the liquid flow through his throat and warm his belly. It was comforting. He'd left the Glock in the taxi, and was relieved it no longer weighed on his conscience. God would protect him. God had to protect him. Hamid had nothing else. If he saw him, the assassin wouldn't hesitate to kill him given the chance. Therefore, he must be unseen.

As he set down his cup, the elevator doors opened. He saw a wide-eyed woman exit with a very clean, well-groomed man behind her. It took him a moment to realize the man was Hamid. He hadn't seen him dressed up before. Shaving had disguised his appearance further. Hamid glanced around, and Demetri leaned back behind the fern, letting the leaves obscure his face. They must have gotten on the elevator right after he had. He clenched his teeth. He'd been careless, spending too much time dithering about the gun. He'd cut it close, almost too close. He stared straight ahead, watching the faint reflection of the couple in the windows. Hamid was checking both directions. He was probably looking for police, ensuring no one had gotten there before him. She was the hostage Hamid had spoken of on the phone.

The monk folded his hands into clenched fists, staring at her. Her face was frozen, expressionless, but her eyes cried out, begging anyone to notice her plight. Something warm and passionate burned in his stomach. He wanted to free this woman, had to, if there was a way. Righteous indignation washed over him, and he frowned. His training kicked in, not allowing passion to overrule reason. Without the woman as a draw, the doctor would not come, would not bring the scroll. And no matter how much his spirit cried for action, he could do nothing until this played out as it must.

If things went as Hamid had planned, then he'd let the woman go without harm. Hamid would have the scroll, and Demetri had no reservations at all about relieving him of it.

Of course, things rarely, if ever, went as planned.

CHAPTER
27

Jon stepped into the elevator and waited for it to ascend. His reflection shone dully in the glass windows before him. The walls on either side felt close, too close, and if it weren't for the open view of the cityscape dropping rapidly beneath him, he'd have felt claustrophobic. The team of mercenaries had taken the elevator just ahead of him, giving them time to take up position before he arrived, and leaving him plenty of time to agonize over what to say.

He swallowed hard and leaned against the back of the elevator, praying. *God, please help me! Help me help Izzy.* He closed his eyes. It occurred to him that he was asking God to help him lie to Hamid. How would God view something like that?

He didn't have the scroll. He didn't know where it was or what had happened to it. And compared to rescuing Izzy from that psycho, he didn't care.

But there was no way he could let the psycho know that. Hamid was expecting the scroll. He'd already shown his willingness to kill in cold blood. In some ways, Jon was surprised Hamid hadn't tried to kill him already, though he probably intended to once he had the scroll. Maybe not having it would give them a better chance.

The gnawing pit in his stomach told him otherwise.

Then there was Sean and his little band of merry mercenaries. What would they do once they learned he'd double-crossed them? Would they listen to reason? *Sorry to break this to you, guys, but I don't have the scroll. I just wanted to rescue the woman. You can understand that, right?*

He shook his head. There really was no way out of this.

Demetri looked up once more as the elevator doors opened again. He frowned. This time the four men he'd tracked to the chapel stepped outside the elevator. They conferred briefly with one another before taking off in opposite directions around the perimeter of the restaurant. Beneath each of their jackets was the obvious bulge of a weapon.

He set down his tea and dabbed at his mouth with his napkin. This was unexpected.

They would be looking for Hamid, taking up positions on either side of him—probably a few tables away to catch him in their crossfire should a gun battle break out. If that happened, a lot of innocent people would get hurt.

But what could he do? He was one man, and he was unarmed. He drummed his fingers on the table, staring at the elaborate, unlit oil lamp in the centerpiece, then leaned back and looked at the ceiling.

Yes, he thought, *that just might work.*

"Excuse me?" he said to the waitress who was passing by.

"Yes, sir?"

"Could I have my lamp lit?"

The waitress patted her pockets and smiled apologetically.

"I don't have my lighter with me, but I'll send someone over."

"Thank you. That is most kind."

"More tea?"

"Please."

The elevator doors opened, and Jon stepped out into the restaurant. He took a few steps forward, looking both directions before spotting a clean-shaven man with dark hair sitting next to an equally dark-haired beauty by the window. Isabel. Scared. Her anxious eyes pleaded with him.

Closer, he saw the blond man and his bald friend sitting two tables away. Behind Hamid, the other pair of mercenaries had taken position.

Hamid waved in his direction, trying hard to look the part of a friend meeting him for breakfast, and apparently oblivious to the four men who surrounded him. Jon took a deep breath—*oh God, here we go*—and started toward them.

"Good morning, Dr. Munro. Please, sit down."

"Izzy? Are you okay?"

She shook her head, trembling.

"Sit down, please."

"Not until I know she's okay."

"Keep your voice down." Hamid looked at Isabel. "Well? Tell him."

"I'm—I'm alright, Jonnie."

Jon nodded and took his seat.

"The waitress is coming over. Order yourself some breakfast."

"I'm not hungry."

"The food here is really quite spectacular. We don't want to raise suspicions. Order something."

When the waitress came, he asked for a cup of coffee and a little more time. She made a note on her pad and offered to check back in a few minutes. When she left, Hamid wasn't smiling.

"What did you do that for? Now she'll be back."

"Precisely." He couldn't resist a smile. "If you're going to kill us, I want there to be witnesses."

Hamid shrugged. "That simply means I may have to kill her, too." Jon's smile faded. "Or we can conduct this business like civilized people, and no one has to get hurt. Now, if you please, the key."

Jon reached into his pocket and slid a slender brass key across the table. Hamid palmed it and put it in his pocket. "And the scroll."

Jon took a deep breath. "I don't have it."

Demetri watched the waiter light his oil lamp and replace the cover. He thanked him and waited until he departed. There wasn't much time. Business was picking up. He pulled the lid off the lamp and unscrewed the bowl that held the oil. He sloshed it onto the center of the table, threw the flowers on top, and dropped the flame into it.

Bright light flared across the table. He drained his teacup and stepped into the elevator.

"What do you mean you don't have it?"

Isabel paled, staring straight at Jon.

"I mean I don't have it. I searched my room for it this morning. Went through all my stuff. It's not there."

Hamid's eyes hardened into shale.

"But even if I did have it, I wouldn't now. It would be in the possession of the four men who surround this table. You didn't see them sit down?" he asked when Hamid's eyes registered surprise. "There's two of them behind me, and two more behind you. They all have guns."

Hamid picked up his knife and held it in front, as if he were cleaning the edge. In its reflection, he saw the two men sitting behind him. One of them glanced his way.

He swore. "I warned you. No police!"

"They're not police," Jon corrected.

Hamid fumed. "Why are you telling me this?"

"'Cus I have nothing to lose. If you try anything, they'll kill you right now. And whether you leave, or Izzy and I leave, they'll think we made the exchange. If this were chess, I believe we'd call that checkmate."

Hamid's lips were set in a thin line. "Obviously you don't play chess."

"Why's that?"

"We all leave together."

At that moment, the fire alarm went off.

Showers of water sprang from the ceiling, dousing everyone and raising shrieks and protests from customers and waiters alike. Hamid ducked as if someone were shooting at him. Jon didn't think. He shoved Hamid and sent him sprawling to the ground. Isabel leaped from the chair, pausing only to kick the downed assassin before turning and running with Jon toward the exit.

Sean rose from his seat and held out his hand toward Jon, reaching for his sidearm. Jon nodded curtly, "Get him!"

Sean looked from Jon to the man picking himself up and starting toward them. Brian and Michael reached him first, planting a foot into his back and pinning him to the floor, a gun pressed to his temple. Sean looked back at Jon, but they were already at the stairs.

"Come on!" he said to William. "He's getting away."

Jon and Isabel burst through the emergency doors onto the stairs. They took them two at a time, leaping down the steps, around the landings, chasing the stairs as they spiraled down the exterior of the elevator shaft. They shoved irate customers out of their way, pushing by with mumbled apologies, thrusting ever further downward to the exits one hundred and twenty meters below.

Behind them were shouts of surprise and anger—voices Jon knew were from the mercenaries in hot pursuit.

"Faster," he panted.

"I can't!"

"You must! They'll kill us! Run!"

An explosion of white paint chips and fragments of metal rang off the side of the staircase. Isabel yelped and hugged the wall. Jon grabbed her hand and pulled her along.

"They're shooting at us!"

"I know! Run!"

Two more shots rang out, spattering uselessly against the staircase. Jon clutched her hand, dragging her forward. They vaulted over the last railing and plunged through the doors.

The crowded shopping center muffled their steps as they surged toward the exits. Jon wove through the human maze, zigzagging to the left and right, putting as much distance between them and their pursuers as possible. Outside a center where children played, he hazarded a glance back. He spotted Sean and William about a hundred feet behind, their eyes scanning the crowd. William pointed at him, and the mercenaries started running.

"This way!" Isabel cried. He followed her down the escalator, turning at the bottom and racing toward the exit.

"Wait! This way!" He grabbed her hand and pulled her down a corridor that said Parking Garage in English and Turkish. Together they ran down the steps onto the lower level, across two rows to where he'd parked the Audi. They clambered inside and gunned the engine, leaving a squeal of rubber on the concrete as the Audi fled toward the ramp.

The windshield broke into spider webs as shots cracked through the car. Isabel screamed and ducked. Jon crouched and tried to peer through the broken glass. The Audi splintered the barricade and surged up the ramp.

A loud boom rang through their ears as the car fishtailed wildly to the left. He gunned the engine and heard the rubber of the back tire flopping against the pavement before it fell free. The Audi's steel rim screamed on the pavement, sending a shower of sparks blazing behind them. A huge bang shoved them sideways into the street, the airbags exploding into the compartment.

Isabel cracked open the side door and pushed herself onto the pavement. Jon followed. Bits of glass showered them as more bullets tore into the car. Jon turned and stared into the car, his eyes drawn by something he couldn't explain.

"I don't believe it," he muttered. More bullets slammed into the car. Distant sirens wailed.

He thrust his hand into the passenger compartment and pulled it out a second later. "Come on!" They ducked between the parked cars on the side of the street, running toward the corner. Windows exploded behind them as more shots missed their target.

They turned the corner and ducked through the stunned and gawking crowd. A bright yellow taxi pulled over toward the curb. Without thinking, Jon hailed it and pulled open the back door. They climbed in and turned just in time to see Sean and William emerge from behind the Audi.

"Go!" Jon yelled. The cab pulled away, disappearing into the flow of traffic.

CHAPTER
28

"Where to, sir?"

"Uh, airport."

"Very good, sir. Did you have any luggage?"

Luggage? He swore. "I left it in the car! No, never mind. Just take us to the airport." He fumbled with his back pocket. His words tumbled out nonsensically. "I still have my wallet. That—that's good. We can buy fresh tickets. Oh, our passports and—the police have our passports. They were shooting at us. Izzy!" He reached over and pulled her into an embrace.

They held each other, saying nothing with words, and meaning every moment. Finally, Jon pulled back and studied her eyes. "Are you okay?"

She nodded vigorously. "You saved my life again."

"We—we've got to stop doing this! Not the saving the life thing, but the getting shot at. That's definitely got to stop." He caught his breath. "I thought I'd lost y…. Did he hurt you? Did he—do something?"

She shook her head. "He tied me up. He threatened me. I think he wanted to, but he didn't do anything. I think he was just mad that I hit him!" She giggled, then cupped his face in her palm. "You're my hero." She bent forward and kissed him. "Thank you."

He stared at her. What was that kiss about? Gratitude? Or something more? He leaned back in his seat. Probably just the stress of being thrown together like this. He blew out a breath.

"What's going to happen now?" she said.

He turned and looked out the window, watching the buildings and houses of the city flash past. "We go to the airport and find out what this key is for." He pulled the key from his pocket and handed it to her. She stared at it.

"You switched it."

He grinned. "Hamid now has the key to my back door, which won't do him any good, as I'm changing the locks when I get home anyway." He turned and held something up. "Look what I found."

She stared at the scroll. "You said you lost it."

"It was in the car. It must've fallen out of my pocket." He chuckled. "If we hadn't had to dive out the passenger side, I never would've seen it." He held up the key. "If what's in this locker is what I think it is, we can get both halves of the scroll, and get out of this country before anyone catches us."

Sean stalked back into the parking garage with William in tow. They met up with Brian and Michael at the van.

"Didja get him?" Mike asked.

Sean replied with an unpleasant suggestion.

Brian said nothing and reached into the glove box, pulling out a GPS receiver unit. Sean leaned over and looked at the read out. "They're heading for the airport."

"We shoulda capped the bugger when we had the chance," said William.

Sean glanced at him and shook his head. He pressed his lips into a hard line. "It was my call."

"Yeah?" William pointed at him. "Your call is what's gonna cost us this operation."

"It's my bloody operation!"

"It's your bloody mess!"

Quick as death, two Berettas flew from their holsters, each pointed at the other person's head. Michael reached for his gun, but Brian put a restraining hand on him. He shook his head briefly. William and Sean glared at each other, cutting diamonds with their eyes.

"Twenty years," William said. "Twenty years we worked together. What's that now? Water under the bridge? You don't like what I gotta say, so you draw out on me? This mission's in the crapper, and mightn't we ought to think 'bout calling the whole thing off? Or are you gonna kill me instead?"

Sean clenched his teeth and lowered his weapon. He blew out a long breath. "You always had bollocks, William. I can't kill you." He pulled the clip from his gun. "I'm outta bullets."

William smirked. "I figured. Me too." He lowered his gun and walked around the van. Sean slammed a fresh clip into his Beretta, and in one smooth motion raised it and held it at William's head.

William went pale.

"Now I can," Sean said. He nodded to Brian and Michael. "Get in."

William stood sweating profusely.

"You're wanting out of this mission, eh? That suits me fine. You done brought the box, but that's been all you're good for. And that's all I'll pay you for. You're fired."

William opened his mouth as if to object, but then closed it again, his face a tight mask of anger. Sean kept the gun trained on him until he climbed into the driver's seat, and started the van.

"This ain't right," William hollered at him.

"Take it up with Employment Appeals!" Sean shifted into gear and the van bolted past the stupefied William.

In the mirror, Sean saw William throw his gun at the retreating van, yelling, "You've got my bloody passport!"

He shook his head and kept driving.

The cab dropped them off at the arrivals level. Jon and Isabel strode through the entrance into the glass, steel and garish rainbow veneer of Esenboğa International Airport. Together they hurried along a winding path of polished tile toward the airport lockers, ducking the gaze of security officers who might be on the lookout for two Americans who were no longer welcome on Turkish soil.

"So what do we do when we get the other half of the scroll? Do you think we can slip them through customs?"

"I don't know, Izzy. I haven't thought that far ahead. I suppose we could always leave them in our pockets and hope they don't check. But that's not the real problem."

"Then what is?"

"The age of the scroll. The vellum is almost two thousand years old. It's already starting to crumble. The longer it is exposed to light, air, and humidity, the more it will degrade."

"Is there anything you can do?"

He glanced at the café they passed by, then turned abruptly. "Yeah," he said, "there is. Come on." He led her down to the café and got in line. "You hungry?"

"I don't know. Probably. I don't remember the last time I ate."

"You should get something. Order a sandwich. Preferably one that comes in a foil wrapper."

"What are you going to do?"

"We'll need a hand wipe to clean it. And then we'll wrap the scrolls in the foil. It's not the best, but it should keep them relatively safe."

"And what about customs?"

"We'll have to take that risk."

After ordering, they took a seat at a table near the exit and unwrapped their sandwiches. Isabel wolfed hers down while Jon scrubbed the foil wrappers with a moist towelette and dried them carefully with a napkin. He pulled out the frail half of the scroll and set it gently in the wrapper, rolling it between the protective foil and folding the ends in until it was completely covered. The second wrapper, he carefully folded and stuck in his pocket.

"Let's go," he said, grabbing his sandwich.

The lockers were set against the wall down a side corridor. Jon took out the key and unlocked the door. "Here we go," he said with a grin, and opened the locker.

It was empty.

He stared into the space, not comprehending. "I-I don't understand. I thought it would be here." He shook his head. "What did he do with the other half of the scroll?"

"Wait." Isabel pulled a yellow Post-It Note off the inside of the door, and flipped it over to reveal six numbers written on the back.

"What is it?"

"Oh, Stephen!" she muttered. "It's the code key to our safe. We have one in the house. Stephen insisted on it. Before he was assaulted, he changed the combination. He wouldn't tell me what it was. He said it was for my own good." She shook her head. "I thought he was hiding something from me. I always believed the worst."

"How do you know it's the code to the safe? You said he changed it."

She smiled and showed him the note. "It's my birthday."

Jon took the note from her and crumpled it up. "So now what? He obviously hid the scroll in your safe, which is at your house—which we can't get to because we're no longer allowed in the country. In fact, if we don't show up soon, they might put out a warrant for us."

"I don't think he intended it to happen this way."

"I don't think he intended a lot of things. He took the precautions he did because he knew he had to." He leaned back against the lockers. "There's got to be a way to do this."

"Perhaps I may assist?"

Jon and Isabel turned, startled. The smiling form of their cab driver stood in front of them, wearing an odd, black cassock instead of regular clothes. His size was startling.

CHAPTER
29

"I'm sorry? Who are you?" Jon exclaimed.

The man chuckled. "You did not think it suspicious to find a cab so quickly in this town? So ready to pick up someone fleeing a gun fight?"

"You-you're the cab driver." He pushed Isabel behind him. The man's eyes flicked from her to Jon.

"I mean you no harm. My name is Demetri Antonescu. I am but a humble servant of God from the Holy Mountain. And sometimes a cabbie."

"What do you want?"

"To go home." He laughed, then grew serious. "But my mission is to protect the autographs. The scroll you seek tells of their location, yes? I only wish to protect them, to ensure they do not fall into the hands of unbelievers or private collectors, such as the man who hired those who have been chasing you."

"How do you—?"

"I was there. Who do you think set the fire and triggered the alarm?"

"That was you?" said Isabel.

"Indeed. And I know Father Bellamy tried to poison your brother. I warned him not to do so. Perhaps I ought to have done more, but I have foresworn the ways of the gun. I rely now on God's power to protect me."

"What do you want with us?" Jon asked.

"As I said, to offer my assistance."

"Why?"

"We can't trust him, Jonnie! We don't know who he is."

"Trust is earned, is it not?" said Demetri. "I have assisted your escape twice now. I am not attempting to stop you or to hinder you in any way. I even know you are carrying half the scroll in a sandwich wrapper in your coat pocket. The other half of the scroll is in a safe in your house, Ms. Kaufman, the combination of which your late brother foolishly set for your birthday, a rather unfortunate obvious selection." He paused and let this sink in. "I could—rather easily, I think—relieve you of the scroll you carry and obtain the other half with only slightly more difficulty. Instead, I stand here offering you my services. I do not need your help, but I think you need mine."

"Why? Why would you help us?"

"Two reasons. I have no wish to violate the eighth commandment, and I cannot read Greek." He folded his hands and smiled patiently.

"What do you want in exchange?"

"A translation, of course. And then your agreement that when you find the autographs, you will bring them to the Holy Mountain for safekeeping. Naturally, we will allow you to examine them for verification purposes. But we must carefully guard all such scientific investigations. The scrolls are sacred. They must be treated as such. We of Mount Athos will safeguard them for the world."

Jon thought a moment and turned to Isabel.

"No," she said.

"We need him."

"Jonnie!"

"We have no other option."

"Oh," said the monk. "And those mercenaries you fled from—the ones trying to kill you? I am entirely confident they are coming this way. I do not believe they will be very happy."

"We have to get out of the country," said Jon. "They've revoked our visas. If we don't leave, the police will be after us as well."

Demetri cocked his head. "So how will you obtain the other half of the scroll?"

"I have an idea. Is your visa valid?" he asked. The monk nodded.

Lieutenant Çapanoğlu glanced up at a nudge from Sergeant Bahar. Several yards away, he spotted the two Americans moving through the crowd. He nodded at Bahar, who spoke quietly into his microphone. Further off, several other plain-clothes detectives waited as the Americans passed, watching for any sign of The Rat moving behind them or toward them.

"Check one?" said Bahar.

The radio chirped. "No sign of him, sir."

"Check two?"

"Nothing, sir."

"Check three?"

After a moment, a voice came back. "No sir."

Bahar looked toward Kahil and shrugged. Kahil ground his teeth. "He's got to be here somewhere. Tell them to keep looking."

"All eyes stay sharp."

Kahil looked up at the cameras scanning the crowd from high above. Each camera streamed video into a central computer running facial recognition software. Each person in the airport was checked and sometimes rechecked against Interpol's database. The software was good, but it wasn't foolproof, especially if someone knew how to avoid the cameras. That's what the detectives were for. He'd had Bahar station them at the most likely places where someone might try to slip through the video web unseen.

And with the two Americans as bait, the odds of luring The Rat into his trap and catching him or killing him outright were exceptionally high.

So where was he?

As Jon and Isabel continued to move toward him, with no sign of The Rat closing in, it became painfully obvious that Hamid Al-Assini was not in the airport. He swore an oath and stepped toward the couple.

Jon and Isabel came to a stop in front of him.

"So," he said, "perhaps you can explain to me what happened to your police escort? Or why you are late for your flight?"

Jon glanced around. "We ran into a little trouble on our way here."

"Trouble follows you like a plague. Come with me, please." Kahil led them into a small room away from the main concourse. Once the door closed, he turned to them and demanded, "Did this trouble have anything to do with the assassination of my four officers? Or with the incident at the Atakule an hour ago?"

"Both, actually."

"And how is it my officers are dead, and you have survived?"

"I don't know."

Kahil folded his arms. "You don't know. What prevents me from arresting you at this moment?"

"Hamid Al-Assini killed your four officers. He did so to kidnap Izzy, Ms. Kaufman, and hold her for ransom. He called my hotel room this morning and told me to meet him at the Atakule for an exchange."

"An exchange for what?"

"For this." He turned over the key to the locker. "There's nothing in it. Hamid believed Dr. Kaufman had left something of great value inside this locker. He was wrong."

"Oh. So you just explained this to him, and he let you go?"

"No." Jon told him about the mercenary team, and about how he'd switched the keys on Hamid. At the mention of Sean's name Kahil grew somber, and he began asking more questions about who was with him and what they were after.

"The same thing as Hamid."

"And what was that?"

Jon shook his head. "Whatever was supposed to be in that dig, I think. I don't know if it's still there or ever was there. But Stephen knew his life was in danger. And so was Izzy's. I think he wanted me to come to protect her, to help get her away from this situation. And if it's alright with you, we'd just like to get onto the next flight and get out of here."

Kahil put a hand on his shoulder and stared long into his eyes. He said quietly, "You're not telling me the whole truth, are you?"

Jon answered evenly. "I've told you everything I can."

"And what are all these people after?"

"They're after an artifact. Hidden in a place called the *Domo tou Bibliou*. It means, 'Home of the Book.' Stephen thought he'd found it. The artifact is a two-thousand-year-old document supposedly written by Saint Paul, which tells of the secret location of the autographs—the original manuscripts— of the New Testament."

Kahil studied his face a moment longer, then started chuckling. "Are you serious?"

"That is what they believe."

"And what about you? Do you believe this?"

Isabel stepped forward. "My brother had a flair for the dramatic. He always thought archeology was about the big find. Like King Tut's tomb. Before coming here, he was convinced the Ark of the Covenant was in Southeast Asia. When he didn't find it there, he tried to manufacture the evidence. He justified this by saying he needed the funding to continue his research, that the real ark still lay hidden. He was found out and discredited. He was fired."

"Even if he's your brother, why would stay with such a man?"

Isabel held back her tears. "We were orphaned together. He was the only family I had."

Kahil folded his arms. "So all this is due to a cleverly disguised hoax?"

"It looks that way," said Jon.

After a moment, Kahil nodded. He reached into his pocket and pulled out their papers. "Your passports," he said. "There is a plane leaving in an hour for Munich. You will have to purchase new tickets, but you should have enough time to make the flight. Come." He led them out of the interrogation room, and walked with them toward the ticket counter. "It is a pity this artifact of yours is not real. A find like that would be priceless. Men would do almost anything to possess it, as we have tragically seen."

He offered them his hand. "Have a safe flight. Please do not take this wrong, but I do not wish to see you in my country again. Hmm?" With that, he turned sharply and left.

Jon bought their tickets and walked with Isabel toward the gate. Their flight would leave in forty-five minutes. They sat down in a row of plastic chairs near the gate. He pulled out his Blackberry, dialing the number of the pay phone where Demetri was waiting.

After one ring, the monk picked up.

"We're going to Munich."

"Once you get there you will need a car. You must go to Bulgaria. There is a town there called Rezovo. It is on the Black Sea. I will meet you there at the chapel of Saint John the Baptist in two days. We will cross the border by boat."

"Rezovo. Saint John the Baptist. Two days."

"God be with you."

CHAPTER
30

"And there they go."

Brian pointed out the window at the 737 leaving the airstrip. In a moment, the tracking chip would be out of range. Sean nodded and checked the time, comparing it to the departures list from the Esenboğa Airport's website. He sighed. "Munich."

"Going home, then?"

"Us or them?"

Brian smirked. "Them."

"I don't know. 'Tis possible, I suppose. An' who could blame them?" He stared quietly out the windshield at the aircraft dwindling into the horizon. In a moment, it would be gone, along with all chance of recovering the scroll.

Beaufort would not be happy. But for all the billionaire had cost him so far in this fiasco, Sean might just pay him a visit and explain it in person. He sucked his teeth. It wasn't Beaufort's fault the operation came apart—a fact he'd doubtless point out when Sean came to collect.

He leaned back in the seat and ran a hand over his face. "Michael, give our man in Berlin a call. Tell him to go to Munich. Tell him who to look for."

"You wantin' him to stop 'em, then? That'll not be easy, what with all the security."

He nodded. "Aye. Tell him to stop 'em if he can. Track 'em if he can't. He's not to harm them. I'll be wanting a wee chat with the good doctor."

Michael nodded and pulled out his cell phone, speed-dialing the number.

Hamid sat back in the front seat of the stolen Peugeot and frowned. He kept the binoculars trained on the dark van, watching the men inside converse. They didn't look happy at all. He lowered the binoculars just long enough to check the traffic in the rear-view mirrors before lifting them to his eyes again. The last thing he needed was a police officer sneaking up behind him to check out the report of a stolen vehicle.

Ever since the men ambushed him in the restaurant, he'd been following at a discreet distance. At first, he'd thought Munro had called the police. When they left him alive and unquestioned in the spray of the water sprinklers, he began to think the doctor had hired some guns to assist his escape. When he watched them destroy the car Munro had driven—his car, in fact—in a flurry of bullets, he realized the truth. The men represented a third party interested in the scroll.

Scratch that. Fourth party. He'd forgotten about the impotent monk.

The key Munro had given to him was not the one the archaeologist had sent to him. It was nothing more than a simple house key. Perhaps even one of his own. It galled him how easily the professor outmaneuvered him. Lying there on the floor with the water soaking his clothes, he'd had an epiphany. He was relying on the wrong skill set. All this time he'd handled the situation like an assassin, when he ought to have been thinking like a thief. An assassin concerned himself with getting close to the mark, perhaps lulling him into a false sense of confidence, waiting for the right time to strike. Controlling the environment as much as possible. A thief avoided being seen by the mark as much as possible—avoided being seen by anyone if it could be helped—and relieving the mark of whatever was desired without drawing any attention to himself. The issue was not controlling the environment, but being completely aware of it, watching for potential obstacles, observers, or other operatives.

Armed with a new determination, he stopped at his Audi only long enough to retrieve the binoculars from the glove box. Then he carjacked a Peugeot from an unwary driver awed by the firefight and followed the team of hired guns to the airport. Now his best bet was to keep them in sight, follow behind at a discreet distance, and avoid drawing any attention to himself. With any luck, he'd be there when Dr. Munro and Ms. Kaufman resurfaced with the scroll, and snatch it away from all of them before anyone even knew he'd been there.

The question of the key made more sense now. It must have been the key to an airport locker. Kaufman intended Munro to retrieve the first half of the scroll at the locker and bring it with him to the chapel for the second half. Munro left too soon, before the key arrived. They were retracing their steps. With both halves, they would emerge from the airport soon, run afoul of the mercenary team, and Hamid would strike before anyone was the wiser.

Something near the entrance to the airport caught his eye. He raised the binoculars again, searching the crowd until he saw him. A man striding toward a yellow cab, dressed head to toe in a black cassock.

The monk.

Maybe not so impotent after all, he thought. He watched as the monk entered the cab's driver side door and started the car. A second job for the father? Offerings must be down. He smirked at his own joke.

So the monk had followed them to the airport. Did he have the scroll now? If not, why was he leaving? He wouldn't have given up so easily.

He wheeled back to the airport entrance, scanning for any sign of Dr. Munro and Ms. Kaufman.

Nothing.

It didn't make sense. The priest wouldn't leave without the scroll—unless it was beyond his reach. Which meant the Americans must have gotten on a plane.

He dropped the binoculars and started the car. The priest either had the scroll, or knew where it was. He glanced briefly at the van where the mercenaries still talked, oblivious to the fact that their objective was slipping away right under their noses.

Somehow, he felt much better.

Isabel slid open the airplane window shade and stared through the oval porthole at the distant and retreating earth. Trees looking no larger than lichens obscured the wrinkled terrain. The red roofs of buildings were a tile mosaic of some Impressionistic vision, conveying an elusive image fading into obscurity. It was all falling away. Her home. Her family. Her life as she'd known it for the past twelve years.

All gone.

She pulled at her lower lip. Maybe she was still reeling from the excitement and fear of the past few days. So much had happened since Stephen's attack. Whatever her normal life had been, the assassin's knife had cut it away, and left it on the ground far beneath her. She felt like a child's balloon loosed from its string and now rising effortlessly and inexorably upward. She was born aloft to places unforeseeable, unknowable, and unable to return to the hands of the one who'd once held her fast. Despite this, she felt neither fear nor exhilaration—only a simple but profound sense of freedom.

And peace.

She turned from the window and looked at the man sitting next to her. Jonnie had his glasses on. He'd rolled his sleeves up to his forearms. He peered over the unwrapped half of the scroll they'd recovered from the buried chapel—the same scroll Stephen had given his life to protect. He furrowed his eyebrows in concentration. Engrossed in the translation and oblivious to its meaning. His lips moved, forming the words etched onto the animal skins by an unknown, long-dead saint.

He looked every bit the part of the frumpy professor she'd always imagined he'd be when she was younger. At the time, the thought of being married to someone so completely predictable and plain overwhelmed her. It was no wonder she'd turned him down. She'd always imagined a husband would offer adventure and romance—with rugged looks and a broad chest, like someone out of a Danielle Steele novel. How could a man like Jonnie have even hoped to compete with that?

She smiled. Jonnie believed in common sense. That was why. Too late, she'd learned romance novels were fictions. Life with Stephen was an adventure, but there was no time left for romance with anyone.

Jonnie was nothing like her brother. At least, not on the surface. He'd been ready to walk away from it all just a few days ago—willing to go back to his safe, quiet life of study. A life he would return to, no doubt, when all this was over.

Yet beneath the surface, Jonnie had shown incredible courage and loyalty. He'd matched wits with Hamid to save her life—had double-crossed men Stephen would have likely bought off instead. Even now he was preparing to steal back into the country with her to finally solve the mystery, and exonerate the reputation of a man who'd sacrifice any sense of honor or self-respect to win a prize.

He was more the man she'd hoped to find than she'd ever imagined. She reached for his hand. His fingers went stiff, not returning her squeeze. She met his eyes. They were filled with questions and doubt. She smiled and pulled his hand in closer before turning back to the window.

Jon felt his heart beat faster. Isabel's hand was warm, and it sent a thrill down his spine to places long left dormant. Did she just want comfort? Was this just friendship? Was it something more? The questions collided off each other, jarring loose memories and moldy fantasies long ago shelved in the attic of his subconscious. It was so easy for Isabel to disturb his foundations, to bring the carefully constructed façade of what he called a meaningful life down upon him. And if she left him shattered again, who'd help him pick up the pieces?

He didn't have time for this. He needed to think! And he needed his hand back. It was hard enough to hold onto the scroll with one hand and make notes with the other. One handed was impossible. He'd at least gained a new appreciation for Hamid. Not that The Rat deserved any.

He could have pulled his hand away if he wanted to, instead of waiting for her to release him. But he didn't really want to. Such thoughts were dangerous, and he shoved them from his mind, forcing himself to concentrate on his task.

The letters mocked him. The language was Koine Greek. The structure of the words told him this. The vocabulary was vaguely Pauline, though he couldn't be sure without the second half of the scroll. He translated as far down as the name *Iohanathan*—Greek for Jonathan—and a form of the word *luō*, a verb meaning *to destroy*. It was guesswork, but it sounded as though this John person was someone Paul was marking out as dangerous, much like he did in Second Timothy with Hymenaeus, Philetus, and Alexander the coppersmith.

Yet for all that, something about the scroll bothered him. Something he couldn't quite put his finger on. He had a nagging suspicion the scroll was fake. Chemical dating of the ink and leather would confirm it one way or another, and he'd happily be wrong.

The thought of having been through all they'd endured these last few days for the sake of yet another one of Stephen's clever forgeries burned him up. How could he possibly stand it if that were the case?

On the other hand, why was he so increasingly certain that it was?

He sighed and gently pulled his hand free. He rolled up the scroll in the foil. There was no way of knowing just yet. Not without the other half of the scroll. Time would tell soon enough.

CHAPTER
31

Heinrich took a large bite out of his liverwurst and cheddar sandwich, swooping up a dangling thread of onion with his finger before it could fall from his mouth and join one or two others already on the floor. Above him, the board indicated the flight from Ankara had arrived at the gate and was presently deboarding. He took a long sip of cola from his straw, burping quietly before encompassing another copious segment of sandwich.

It was unfortunate. Liverwurst and cheddar with onions was a meal to savor. Especially when someone else paid for it. He hated to rush it. However, MacNeil's instructions were quite explicit, and as the sandwich was on the Irishman's dime anyway, he'd best not miss his marks because he spent too much time eating it. He raised his right wrist briefly, glancing at the wallet-sized photographs he'd strapped there. The photos were black and white and a bit grainy, but each person was recognizable enough.

In his wallet, he carried a fake I.D. It was stolen, actually, from a Munich detective some years back who'd spent too much time in a certain bordello Heinrich happened to own. The detective had been too ashamed to admit the badge was missing, until Heinrich offered him a convenient excuse. Even now, he chuckled to think of it. The detective actually paid Heinrich to have a couple of thugs beat him up, so he could claim his wallet was stolen, along with his identification. Heinrich found a pair of skinheads who were more than willing to do the job for free—and with a gusto which surprised even the detective. He spent six weeks in the hospital with three broken ribs and a deviated septum. Heinrich pocketed the money, kept the badge for situations such as these, and ingratiated himself to the detective all in one sweet maneuver. The only downside was the fact that he lost the wages his girl might have earned from the detective while he recovered instead.

He had to be very careful with the badge. If any real police ever discovered him with it, the whole fiasco would blow up in his face. He'd drag the detective down with him, but he was equally confident it wouldn't matter much.

He finished the last of his sandwich as the two marks emerged from the terminal. He took a last sip from the cola, then dropped it in the wastebasket and fumbled for the badge as he approached them both.

"Excuse me," he said, holding up the I.D. The couple paused, exchanging furtive looks. "You are Doctor Jonathan Munro and Ms. Isabel Kaufman? You will come with me, please."

"What is this about?" Jon said.

"I think you know," Heinrich lied. "Please." He turned and waved them forward with his arm.

"Jonnie?" said Isabel.

"Come on," Jon replied. "We'd better go with him."

Heinrich smiled. This was working better than he'd hoped. Once he got them outside the airport and into his car, he'd have them for sure. Even with the badge, he didn't dare bring a gun through security. He flashed the I.D. at the security checkpoint, and put it away again.

"I demand to know why we're being taken into custody."

"Really, Dr. Munro. Do you wish to be discussing this here?" Inwardly he cursed MacNeil for not giving him more information. It would be hard to keep this up for long if the professor kept asking questions.

"It's just that we're doing what we were told. Lieutenant Kahil asked us to leave Turkey and return to America. That is all we're trying to do."

"Ah, but that was Turkey. Here in Germany, we have our own rules."

"But we haven't broken any laws!"

Heinrich stopped and faced him. His face reddened with frustration. His car was a scant two hundred yards away in the parking garage. Couldn't this man shut up long enough to get that far? "Seriously, Dr. Munro, if you persist in resisting, I shall have to put the cuffs on you. Is that what you want?" He hoped this would quell him into submission. He hadn't thought to bring the cuffs with him.

Munro stood his ground. "I want to talk to my embassy. I'm an American citizen, and I'm tired of getting treated like this."

Heinrich laughed. "You Americans! You call Germans arrogant, yet you persist in demanding we treat you with special deference. You'll have an opportunity to contact your embassy once we reach the station, I promise you. But for now, will you please just come along quietly?"

The two Americans exchanged a glance and followed. Heinrich trudged along in front of them, muttering an insult in German. He considered sending Sean a bill for additional expenses, just for the frustration of putting on this charade. He'd only worked with the mercenary twice before. Once, handling a delicate matter of relieving an American military attaché of his flash drive, deleting certain files, and then returning it before the man knew it was missing. A pair of his ladies proved more than the hapless American could handle. The other time was during a misunderstanding in the Balkans over a particular arms shipment that went to the wrong side. That was a simple courier job, and the only time he'd met Sean face to face. Altogether, it was an agreeable arrangement. Sean paid well for his services, and Heinrich performed them with an alacrity the former IRA agent found refreshing.

He'd never hit him up for more money, though, and wasn't quite sure how the man would take it. Sean was unlikely to do anything beyond simply refusing to pay it, but it might put a crimp in their business dealings. Given the dubious and rather difficult nature of his present assignment, however, that might not be a bad thing.

They crossed into the parking garage and Heinrich pulled out his keys, unlocking his Benz. He turned when he noticed the two Americans had stopped.

"Nice car," said Jon, staring at him oddly. He smiled and nodded, opening the back door for them. Jon ushered Isabel into the rear seat, then stopped again. *What was it with this man?* Heinrich thought.

"Your car doesn't have a radio," Jon observed. Heinrich furrowed his brow. What was he getting at?

"No," Heinrich muttered. "It's my personal vehicle. Please. Just get in."

Jon closed the door. "Why did you bring your personal vehicle?"

Uh oh. This isn't good. Heinrich opened his door. His gun lay just under the front seat. "N-no reason. Just convenient, I suppose. I came from the house."

"And how does a detective in Berlin earn enough money to buy a Mercedes Benz?"

Heinrich shrugged. "I get paid well."

Jon nodded slowly. "I bet you've been paid well. You're not a cop. Or if you are, you're on the take. We're not going anywhere with you."

Heinrich lunged for the front seat, feeling around for the gun. His fingers closed around it. Just then, he felt an incredible pain shoot through his knee. He cried out, falling backwards as Jon yanked him out of the car. The gun flew from his fingers and skittered across the pavement.

A second sharp pain burst through his abdomen. Jon reared back and kicked him again. His keys fell to the ground. Through tears, he saw Jon pick up the keys and jump in the front seat. A moment later, his car was speeding out of the parking garage.

He lay there a moment, catching his breath, feeling around for anything broken or ruptured—anything for which he could bill Sean MacNeil further. If he was going to get physically beat up, at least Sean should pay for it. Finally, he rolled to his feet and stood, wincing as he put pressure on his knee. Munro must've slammed the car door on his knee when he went for the gun. *You're a stupid fool, Heinrich, that's what you are. Should've seen that coming.*

He spotted his gun lying several feet away. *And perhaps next time you can leave your weapon somewhere more accessible than below the front seat!* As he retrieved his gun, he pulled out his cell phone and made two calls. The first was to an employee to bring round a car and pick him up at the airport. The second was to Sean MacNeil.

"Go," said Sean.

"I had them, Sean."

"Had them," Sean repeated.

"The American surprised me. Before I could get to my gun." He winced in pain. He tasted blood.

"Unbelievable. I asked you to do one simple thing. Is there no one who can do this bloody job?" Heinrich heard Sean sputtering something unintelligible. "How hard can it be to follow two dumb Americans?"

Heinrich caught his breath and sank down against a building support. "Easier than you think, I suppose." He fumbled for his wallet.

"Now what's that supposed to mean?!"

"They took my car." He started laughing. "My Benz. I have a GPS chip installed—in case it's ever stolen!"

Sean was silent.

"Most fortuitous, yes? You can track them remotely—and they'll never even know they're being followed." He laughed again, and winced as the ache in his stomach doubled him over in pain. "That worked better than I could've hoped." He gave them the code and hung up.

He wondered if he could charge Sean for the car.

"Jonnie, you are incredible!"

He glanced in the rear-view mirror. Isabel was in the back seat, beaming. He ran a hand across his brow. *Am I, really?* He pushed to one side as Isabel climbed over the console into the front. She slid down into her seat, then leaned over and kissed his cheek.

"I don't know, Izzy. I—" he pressed his lips together. "I think I hurt that guy pretty bad."

"So? He had it coming."

"Did he?" He shook his head. "I've never tried to hurt someone in anger before."

"Yes, you have."

"Well, okay, but not like that. I was just really angry. This whole thing—it's just crazy, you know?"

She smiled at him. "You are a man of action, Jonnie."

"Action?"

"Yes. You are risking everything to retrieve this piece of our history, our heritage, and you don't even know for certain it is real."

"A lot of people seem to think it is."

"True, and in a few days, we will retrieve the other half of this scroll. We will put the two together. And we will know. We will have one of the greatest treasures of all time."

He flexed his fingers on the steering wheel. Isabel settled into the passenger seat and began programming their destination into the console's GPS. He watched her for a moment. She was so excited. Did she really know what it was all about? Or was it simply the adventure of it all? Finding the autographs would be incredible. Yet would they produce faith in anyone except those who already believed? And what about Izzy? He'd never really asked her. What were her beliefs? And if she didn't yet believe, would the autographs convince her?

Were they even real? A nagging doubt about the scrolls teased the edges of his consciousness, fraying his confidence. What would happen when they put the two halves of the scroll together, and he'd know beyond a doubt the whole thing was a fake? Would it then be worth all the risk and sacrifice?

CHAPTER
32

The trip from Germany through the Czech Republic, Slovakia, Hungary, and Serbia was met without incident, nor even so much as a border check—thanks to the European Union. They stopped at a hotel in Belgrade, bought a change of clothes at a local shop, and ate dinner. According to the GPS system in the Benz, they were making excellent time. Jon suggested they ditch the car—if only because of the border check they'd meet at Bulgaria. What really bothered him was the fact they hadn't encountered any police—despite the stolen car. Surely, that fake cop must've reported it by now.

Unless he'd hit the German harder than he'd thought. Somehow, he couldn't shake the thought he might've seriously injured the man—or even killed him. He hadn't meant to. He didn't even know what he was going to do until he'd grabbed the car door and slammed it into the man's knee. After that, he barely remembered anything except how angry he was that yet another person was pointing a gun at him. He tried praying about it, but found very little peace. Instead, he could only swallow the guilt and concentrate on the task ahead. They found a suitable car rental near the airport and picked up a Fiat before returning to the hotel.

The room held two double beds, but little else. Isabel changed in the bathroom, and Jon studied the fragment of scroll, trying to recall what it was about the document that bothered him still. He waited with the television tuned to CNN. He was hoping to catch any news from either Germany or Turkey on their recent adventures, but it was difficult with the broadcasts given entirely in Serbian with English subtitles. He found the effort to constantly look up and check the translation rather distracting from his study of the scroll.

He was somewhat more distracted when Isabel came out of the bathroom, dressed in a thin, white nightgown accentuating the curves of her torso.

"Jonnie?"

"Huh?"

"You're staring at me."

He pressed his open mouth into a sheepish grin and forced his eyes away. "Sorry," he mumbled. She crawled into the bed opposite him, pulling the covers up to her shoulders. She propped her head on one elbow.

"I didn't say I minded," she purred.

His pulse quickened.

A nervous laugh escaped his lips. He glanced from the scroll to the sister of his former best friend, the one woman he had ever loved.

"Izzy—" he began.

"What?" Her eyes twinkled.

"Nothing."

"What is it?" She smiled again, her lips parted just enough to show her teeth. "You can tell me."

"I—I can't do this."

Her smile faded, the softness in her eyes fading as she grasped his meaning. Finally, she said, "Well, who said we were doing anything?"

She rolled over, turning away from him. He stared at her back. He put down the scroll. "Izzy?"

"I think I'd just like to get some sleep now."

He studied her silently, and then climbed into the other bed. He stared at her back until he fell asleep.

She said little to him the next morning. Their conversation was curt, perfunctory, and related solely to the task of getting on the road again. About a half hour into the drive, Jon said, "I'm sorry if I offended you."

She continued to stare out the window.

"Are you mad at me?"

"I don't know what you were expecting."

"I wasn't expecting anything."

"Then why would you say that? You said, 'I can't do this.' What did you mean?"

He didn't answer.

"Did you think I was offering myself to you?"

"No." He answered too quickly.

"I don't offer myself to just anyone who comes along."

"I know."

"Well…good."

He vented his breath, trying to form his question the right way. "W-were you?"

She jerked her head around, staring at him hotly. "No! God, no! How could you think that?"

"I—wow. I don't know how to…do…this."

"Do what?" The question sounded like an accusation.

"Talk. About whether or not I want to be with someone. Or I don't know how to know if someone wanted to be with me—I wouldn't know. I haven't been in a relationship with anybody in twelve years." He was talking too much. He felt unhinged.

She smirked. "How could you do that?"

"What?"

"Just cut yourself off from love?"

"I don't know. I guess there just wasn't anyone after you."

She turned away. "Don't do that."

"What?"

"Blame me. You could have loved someone else."

"I suppose so. But there wasn't anyone."

"Now you're acting pitiful."

"I'm sorry."

"Just stop apologizing."

"Okay."

They said little else as they drove. At the border, Jon found his caution rewarded. The inspection was cursory, but he felt much better about showing the rental papers to the guards than he would have trying to talk their way through in the Benz. Once on the other side, they drove another five and a half hours through gently rolling hills, small towns nestled in quiet valleys, and around sprawling cities dotting the countryside until they came to the coast of the Black Sea. Here they turned south through the coastal city of Burgas, driving through a wharf of small shops and homes strung across a narrow isthmus between the Black Sea and Burgas Bay.

The sun was drawing down to the horizon now, casting languid rays across the blue waters of the bay and turning the wharf houses a brilliant tangerine. On the far side, the whitecaps of the waves reflected the light, driving it back toward the shore in an endless glimmer. For a time, they forgot all sense of what they were after, what the last few days had been, or what the future might hold, and instead simply drank in the idyllic beauty offered them.

They followed the coast of the sea as the town disappeared behind them and the sun slid beneath the horizon. Jon rolled down the window, and above the rhythmic hum of the engine, they listened to the gentle rush of the waves driving toward the shore, the cry of seagulls calling to the deep. The towns and villages they encountered now were an interruption to the endless stretch of beaches and craggy cliffs overlooking the water.

An hour passed before they finally arrived in the village of Rezovo. Jon and Isabel drove straight for the church of St. John the Baptist, a small white chapel with a red tile roof overlooking a grassy knoll. As they climbed out of the car, Isabel wrapped a silk scarf around her head, then took his hand and walked with him toward the entrance. Before they reached the front door, it opened and a large man in a black cassock stepped out.

"Welcome to Rezovo," said Demetri. "I'm afraid I have some bad news."

The Lost Scrolls

CHAPTER
33

They stared in stunned silence.

Demetri smiled. "Forgive me for greeting you this way. You must be tired from your long journey, yes?" He turned and led them away from the chapel down a flight of stairs to a pier by the water's edge. When they reached the bottom, another monk waited for them. Tethered to the mooring was a small rowboat, with just enough room for the three of them.

"Blagodarja vi za vashata usluga, Pit'r," Demetri said to the man. *"Molja dajte tjahnata kola pod naem. Vizhte, che to e zaredeno v mojata smetka."* He then turned to Jon. "Give him your keys. He will return your rental car."

Jon handed over the keys, thanking Pit'r, and asked, "You said you have bad news?"

"Yes." Demetri climbed into the rowboat and picked up the oars, inserting them into the rowlocks. "Please, come in."

They climbed in and sat down, feeling the watercraft shake and bob in the water. Demetri untied the line and pushed them away from the pier. Through heavy strokes, he said, "The men who were following you have staked out your house, Ms. Kaufman. They've been there since yesterday."

"So we're walking into a trap?" said Jon.

Demetri grimaced. "It is only a trap if you do not know it exists. I had hoped leaving the country would throw them off your trail."

"How did they know we were coming back?" Isabel huddled close to Jon, trembling.

Demetri paused his rowing, studying them both in the darkness. The lights from shore barely illuminated their faces. "That is precisely what I wish to know. Perhaps one or both of you could offer up an explanation?"

"What are you suggesting?"

"You are being tracked. I wish to know how. Perhaps one of you is not what you seem?"

Jon stared at the man. This didn't make sense. There was no way Isabel could be working for those men, was there? Demetri waited patiently.

"Izzy?"

"I do not understand this," Isabel said. "I have been with you the whole time. You never so much as made a phone call."

"Me? Are you accusing me?" She couldn't be serious.

"No. I'm not accusing you. But Demetri is right. There must be some explanation. How else could they have known?"

"The man waiting for us in Munich. He knew we stopped there. He knew we didn't make our connection. He ensured it. But how could he have known where we.... The car!" Briefly, he filled Demetri in on their encounter with the man in Munich, including how far they had driven the Benz. Demetri nodded and resumed rowing.

"That is it. The Benz was equipped with GPS. That is why there was no report of it being stolen. They used it to track you. You were wise to abandon it."

"We shouldn't have taken it in the first place."

Demetri shrugged. "Regardless, once you did not make your connection, they would easily have guessed your purpose."

"So how do we get around them?"

The monk chuckled. "We shall have to think of something."

Demetri rowed them a mile past Rezovo, bringing them onto shore just outside of Beğendik. Here they walked for several hundred yards to the car he'd left for them, then climbed in and drove along the winding back roads until they reached the major highway that ran past Istanbul, Adapazari, and Bolu before dropping south toward Ankara. It was a six-hour trip, and both Dr. Munro and Ms. Kaufman slept through most of it. Demetri drove in silence, not wanting to disturb them until they reached the capitol.

The explanation Dr. Munro had offered him made sense, but could he trust it? It felt too convenient. Was Dr. Munro working with those men? After all, he did bring them to the Atakule. Or was the explanation too convenient because he was protecting the woman? He obviously loved her, but would he lie to himself? One or both of them could have been playing him, using his efforts to bring them across the border back into Turkey without any intention of keeping their side of the bargain. Or was the failure of the mercenaries in Ankara less the result of incompetence, and more a deliberate ploy to throw them off balance?

On the other hand, Dr. Munro and Ms. Kaufman's continual escapes could be nothing more than dumb luck—or more likely, the hand of God. In which case, he must help them and trust the Divine hand to bring the scrolls to the Holy Mountain as He must surely do—for what other possible reason could there be for Providence acting on their behalf? It made little sense, the Lord using such people to do His will. But his own salvation made even less sense, and the mysterious ways of God were not his to debate.

Demetri woke them on the outskirts of Ankara. The morning sun was just peeking over the horizon. They stopped by a fast food restaurant so they could refresh themselves. Demetri ignored the food, settling for a small cup of tea. After they ate and were fully awake, he drove them to the neighborhood where Isabel used to live just days before. He pulled up to a corner several blocks from the house and reviewed the situation with them.

"I count three men. What happened to the fourth, I do not know. One watches the front from a car across the street. The other two keep watch on the back of the house and either side street from the alleyway behind. They rotate every four hours, and have set up motion detectors as well. It will be very difficult to breach the perimeter, except when they exchange positions."

Jon studied the row of houses on the street. Most were terracotta with red tile roofs. Waist-high walls of stone encompassed front yards in which vegetable gardens grew rather than grass. A tiny iron gate in the center of each wall hung over stone walkways that led to the front stoops.

"Okay, so what's your plan?" Jon asked.

"They rotate counter-clockwise. We must come up behind the one moving toward the front of the house, which is the least guarded. I will deal with the guard. Ms. Kaufman, you must enter and retrieve the scroll from your safe. When you do, bring it back here and put it in this." He pulled out the safe box from the back for them to see. "It will keep it secure. Protect it from the elements much better than a sandwich wrapper."

"Wait, what about the motion detectors?"

"Oh. There are two of them, one mounted above the front and rear entrances. The range is about three meters out. You'll need one of these." He reached onto the passenger seat and handed Jon a small laser pointer attached to a tripod, with a scope mounted on the top.

"What do I do with this?"

"It is not hard. The motion sensors are infrared. Point the laser right in the center of the sensor to disable it. This way you will not alarm our friends in the back that we have arrived."

Jon stared at the contraption. He'd been considering installing just such a security system on his home, but Demetri's explanation of how to disable it so easily removed whatever confidence he'd had. The monk was completely casual about it, as though it were common knowledge.

"It is time," said Demetri. They watched as one man moved toward the side street, just as someone else came forward and leaned back against the tree across the street. Jon peered through the windshield, recognizing him as Michael. Michael bent his head briefly. An orange light flared from his cupped hands. He leaned his head back and blew out a puff of smoke.

Demetri had parked on the side of the street behind Michael's position. He climbed out the passenger side door, leaving it open. "Wait for my signal," he said.

Jon and Isabel stayed on the edge of their seats, watching. Demetri slipped casually along the sidewalk, moving behind the tree where Michael kept watch. He disappeared for a moment. Jon saw Michael turn his head sharply to one side and lean forward. A long arm snaked out and grabbed his hair. His forehead collided with the tree. His legs buckled. He crumpled to the ground.

Demetri stepped into view and waved them forward.

"Glad he's on our side," Jon muttered as they swept toward the house. They passed the gate into the yard. He stopped a few yards away from the front step and set up the tripod, aiming the laser pointer at the motion sensor clearly mounted above the doorway. Isabel glanced back at the monk, tapping Jon's shoulder. He turned to see Demetri pull Michael out of the street and toss him over the stone wall of another house.

"Don't be too sure about that," she muttered.

"What do you mean?"

She shivered. "The sooner we get away from him, the better I will feel. He is not what he seems."

Jon switched on the laser. A tiny red dot flashed onto the motion detector. He glanced at Isabel. "Ready?"

She held out her key. Taking it from her, he grabbed her hand and rushed up the stairs. He pushed the key into the lock and opened the door. They went inside.

Above them, a tiny light on the underside of the motion detector flicked on.

CHAPTER
34

Officer Gani Sahin raised the microphone to his lips a second time. The first had been when a large, black-garbed man had clearly assaulted another foreigner on the street. He'd been ready to call in for backup right away rather than risking his neck confronting the man alone. But the sudden appearance of two others who came forward at the large man's signal made him hesitate—if only to assess the situation more clearly.

Lieutenant Çapanoğlu had insisted they keep watch on the house. Apparently, for good reason. He watched the couple hasten through the yard, pausing briefly before dashing up the front steps, while the large man slunk away beside the wall where he'd just tossed the foreigner. The man crouched down to wait, almost out of sight.

They didn't have the manpower to keep the house under constant surveillance as Kahil had insisted. Random patrols were the best they could do. The Gendarmerie officer hadn't been pleased with this answer, but as he'd been operationally responsible for the deaths of several police during recent events, there was little concern at the station for what pleased Lieutenant Çapanoğlu.

Nevertheless, this would surely satisfy the man. Sahin spoke quietly into the mic. "Dispatch, this is Officer Sahin. I am at the house the Gendarmerie asked us to watch. Patch me through to Lieutenant Çapanoğlu, please."

A moment later, Kahil's voice crackled over the radio. "Çapanoğlu here."

"Lieutenant, you have company. A large man in black is lurking outside, and a foreign couple has entered the premises."

"Excellent work, officer. Can you hold them there?"

Sahin chuckled. "Of course. With a regiment or two under my command, I am sure I could manage it myself, but alone, perhaps not so easily. This man in black is quite sizable, and he moves rather fast. I am confident he is armed."

"Understood, officer. We are sending backup."

Sahin kept his thumb off the mic as he muttered, "Perhaps you could include a tank as well." He settled back into his car to wait, hoping he was safely out of sight.

Sean licked his lips and studied the back window of the house. Something wasn't right. The alarms hadn't gone off, but the one on the front door was malfunctioning. Cheap Chinese electronics.

But this wasn't what bothered him. It was something else. Something different about the house. He looked at the back door. Still locked. The lower windows dark. His gaze traveled upward. The windows on the second story were dark. Then he saw it. A faint deepening of the shadows. A movement from left to right. He picked up his binoculars and studied the window. After a moment, he set them down again, seeing nothing.

Had someone found a way inside? He picked up his radio. "Brian, Michael. Check in."

"All clear," came Brian's ready voice.

He waited a few seconds. "Michael, check in."

No answer. He clicked twice on the radio. The signal to move in. Someone had gotten by Michael. Someone was inside the house.

"Here it is," said Isabel, quickly opening the safe hidden in a back closet of her brother's bedroom. She pulled out a slender box and carried it to the bed; inside laid the other half of the scroll.

Jon carefully unrolled it, laying the first half from his pocket beside it. "We have a match." He pulled out his notebook and began transcribing the rest of the message. He furrowed his brow. This wasn't right.

"You have found it, yes?"

They looked up, startled. Demetri came into the room. "Yes."

"Then you will hand it over to me."

"It's not what you think," Jon said, looking again at the scroll.

"You will hand it over to me, as we agreed."

"Wait a minute, we made no such agreement! We were to find the autographs together. You were going to allow us to verify them."

"Alas, I am afraid I cannot take that risk. The autographs must come to Mount Athos. And I do not believe I can trust you. Not now that those men have followed us here."

"What about not breaking the eighth commandment? What about a translation? You can't read Greek!"

"I am sure I can manage." He chuckled. "Mount Athos is, after all, in Greece. And as for the commandment—it is not stealing to simply retrieve that which is rightfully ours. Now, if you please."

"Jonnie, don't!"

"I do not wish to resort to violence. Hand them over. Now."

"You'll keep your word? You'll let us study them?"

Demetri smiled. "Once the scrolls are safely at Mount Athos, we would be honored to have your expertise."

Reluctantly, Jon placed the two halves of the scroll into the box and closed the lid. He handed it to the monk.

"I am sorry for this," Demetri said. "Truly." With a sad smile, he turned and left the room. Jon turned to Isabel, who turned from him, fuming. He touched her shoulder, but she pulled away. A second later, the downstairs exploded.

Brian tapped Michael on the shoulder, letting him go in first. He'd found him struggling to his feet on the other side of the street, a bleeding welt on his forehead. There was a dangerous gleam in the young man's eyes.

"Found him," Brian had said over the radio. "Looks ticked."

"I am ticked," Michael had retorted.

"Go get 'em, Tiger," Brian said now.

Michael tossed the grenade and burst through the front door seconds later as the debris fell and the dust settled. Brian shook his head gleefully and followed.

Demetri lay collapsed at the bottom of the first landing on the stairs, his ears ringing and his eyes blurry from dust and the glaring afterimage of the explosion. Fire seared his chest and legs. He coughed, a futile effort, as there was almost no air in his lungs. He tried to raise his head, but found he could not. He felt nothing below his waist.

A face appeared above him. Dr. Munro.

"Help. Me." His voice was little more than a croak. He licked his lips, tasting nothing but blood. He fumbled for his prayer beads, thrusting them in Jon's hands. "Pray...!"

Demetri coughed again. A shuffling noise came from below. Dr. Munro looked up. Someone was coming. Quickly, he clasped Demetri's hand, praying silently, and then dashed up the stairs, leaving the monk staring hopefully toward heaven.

Sean caught sight of Brian and Michael making a room-to-room search on the first floor. They each held a flashlight in the left hand, crossed under their weapons in their right. Just like he'd taught them. He relaxed a bit. It was good to see some competence for once.

Brian caught his eye and muttered, "All clear."

He nodded and aimed his light at the stairs.

"Got something," said Michael. Sean watched him leap up the stairs, straddling a dark form that lay there. He tossed a box down to them. Brian caught it and flipped it open. "We've got 'em," he said.

A loud smack broke the silence. Sean and Brian stared at Michael, who gripped the priest's torso and backhanded him in the face. "How d'you like it? Hit me again, why don't ya?"

"Michael!" Sean barked. "Go find the other two." He took the box from Brian and pulled out his cell phone. Beaufort would be pleased.

Sahin dashed across the street as a parade of at least a dozen police cars swept down the street from both directions. Now that his regiment had arrived, there was no way he was going to let that Gendarmerie lieutenant steal credit for his arrest. He tripped over the laser on its tripod as he rushed the front walk, sending it skittering across the lawn. He stared at it a second, wondering what it was, then turned and leaped up the stairs to take a position outside the front door.

Jon grabbed Isabel's wrist, ducking with her into the closet in the master bedroom. Together they pushed their way through the clothes, retreating as far as possible into the back. The closet grew hot and still.

"God," Jon whispered, gripping Demetri's prayer beads, "please help us. Please don't let those men find us."

Isabel squeezed his hand.

The proximity alarm went off on Sean's wrist. He swore and closed the cell phone.

He hollered up the stairs, "We got company, boys!"

"Sahin!" His radio crackled. "Get back here!"

He spoke quickly. "Sorry, Lieutenant, I don't take orders from you!"

A moment later, it crackled again. "Officer Sahin, this is Sergeant Bahar! Stand down!"

Sahin swore and stepped away from the wall. A second later, two bullets tore through his chest. He staggered, staring in wonder at the wound before falling to the ground.

A storm of gunfire erupted into the house. Windows shattered. Siding and plaster exploded in clouds of debris. Bullets rained into the rooms from every conceivable angle for a full minute before Kahil raised the command, "Cease fire! Cease fire!"

When all was still, he lifted the megaphone to his lips. "We have you surrounded! Throw down your weapons and surrender!"

The Lost Scrolls

CHAPTER
35

Brian swore. He slumped against the wall, below the level of the windows. He'd been hit in the shoulder, leaving his right arm slightly less than useless. A second round had penetrated his abdomen. He peeked at the flow of blood and closed his eyes, coughing. Every movement sent fire scorching across his chest.

He turned to Michael, who lay on the floor not too far from him, a long sliver of glass protruding from his thigh. He was losing blood rapidly.

Brian's radio crackled. "Status!"

He winced. "I'm hit in the shoulder. Not bad." He stared at the wound in his stomach. "I can manage." He coughed more and tasted blood on his tongue. "Michael's losing blood. Got himself a nasty leg wound. We can't hold out much longer."

"Copy that."

"Go on, Sean. Get out if you can. Just take care of me daughter, will ya?"

"I'll be sure she gets your share."

"Think Turkish prisons are as bad as they say?" After a moment's silence, he said, "That's what I thought. Out."

He crawled over to Michael. The young lad's face was going pale. Brian unbuckled his belt and slipped it off. Michael grabbed his hand. "I don't wanna go to prison."

"There, there. Now be a good lad and let me put this on ya." He slipped the belt around Michael's wounded leg, cinching it as tight as he could muster. Michael screamed.

"Take it off!"

"Not a chance. It'll save your life." Cough. Cough.

"I don't want to live."

"Shut up."

He glanced up as the figures of Jon and Isabel emerged from the closet in the master bedroom. Jon shielded Isabel with his body, shuffling sideways around Michael.

Brian coughed, trying to raise his gun. "Dr. Munro. Ms. Kaufman. Nice to see you." The gun felt heavier. He dropped his hand. "There you go again. Everything's all shot to hell, and you without a scratch on ya. Wish I had your bloody luck."

"Are you gonna kill us?"

He shrugged. "Was. Don't see much point in it, now." Jon and Isabel inched around him toward the stairs. Brian said, "Hey, do me a favor? Tell 'em to send a medic up here."

Jon glanced back, and then disappeared around the landing. Brian leaned against the wall and closed his eyes, enjoying the warm sun on his face.

What a day.

Kahil stared at the front of the house, silently daring anyone to step outside. Sahin's body still lay on the front steps. Another good officer cut down in the line of duty. First the hospital. Then the shoot-out at the Atakule. Now this. And all he had to show for it was a pointless interrogation and a failed trap at the airport. Whatever hope he'd once had of a lengthy career in the anti-terrorism unit was evaporating quickly. Tabak was still running interference for him, but how much longer could the captain hold out?

The general directorate of security was already calling for his head—even suggesting bringing him up on formal charges. They were intimating something more than incompetence. He'd learned through a concerned friend that they were developing a theory to explain it—that he, Kahil, was in the service of the rebels themselves—a traitor using his position to delay and frustrate the investigation.

It was all untrue, but what difference did it make? Someone had to pay for this. And if it wasn't going to be the bad guys themselves, then it might just as well be him.

He grit his teeth and prayed they would find The Rat holed up within—perhaps full of bullets or some other appropriate fate. Even then, it might not resuscitate his career. Nonetheless, it would give him some measure of satisfaction.

Sean peered out the kitchen window. Police leaped over the fence, filling the back yard and closing in on the house. He fingered the box containing the scrolls. Some force was against him. To have come so close yet again….

He wasn't out of it yet. If he could get onto the roof before anyone saw him....

He turned around as two figures fled down the stairs and aimed his gun at their backs. They thrust themselves toward the front door.

He lowered his gun. This might buy him some time.

"We're coming out," Jon shouted.

He and Isabel raised their hands above their heads, moving cautiously onto the front porch. Turkish police in full battle gear drew down on them.

"Turn around and put your hands on the wall!"

They did. A moment later, they were cuffed and hustled off the front porch, back around the wall, and behind a pair of police cruisers. Kahil met them on the far side.

"How many more?"

"There's three of them, one on the stairs, another two upstairs," Jon replied. "The guy on the stairs is a good guy. He's hurt pretty bad. The others, I don't know. One of them is asking for a medic. I think they're surrendering. There's at least one more. I don't know where he is."

Kahil turned to Bahar. "Take the house. I want them alive if you can."

Bahar nodded and gave the order. Policemen surged into the house. Kahil frowned. "Why am I not surprised to see you two again?"

Sean pushed up the stairs, pausing at Brian and Michael lying there. Michael was unconscious now. Brian was failing quickly. He slapped his cheeks. "Hey. Brian! Stay with me, now."

Brian opened his eyes. "Sean. Get out. You're no good here."

"Are you hit bad, mate?"

"Aye." Brian winced. "Go. I'm no use to you, now."

"Michael?"

"Tried to save him."

Sean clenched his fists. "I'll find a way to get to you."

"Just go."

He pushed his head against Brian's forehead, embracing his neck. "I'll find a way." Commotion below told him the police were closing in. He slipped into the bedroom behind Brian and Michael. The window there overlooked the side of the house. He pushed it open and climbed onto the ledge, cradling the scroll box against his chest. The roof was just within reach. Beneath him, the Turkish police pawed through the bushes and combed the alleyway on the side of the house. He flung himself out the window, his fingers finding purchase on the roof.

He pulled up, but couldn't lift himself one-handed. Grunting, he swung the box up on top of the roof tiles, put both hands on the edge, and hauled his body upwards. Below him, he heard the officers rush into the room.

He pulled his foot clear and lay panting on the tiles. Above him the cobalt sky surged endlessly upward, and for a moment he felt as though he could push away from that roof and float forever into its depths. He rolled over and reached for the box. His fingertips touched it and it slipped, skittering down the tiles to tumble off to the ground below. He reached after it, his fingers closing on nothing.

He grimaced and scrambled into a crouch, hugging the peak of the roof. He stuck his head over the side, scanning the alleyway. It was empty now, but policemen still roamed the front and back yards, establishing their perimeter. On the street below a crowd was gathering.

The building across the alley was a scant eight feet away. He retreated half again that distance, then rose to his feet and ran at full speed toward the edge, thrusting off at the last moment.

He hit the other side with a loud smack, his hands barely gripping the peak as his body swayed wildly to one side. His forearms stung and bled from the impact. Quite suddenly, he lost his grip and slid downwards, tilting over the edge and dropping to the ground below. A large pine bush broke his fall, bruising his ribs for good measure. He rolled free onto his hands and knees and hobbled across the backyard, where he disappeared over the far wall.

Hamid watched Sean drop over the wall. Shaking his head, he adjusted the riot gear he wore and moved closer to where he'd seen a small object fall from where the mercenary had hidden on the roof. The police officer he'd murdered to steal his uniform hadn't quite been his size, but he hoped with the confusion no one would notice—or see the bloody stain in the back of the shirt, where he'd lacerated the cop's kidneys.

Whatever it was Sean had dropped must've fallen near the shrubs lining the back porch. It didn't look like it had been a grenade, and the way the mercenary had reached for it suggested it wasn't something he wanted to lose. It was quite possibly that it was the very something Hamid was looking for. He spotted it lying about five feet from the edge of the house. As he moved in to retrieve it, another officer stepped in and picked it up. Hamid stopped. He could do little else.

The officer spoke quickly into his radio. "Sergeant Bahar, I've found something. Looks like someone might've tossed it from an upstairs window."

"Bring it around. Kahil will want to see it."

"Yes sir."

Hamid ducked his head and followed.

Kahil watched the men storming the house, their weapons held in front, and legs moving in a low crouch. He nodded in satisfaction. Once they took those inside prisoner, the subsequent interrogations would help him finally corner The Rat and put this whole mess behind him. He might even receive a commendation out of it.

He turned around to face the two Americans. As he did so, Bahar approached him with a small box he'd found in the back yard. Kahil frowned. Unlatching the box, he opened it carefully and peered inside. Two halves of an old scroll lay side by side in the velvet interior.

His smile broadened and he brought the box over to the Americans. "Get them up," he said. The officers lifted Jon and Isabel to their feet. They turned around and faced the Gendarmerie.

"I thought I told you to get on that plane."

"Well, we did."

"Then what are you doing here?"

CHAPTER
36

"You have entered my country illegally. Did you come back for this?" Kahil reached in and lifted out one of the scroll halves.

"Gently, please. It's very old."

Kahil unrolled it cautiously. "So. Is it what they say it is?"

Jon shook his head. "It's fake. The vellum itself is quite old. Second century, I believe. But you'll find the ink is less so. Of course, I haven't tested it. But it's very dark. Not faded. And it's written in minuscules. Saint Paul had poor eyesight. He wrote in large letters. Uncials."

"A not-so-clever forgery, then."

"Not even that. A red herring for some. A clue meant for me. In the center of the text it reads: '*Iohanathan*'—that's probably me—'did you think I would destroy it? I hid it with style.'"

Kahil raised an eyebrow. "Do you know what it means?"

A small grin crept over Jon's face. "I think I might. If your antiquities people remove the ink, I am sure they will discover just what this ancient document really was. The acid from the ink would have burned into the vellum, allowing it to show up with a spectrograph. There's bound to be some value to it."

"An elaborate ruse." He looked at Isabel. "Perhaps your brother found what he was looking for, then? Hmm?" He closed the box. "You will tell us what you know. If you cooperate, you might get off easy."

Brian felt the world spin around him. Michael was dead. He would be, too, in another minute. But he might just be able to buy Sean some time. He pulled out the pack of grenades and set it in his lap.

Kahil was instructing an officer to put Jon and Isabel into a car when the top half of the house exploded. Shards of glass and splinters of wood sailed heavenward. Cries of alarm erupted from the police line as the men instinctively dove for cover.

Jon saw Isabel turn to run. "Izzy, wait!" She looked his way. He led the way around the police car, ducking out of the cops' sight.

"Front pocket, Demetri's prayer beads."

"You want to pray?"

"He has a handcuff key on them!"

"Oh God, I do believe in miracles," she muttered. She turned around and reached into his pocket, pulling out the beads key first.

"Careful! Don't drop it." He turned around so she could reach his cuffs. After a moment's struggle, he was free. He reciprocated quickly.

She followed him close behind, dodging past the cops whose eyes were trained on the explosion. In a moment, they were back in Demetri's car. A few seconds later, they disappeared down the street.

Sean watched them from the front seat of his van two blocks up. His arms, legs, and ribs hurt like hell. They climbed into the front seat of a sedan parked a few blocks away, then pulled out into traffic and drove past him. He started the van and turned after them.

He let them stay three car lengths ahead. He would not risk losing sight of them, but following the car alone was a difficult endeavor. Under normal circumstances, he'd have used a three-man team with multiple vehicles to maintain surveillance.

But these were far from normal circumstances. An image of Michael's body leaking his life onto the floor of Isabel Kaufman's former home howled into his mind, a gale-force blast of grief shaking the windows of his composure, threatening to burst forth and drown his consciousness in guilt and anger. Brian's words fluttered in his mind, accusatory whispers of what he ought to have done differently. He saw him now too, the crimson wound in his stomach threatening to swallow him whole. He steeled himself against the onslaught, pushing the memories down into the recesses of his psyche, knowing they would haunt his nights like other phantasms of unforgotten, unremediated loss.

He hit the steering wheel with his palm, the quiet shock of pain centering him in the present moment, pushing the storm further from his mind. There was no time for anything else.

They were two car lengths ahead—the couple whose continued presence on this planet was an affront to everything Sean ever thought himself to be. None of it made any sense. They'd bested him at every turn. He stared at the cab, his eyes burning holes in the trunk. Had they been professionals themselves, or even government agents, he could accept it. But these two weren't even amateurs! They stumbled through his traps and intrigue with something more than dumb luck—and something far different from skill. None of it made sense. It was almost as if—

He shook his head. This was pointless.

The thought persisted, breaking his defenses and confronting him with stark possibility. It was almost as if an unseen hand were guiding them, defending them. Protecting them. He wasn't superstitious. The faith of his grandmother was useless but for identifying Protestants, Royalist sympathizers. Those who believed in Providence were no different from the drunks in Killyleagh warbling about the little folk.

But this was different. And if something were guiding Dr. Munro and Isabel Kaufman, he was a fool to pursue them.

"You're losing it, Sean," he muttered. "There's nothing more to these two than dumb luck, make no mistake." At this point, there was little else he could do but follow.

Farther back, Hamid put on the Bluetooth earpiece and answered the phone. He was dreading this call.

"What is going on?"

His employer was growing impatient. He shifted in the Peugeot's seat and forced himself to relax. "I am following one of those mercenaries hired to obtain the scroll. He himself is following our good doctor and the archaeologist's lovely sister. All is going well, I think."

"Going well?!" There followed a string of epithets. "Have you seen the news? Your face! Their faces! The whole country is after you!"

"What is the problem?"

The man momentarily lost his vocabulary. Hamid had considered letting the call go directly to voicemail. Now he wondered if he should have. He shook his head. For what he was paying, the man deserved an update on the chase. "Did you not tell me to do whatever it takes?" he asked. "Here I am. Doing whatever it takes."

There was a moment's silence, then, "And I suppose I shall be billed for the expenses of this course of action."

"But of course," Hamid replied smoothly. This had been his primary reason for answering the phone. "It cannot be helped. Unless you no longer wish to employ my services. I assure you, the scroll you seek is of no interest to me in the slightest. Except, perhaps, as an item to sell to the highest bidder."

There was another curse. "How much longer?"

The dark van was still four car lengths ahead. Hamid suspected the man had no idea he was being followed—a situation he would turn to his advantage as soon as he could. For now, let the man incur the risks of tailing the doctor and the woman. Hamid had plenty of time to react from this distance. Even if the tail were lost, he'd still be able to find them. "Not so much, I think," he replied.

"See that it isn't."

"Unbelievable," Isabel muttered.

"What?"

"Stephen forged the scroll all along?"

Jon shrugged. "Well, that one at least. But I think there's an original. He found it. He must have realized what it was worth, what men would do to possess it. In fact, he probably knew they were after him. It. So he concocted this elaborate ruse to divert them. He meant for us to find the scrolls, to find the *Domo tou Bibliou*—but if they followed us there and forced us to surrender what we found, he prepared for that. The scroll was never hidden in the *Domo*—not after Stephen found it, of course."

"And you know where it is?"

"More or less. Give me a second." He pulled out his Blackberry and dialed. A moment later, Leon answered the phone.

"Dr. Munro? Good Lord, man! What's happened to you?"

"I'm alright, Leon."

"We've been watching the news reports out of Turkey. So much violence there. Stephen's face has been splashed all over the news, along with you and Ms. Kaufman."

"Uh huh."

"They're saying you're connected to terrorists."

"Relax, Leon. It's nothing like that. We ran into 'The Rat,' but we're alright. We gave him the slip, I think."

"You need to come home."

"Can't do that. Not yet. Leon, I need you to do something for me. Send me everything you can about St. Simeon."

"St. Simeon? Hang on. Okay, wait, there were two of them."

"Send me everything you have."

"Okay. I'll send you the link."

"Good enough."

Isabel was on the edge of her seat. "St. Simeon? Where is the scroll?"

"Exactly where Stephen said it was. He hid it with Style."

"Style? I don't...Simeon the Stylite." Isabel managed a wan smile. "'I hid it with Style.' Those were his last words. I should have known. St. Simeon, of course! Stephen always had a morbid fascination for a man who'd spent his life on a column. His church is the oldest in Syria. It is thirty kilometers northeast of Aleppo."

"I know. I wrote a paper on Simeon in college. Stephen plagiarized it."

"Great. We've been there. We took a trip there not three weeks ago…my God! He must have had it with him!"

"He assumed you'd remember. That's what he told you in the hospital. He was trying to spare us the trouble." He frowned. "Except—"

"Except that he wanted us to go to the *Domo* first!"

"Right! Why?"

"So you'd know it was real? Was it a test of faith?"

"No. That doesn't work. He knew I'd spot it as a forgery. He didn't even try to hide it that much. The scroll was obvious—too obvious. What? What were you doing, Stephen?" He slammed his fist against the steering wheel. After a moment he said, "There's something we're missing. A piece of the puzzle we don't have yet."

"I think we should trust him. He's trying to show us where it is. How to find it. The answer may be waiting for us in Aleppo."

"You're right. We have to go to Syria."

CHAPTER
37

"You mean all this time it was a fake?!"

"Relax, MacNeil. We know where the real one is now."

"And if you'd done your bloody research, we could've had it in possession a long time ago."

Beaufort's voice was smooth. "Don't worry about it. I'm good for whatever expenses you've incurred."

Sean stared at the car with Dr. Munro and Ms. Kaufman. Another mile marker flashed by. He shook his head. "You have no idea. I've lost two—no, three men because of you."

"You can hire more men."

More men. Did he have any idea? William had been useless, but Brian was irreplaceable. And Michael? What was he going to tell his sister? How would he explain her son's death? He forced himself to speak in even tones. "That won't be as easy as you might imagine."

"Look, just do whatever you have to. They're on their way to Syria now. Some place northeast of Aleppo." Beaufort's tone told him the man was losing patience. Beaufort never wanted to know the details. He only wanted to manipulate others, to give commands and acquire his treasures. Who got hurt in the process or whatever it cost did not matter to him in the least.

Soon, Sean promised himself. Soon it would matter to Beaufort very much. He would make sure of it.

"Syria, is it? I have a contact there. Yesoph Panikkar, but he only responds to email."

"Okay," said Beaufort. "You want me to set up the meet?"

As if he'd do it personally. The man was unbelievable. Sean gave him the address. "Just tell him…" He checked his GPS. "Just tell him I'm coming, and to meet me in A'zaz."

"Meet Sean in A'zaz. Got it. Anything else I can do for ya?"

"Bloody hell," Sean muttered, hanging up on him. It was the least the man could do.

The trip from Ankara to the Syrian border was a long one. Demetri's GPS gave them the fastest route, but even so the drive still took them more than six hours before they arrived in the town of Kilis, a scant ten kilometers from the Syrian border. Jon drove them to the border and took a side road away from the checkpoint. They saw the remains of a minefield that Turkey had lain down years before, and beyond, a thin, barbwire fence that marked the border between the two states. After several miles following an endless fence, with olive trees and other farmland growing on either side, he turned the car around and headed back to town.

Kilis was a moderately sized urban center with large shops and spacious streets, along with narrow alleys between decaying stone buildings. The town sprawled in a valley surrounded by vineyards and olive groves. Tall minarets spiked the sky in various locations, pinpointing the different mosques serving the religious needs of the seventy thousand people who called the city home. Residents in Western attire sped by on motorbikes or in rickety cars; one or two rode in ramshackle carts drawn by tired horses. Many of the shops featured artisans creating their wares right on the street. Jon and Isabel witnessed a cobbler threading his needle through a red shoe, while dozens of other shoes hung like banana bunches around the front of his store. Across the street, a weaver worked her loom, her head covered by a beautiful scarf. Others sold fresh bread, hand-sewn quilts, or tin cooking pots beaten into shape over a wooden form.

Jon's phone was out again. He parked the car near a roadside café offering free internet. Isabel purchased a headscarf and quickly fastened it in place before they went inside. After ordering a light dinner, Jon found an available computer and uploaded a mapping program.

"How do we get to the basilica? Syria won't let us through without authorization from our embassy, and I don't think we're going to get it. We're in Turkey illegally."

She giggled. "You know what that makes us?"

"What?"

"International fugitives."

"International criminals, you mean."

"So what's one more country? The border is guarded, but not well, I think." She turned the computer to see. "The last time we came through the checkpoint it took us two hours because one of the men who needed to sign our papers was sleeping. Look here, there is a small road running to the west of the highway. It looks like it crosses the border here." She pointed at the screen. Jon zoomed in until the image resolution was lost.

"Is that a road?"

"Might only be a farmer's trail. We won't know until we get there. We'll have to make a run for it."

"Great. More people shooting at us. Even if we get through, they'll radio it in. All of Syria will be looking for our car." He ran a hand through his hair. "This isn't a good idea."

"What choice do we have?"

"I...I don't know. Leave?" She glared at him. "No. I guess we're in too deep to do much else. You know what'll happen if they catch us, though." An impression of what a Syrian prison looked like flashed into his mind. He paled at the thought. Isabel squeezed his hand.

"Then we don't get caught."

"And how do we manage that?"

They fell silent for a long moment. Then Isabel brightened. "I have an idea."

"Okay."

"We can't change the fact they'll see us cross. But we can always change what they see."

Jon furrowed his brow. "What did you have in mind?"

A few minutes before sunrise, two guards at the checkpoint a mile past the border slouched languidly in the guard shack. The crossing gate had "No Entry" signs in Turkish, Arabic, and English clearly marked on it. The guards took turns gazing into the endless expanse of wasteland. One of them rubbed his eyes and stared down the road. He tapped his companion.

Something resembling a large parade float barreled toward them. Shiny orange quilts and dangling tassels covered most of the vehicle, with several bunches of red ladies' shoes hanging from every conceivable place. On the hood, a pair of oversized sunglasses sat above a huge mouth made of red shoes fastened onto the grill. Behind the part of the windshield not covered by blankets or shoes, it looked as though no one were driving.

The two guards gaped at this bizarre creation before rising from their seats and taking a stand in front of the gate. They motioned for the unknown driver to stop. Fifteen feet from the gate, the car lurched forward as the driver pressed the accelerator. With a cry, the guards flung themselves out of its path.

The float crashed through the gate, sending splinters of wood flying in all directions. A portion of quilt tore free and drifted to the ground by the guardhouse. The guards scrambled into firing position. They let loose several rounds at the retreating car, then dashed into the guardhouse to phone in a description of the impossible scene to their commanding officer.

Once over a rise in the road, Jon pulled the car to the side. He and Isabel leaped out and quickly dropped the quilts, shoes, and sunglasses to the ground, kicking them into the ditch on the side of the road. They jumped back in the car and gunned it, creating a large cloud of dust behind them.

Several miles and turns later, they began to relax. "I think we're clear," Jon muttered. Isabel nodded and took his hand. "That was a good idea."

"It'll buy us some time, at least. We still have to figure out how we're going to get back across again."

"Assuming we go that route. I guess we could go to the American embassy and claim we were kidnapped."

She smiled. "It's not too far from the truth."

"No, it's not. This trip has been a lot more than I thought it would be. I'll be happy to be back in the States again."

She feigned hurt. "And miss all this adventure?"

He laughed nervously. "I don't know how much more of this adventure I can take."

"You get used to it. One time when Stephen and I were going to Ararat, we got caught in the crossfire of the Gendarmerie and some Turkish separatists. It didn't help that our guide was a Kurd, or that we didn't exactly have permission from the Turkish government to explore the site. Stephen was determined to see the anomaly."

"The anomaly?"

"Oh, you've heard of it! They had satellite photos of it. Lots of speculation that it might have been the Ark."

"I thought that turned out to be a rock or something."

"Maybe. Stephen wasn't convinced. He wanted to see it for himself. We got about halfway up the mountain when the Turks showed up. Helicopters flying overhead. Guns blazing. Evidently, there was a separatist stronghold in the mountains. Our guide was leading us right to it."

"Why?"

"Oh, to resupply, I suppose. Meet old friends. Who knows?"

"Hold you for ransom?"

"You're so untrusting."

"So what happened?"

"Well, after our guide was shot, we turned the jeep around and got the heck out of there. We never did get to see the anomaly. It's a pity, too."

"I imagine. What would you have done had you seen it? I mean, had it been the Ark?"

"Are you kidding me? Of course, we'd have documented it and taken photographs and video. Then there would be the books and the tours and the speaking engagements. We'd have been quite busy."

"I see."

"What? You don't sound excited."

"Oh, it's just—well—I don't really think about it in those terms."

"What do you mean?"

"Well, you're talking about finding Noah's Ark. I mean: *Noah's Ark*, right?"

"It's one of the enduring mysteries, Jonnie. Don't you want to know whether or not it's true?"

He grinned, pointing with his finger. "See, that's my point right there. I already believe it's true. I believe it because the Bible says it happened. I don't need to see it."

"That's strange. Coming from you, at least."

"Why?"

"You're a scientist."

"Well yeah—my science has done nothing but prove the Bible to be true and accurate in all its claims. It has been doubted over and over, but never disproven. No archaeological discovery has ever contradicted a Biblical reference. Not once. It is completely reliable."

She shook her head, clearly enjoying the conversation. "What do you mean by that?"

"I don't understand."

"Well, you keep calling it 'reliable,' but what do you mean? You think we should just drop everything and start going to church or something?"

"Well, no, not exactly."

"Then what do you mean?"

CHAPTER
38

"Well, I guess what I'm asking is: What's the point of looking for Noah's Ark, or the Ark of the Covenant, or the autographs, for that matter, if you're not going to believe the story?"

"But what does it mean to believe in it?"

"Well—"

"I mean, do you actually, like, *believe* believe?"

"Well, yeah."

She laughed and shook her head. "You don't seem like it."

His mouth hung open. "What's that supposed to mean?"

"I-I don't know. You'd be different. You know—holy or something. I just didn't think you were like that."

He frowned. "What am I like?"

"You're normal."

"Of course!" he laughed. "You think I have to be a fanatic or something?"

"Well, no, but normal people don't believe this, at least, not the way you're talking about it." She shook her head, frowning now. "I mean, you're talking about this stuff like it's true—all these spiritual things—and the miracles and God and whatnot—you know, not just metaphors, but true, like there really was some guy named Jesus who rose from the dead—and maybe something like that did happen, but not the way it's portrayed. I mean, it can't really be true, can it?"

"But it is."

She shook her head. "No. You don't really believe that. You can't!"

"Why can't I?"

She stared with her mouth open. "Y-you're a scientist! You can't really believe this stuff. I mean, the Bible talks about things like giants and stuff. It's myth."

"It's fact," he insisted.

"I don't believe you. I don't think you really believe what you think you believe."

He was silent a moment, staring ahead at the olive trees that flashed by on either side of the car. When he spoke, there was an edge to his voice. "So you're saying I'm a hypocrite."

"Could we just drop this?"

"I don't want to drop it. You basically said that because I'm not a monk or something that I don't really believe. I don't think that's fair."

"Okay. I just don't want to argue."

"I may not be the best Christian that's out there, but that doesn't make me a nonbeliever."

She made no reply. Jon let the conversation drop.

After two hours at the border, Sean cleared customs and headed south for A'zaz. To the border guards, he'd presented himself as Jackson Peters, a convert to the Muslim faith on a cross-country pilgrimage. That he'd dressed the part added to the guards' amusement, but they let him through. He tossed the *keffiyeh* on the seat, but kept the *thobe* on. The white gown was amazingly comfortable, and it would likely ease any hesitation the locals might have about a blue-eyed foreigner passing through their country.

A scant five minutes later, he entered the town. A'zaz was a small community of about twenty-nine thousand. Most of the town consisted of single story dwellings built of the same rock as the surrounding countryside, giving the place the semblance of having risen whole from the desert. The streets were a maze of narrow alleys, with scant room for two vehicles to pass. Various stalls spilled their wares onto wooden tables beneath brightly colored awnings, further constricting the streets.

Sean slowed the van to a crawl and navigated the maze until he came to a tiny shop at a nondescript corner. He parked the van and donned the *keffiyeh* before stepping out into morning blaze. At a table to the left, three men sucked languidly on their water pipes, eyeing him quietly. He walked up to them and addressed them in Arabic.

"*A salaam aliekum. Ana at'la' l Yesoph Panikkar.*"

From behind, someone pressed the barrel of a gun to his temple. Sean closed his lips and straightened. "And you have found him," said a voice in English. "But this is not the Sean MacNeil that I know. The man I know would never let himself be taken so easily."

Sean chuckled, and dropped like a stone. His rear leg wheeled behind, catching the gunman at the ankle and sweeping him off his feet. Sean pounced on the man, his hand at his throat, his knee pinning the gun hand to the ground. "Would this be hard 'nough for ya, then?"

The gunman laughed and nodded wearily. "It is good to see you again, Sean. What brings you to Syria?"

Hamid parked the car on a side street and stared out the windshield at the meeting that took place around the corner. He frowned, wishing he had a parabolic mic handy. He settled for his binoculars, studying the meeting through the double circles.

After dropping the gunman to the ground, Sean had helped him back up again. The two embraced like old friends before taking a seat at the table with the pipe smokers. The gunman made what looked like introductions, then they got down to business. Hamid dropped the binoculars. They were useless. He could read lips in Arabic well enough, but English was another matter.

It was possible Sean had given up on following the Americans, though it seemed unlikely. Hamid had only assumed the Irishman was trailing them. So either he had given up the chase, or he already knew where they were headed. It meant he was in A'zaz to gather a new team.

Hamid leaned against the door and grimaced. There was nothing else to do but wait.

"It's settled then," said Yesoph. "When do we leave?"

"Immediately," Sean replied, taking a sip of *kahvesi*. "The Americans must already be at the basilica. We have no time."

"And what of this man who is following you?"

Sean smiled. Yesoph was still trying to get one up on him. "He's nothing. A sand fly. You swat him if he tries to lunch on you."

Yesoph smiled.

"His real name is Hamid Al-Assini. You can collect the bounty on him if you wish. You'd be doing the world a favor."

Yesoph set down his cup. "Under normal circumstances, I do not collect bounties. Otherwise, I would have handed your head to the authorities a long time ago and retired. But in this case, I make an exception. We shall consider it a 'bonus' for the urgency of your request."

"He's all yours. But mightn't you wait a wee bit, till after we have the scroll?"

"Of course." Yesoph turned and spoke a few short words to the other men at the table, then barked an order to someone inside the house. A moment later, a woman hidden beneath a colorful *hijab* appeared and gathered the *hookah* pipes. She returned a moment later with four Kalashnikov rifles slung over her shoulder and two boxes of ammo. She handed these to Yesoph, then disappeared into the building again.

"New wife?" Sean asked.

"Eldest daughter." Yesoph handed out the weapons.

"Little Aabida?"

"Not so little anymore, eh?"

"Yesoph, my friend, we are getting too old for this."

Yesoph clapped a hand on his shoulder. "I knew that before you tossed me to the ground. But thank you for reminding me just the same."

Hamid watched them climb into Sean's van, then pull ahead into the street. He frowned. One of the men had glanced his way. He looked directly at him, as if he knew who Hamid was.

Had he been made? It made little difference. He had no choice but to follow—even if it meant he were driving into a trap. He'd simply have to watch carefully, and strike only at the right moment. He started the car and slipped quietly behind them.

CHAPTER
39

Jon and Isabel said little else to each other as they drove southeast toward the Qal at Simân, a fifth-century church erected in honor of the man who climbed and lived atop a pillar in order to be closer to God.

Isabel stared out the passenger side window. Jon watched as the barren scenery flashed by, revealing little. It was impossible to tell from the lay of the land how far they had gone, or how much further they had to go. He wanted to talk to her more, to defend his beliefs, but he was out of arguments. What did it say about him that he couldn't demonstrate his faith? That it wasn't obvious to someone like Izzy?

Was he a practical atheist? He'd accused others of it before, saying they intellectually agreed with faith, but refused to do anything about it with their lives. But was he the same way?

When he honestly looked at his life, what could he point to that would convict him of his faith? Sure, he attended church and did "religious" functions, but was there anything resembling any kind of relationship with God? He knew God existed. He knew the Bible was true. But this was nothing more than intellectual assent. Izzy seemed to expect that faith would make a practical difference in his life, and the simple fact was that it didn't.

His faith was as dry and dusty as the ancient scrolls he studied under microscopes—keeping the truth at arm's length while comforting himself with a firm belief in the facts of the matter.

The distance between his faith and that of the men who wrote the New Testament was as broad as the distance between heaven and earth, and just as insurmountable. The authors of the autographs he was seeking had centered their lives on God— attaining through Him an experience of life and a historical permanence far surpassing that of their contemporaries. Even St. Simeon himself realized this. His pillar still stood after more than fifteen hundred years, mute testimony to his desire for the Divine.

Why didn't he have that desire? If all this were true, why didn't he want it more?

With these questions flitting through his mind, they approached the ruin from the south, having driven past it on the road below and turning at the base of the mount to climb several hundred feet to the shelf on which the ruins overlooked the valley. Sheer cliffs of sandy rock peeked out beneath patchy, browning vegetation. The road up was pockmarked and broken, with slaps of pavement crumbling into powdery holes or sliding off the edge to tumble down the hillside below. After a difficult and jostled climb, they drove the sedan onto a large expanse at the top of the hill. There were no other cars there.

They stepped out and walked toward the expansive basilica, for the first time really appreciating the size of the ruin. It consisted of four churches built away from an octagonal court, covering the four points of the compass and forming a large cruciform. In the center of the court was St. Simeon's style. Tall arches of crumbling stone and broken columns surrounded the style. The column was little more than a boulder set on a tall, rectangular block worn down by ages of weather and adoration.

The top and sides were rounded and smooth, and only a scant two meters remained.

Isabel shook her head. "Where should we start?"

"Your guess is as good as mine. Let's start with the churches." They looked across the courtyard at the stone ruins arrayed at the points of the compass around the column. "North, south, east, and—" he pointed behind them, "west."

"Which one?"

"Ah. I have no idea. Can you think of any one he preferred? I mean, you were here before, right?"

She looked around at the churches and shook her head. "I don't know. Nothing stands out."

He pointed at the northern church. "Let's split up. You take the south. I'll go here. If you find anything, give a yell."

She shrugged, and they took off in opposite directions.

After several hours, they returned to the center of the ruin. Jon lifted his hands helplessly. "I don't get it. It should be here."

"And I hope, for your sakes, it is."

They turned abruptly as Sean entered the courtyard, his Kalashnikov leaning casually against his shoulder. Jon put himself in front of Isabel. Sean smiled.

"Chivalrous, isn't he?"

"What do you want?" said Jon.

"We had a deal, you and me. I kept my end of the bargain. Time for you to do the same, yeah?"

"What is he talking about?" Isabel asked.

"I'd say our deal is off."

"Now that'd be a pity, as it's the only thing keeping you alive."

"What deal?"

"I was to give him the scroll to save your life. But that was back at the Tower," Jon added hastily.

"Aye, that's 'bout how I remember it, too. So how 'bout it? Where's the scroll?"

Jon pressed his lips together. "I don't have it!"

"An' I done guessed that already. Why else would you be standing here? Tell me where it is." He raised the AK-47. "Or I undo my part of the bargain."

"A bit premature, don't you think?" The voice came from behind Sean.

Sean stiffened. Jon and Isabel looked for the source of the voice.

"Put down your gun. Kick it behind you, please."

Sean sighed and set the gun down. "You're making a mistake, my friend."

"I think not." Hamid came out from behind the wall, his weapon trained on Sean's back. Sean glanced behind and watched him approach. Hamid bent down and expertly picked up the weapon's strap with his prosthesis, slinging it over his shoulder. "We are all after the same thing. The same treasure. You were about to shoot the only two people who can tell us where it is."

"That's where you're wrong, friend. I was only going to shoot one of them."

Hamid made a clucking noise with his tongue. "Such violence. But now, go ahead and ask your question. I'm sure we're all very eager to hear the answer."

"You're carrying the gun, friend. You can bloody well ask him yourself."

Hamid chuckled. "As you like." To Jon he said, "Where is the scroll?"

"I-I don't know where it is."

"I think he's lying to us."

"Aye. You're a brilliant one, aren't you?" Sean half-smiled.

"Have you no sense of gratitude?" Hamid asked them. "I am the one keeping him from killing you."

"I don't know where it is!"

"Still lying," Sean drawled.

Hamid snorted and addressed Jon. "You don't know where it is, and yet you knew to come here. Why?"

"Sightseeing."

Hamid fired. Jon and Isabel yelped as the bullet broke against St. Simeon's column. Fragments of rock pattered against the ground.

"Alright! Alright!"

"Why did you come?" Hamid repeated.

"It was the only clue we had!" He looked helplessly at Isabel. "Just before he died, Stephen told me he hid it 'with Style.' He repeated the same thing on the forgery he made...the scroll he left in the *Domo*. He hid the real scroll 'with Style.' This is the basilica of Simeon the Stylite. This," he pointed at the column, "is Simeon's style."

"So where is it?"

"We looked everywhere," he shrugged. "We've checked the entire compound."

"And yet you haven't found it."

"No."

He raised the gun, alternating between Isabel and Jon. "Perhaps you are not sufficiently motivated."

"Well, where else would it—" Jon's eyes widened, "—be," he whispered.

Hamid smiled. "You know where it is."

Jon dropped to his knees and started probing around the edges of the column, searching the dust. The ground around it was hard-packed earth, but for a small depression on one side. "Here," he said. "Izzy?"

She bent down and started digging with him, pushing shovelfuls of dirt out of the way. After several minutes, Jon felt something hard and smooth beneath his fingers. He glanced at Isabel, who gave him a wary look.

"You've found something, yeah?" said Sean, peering around the column. Hamid clucked his tongue, waving the gun at him.

Jon grimaced and pulled out a small, slender box, very similar to the one they'd retrieved from Stephen's safe. He opened it, gently removing the scroll inside.

Hamid turned to Sean. "I guess we have no more need for you." He raised the gun. A sudden spurt of blood erupted from his forehead. Hamid's eyes went blank as he fell backward into the dust.

Isabel screamed.

CHAPTER
40

"Took you bloody long enough!" Sean bellowed. He bent over the assassin's lifeless body, struggling to free the Kalashnikov.

Jon grabbed Isabel's hand and jerked her away from the courtyard. Bullets lanced the ground near their feet. Clouds of dust exploded upward. They ducked around a wall as fragments of stone splintered from it.

Sean ripped the AK-47 free, untangling it from the unwieldy plastic of Hamid's prosthetic arm. He tossed the arm to one side and tore after them.

Rounding the wall, he caught sight of two figures disappearing into the parking lot. He fired a burst over their heads. They ducked and kept on running. He gripped the gun, sighting along their backs. His finger tensed on the trigger.

A scream erupted from his throat. He turned and kicked over a stone, bellowing curses.

Yesoph came up behind him. "You are unhurt?"

"I'm fine," he hissed. He stalked toward the courtyard.

"All is well, then."

Sean abruptly about-faced and grabbed a fistful of Yesoph's robe. "All is not well! They're getting away!"

"And we will pursue them! Do not fret, my friend. *Inshallah*, we will find them."

"*Inshallah*, we'd bloody well better!" He released him and strode into the courtyard. Yesoph's men were busily trying to heft Hamid's body toward their van.

"Leave him."

The men looked from Sean to Yesoph. Yesoph spoke to them quickly in Arabic. He turned to Sean. "No, my friend. We had an agreement."

Sean glared at him. "Unless we catch them, we won't find the scroll, and you won't get paid."

"I understand. I accept this."

"I won't get paid, either. And that is unacceptable."

"You gave your word. These men are entitled to their bounty. And besides," he pulled a GPS tracking unit from the folds of his robe. "I do not think finding them will be a problem."

Sean took the unit from him. He stared at the tiny dot pulsing on the screen, moving further and further away. His expression softened. "Alright then, let's get this piece of meat in the truck."

"Anything?"

Isabel stared out the rear window, trying to see past the dust that flew behind them. The car jostled and shook on the road, making her teeth chatter. Jon sounded as frantic as she felt.

She turned around, bracing herself in the seat. "Nothing!"

His lips were set in a grim smile. "They won't give up that easy. We have to put some distance between us."

He pulled out his Blackberry, glancing at the screen. He dropped it uselessly on the seat. "I need a signal," he said. They came to the end of the driveway, pulling onto the road in a spray of gravel and dust. Jon turned the car south, heading toward Aleppo.

"Where are we going?" Isabel looked from Jon to the rear-view to the landscape slipping by.

"I told you, already."

"No, you didn't."

"I did so! Now shut up!"

She stared at him, open-mouthed. He was sweating, feverish, focused on the road. "Hey," she said. "Hey!"

His eyes flickered in her direction.

"What is wrong with you?"

He blinked languidly and turned back driving.

She narrowed her eyes. Then she saw it: a stain of red welling across his left leg. "Oh my God, you've been shot!"

His hand strayed to cover the wound. "It's nothing."

"We have to get you to a hospital."

He waved her off. "I'm alright. I think it just grazed the skin."

"We have to stop! We have to treat that. Y-you could get infected!"

"So now you're an expert on bullet wounds?"

"What? And you are?"

He shook his head. "Can't stop. We have to get away. They'll catch us..."

She put her hand on his shoulder. "At least let me drive."

He glanced once more in the rearview mirror, then pulled the car to the side of the road. Isabel flew out of her seat and rounded to the driver's side, where he was still opening the door. She put his arm around her shoulder and lifted him up, surprised by how heavy he was.

"Come on," she said, "help me out, now."

He took a step and cried out in pain, falling backwards against the door. She pulled him upright again. "Better let me take a look at this."

A ribbon of blood trailed down his leg. She pulled away the sticky fabric of his pants, shredding the fabric up to the knee with a loud rip. An ugly, dark wound lanced his calf muscle. "Oh, Lord. It did more than graze the skin. Looks like the round is still in there. Sit down."

"What? No, there's no time."

"Shut up and do as you're told. I have to get the bullet out, and stop the bleeding now." She dabbed at the wound with the remains of his pant leg. Jon winced and collapsed into the front seat.

"That hurt!"

"Of course it did." She pulled out her knife.

"You did it deliberately!"

"Gonna do a lot more, too. Better bite down on something."

Jon grabbed the shoulder belt. A throaty scream erupted from his lips as she dug the knife into his leg. He gripped the sides of the door frame, pushing himself up in the seat. Isabel ignored his protestations, pushing deeper until she saw the round head of the copper bullet. "Almost there." She grit her teeth and dug further. Jon writhed in the seat. "Hold still! Got it!"

The bullet dropped into her open palm. She held it up for Jon to see, but he'd closed his eyes, lying exhausted in the front seat. Isabel let her eyes linger on him a moment, then cut his pant leg off the rest of the way with her knife, tearing it into small strips, which she tied together before looping the makeshift bandage around his leg. He moaned when she tightened the knot. At least he was still alive.

"Come on," she said, pulling him upright. "Let's get you situated and get out of here."

A moment later, she shut the door on her passenger, climbed into the driver's seat, and spewed gravel as she tore off down the road.

Sean glanced in the rearview mirror at the body lying on the floor of his van. The men surrounding the corpse were quieter now. They had their bounty, per Yesoph's interference, but the stoniness in their eyes and muttered voices warned him against trusting them further. He wondered if it would be prudent to drop them off where he'd found them.

Yesoph would demand full payment for their services, even though they'd totally blown the operation. He might be able to argue him down to seventy-five, but he doubted he could go lower.

On the other hand, he'd add this to Mark Beaufort's bill, so there was no real gain or loss to him either way. No, the only loss he'd incurred was his willingness to fully trust in Yesoph Panikkar again, and that was a price almost too high to pay. Good help was hard enough to come by as it was. Help that wouldn't turn around and stab you in the back for an extra euro was even harder to buy. He'd thought Yesoph belonged in this latter camp.

Yesoph's only redeeming action had been installing the tracking device on the American's car. Without it, Sean would have already given Mrs. Panikkar something to cry about. He looked at it now. The glowing red dot indicating the car's position had been stationary for several minutes. He frowned. Was this another screw up?

"Where exactly did you place this tracking device?"

Yesoph was watching the screen as well. "Under the hood."

"Could it have fallen out?"

"I do not think so. The mount is a ceramic magnet. Very strong."

Sean eyed his associate. Yesoph was pinching his lower lip. So it could have fallen out. Terrific.

"Perhaps they've stopped."

"And why would they do that?"

"I do not know. Maybe we can ask them when we catch up to them."

"If we catch up to them. And if that chip is lying on the side of the road—"

"Look!" Yesoph pointed at the screen. "It is moving again."

Sean watched the red dot pulsate, the GPS map scrolling beneath it. "They did stop," he muttered. Why would they do that? He shook his head. Not that it mattered. "We're not as far behind as we thought. We're still in this, boys!"

He hit the accelerator. The van surged forward down the road.

CHAPTER
41

"Where are we going?" Isabel glanced from the road to her passenger. Jon was slouched in his seat, his head leaning against the window. His eyes were open, but unfocused.

"Civilization," he said thickly. He held the Blackberry in a limp hand. "I have to get a signal. Head for Aleppo. Best chance we have for a cell tower."

"Okay. And after that?"

He shook his head. "I don't know. I have to translate this." He winced as he sat upright.

Her gaze flickered to the rearview mirror. The smile evaporated. She swore.

"What is it?" Jon sat up, frowning.

"We've got company."

He turned around to look out the back window, then dropped into his seat. "Told you not to stop."

She thought up a retort, but let it die on her tongue. Instead, she depressed the accelerator.

"There they are!"

Sean smiled grimly, not quite sharing Yesoph's jubilation.

He glanced at the speedometer. He'd already buried it at 145 kilometers per hour. The steering wheel shook in his hands, sending a violent shiver through his body. He clenched his teeth and pushed the pedal to the floor.

The tires protested the acceleration, skidding over stones and sand, threatening to fishtail the van out of control. Reluctantly, he backed it down.

"You must go faster, my friend."

"D'you wanna drive?" The van hit a deep pothole, jostling his passengers and causing Hamid's body to fling upright. One of the men cried out in Arabic, raising his weapon at the corpse. The gun fired, blasting a hole through the roof.

"Safeties! Safeties!" Sean bellowed. He glared at Yesoph, who translated the command. "When are you people gonna learn how to pave a bloody road?"

Yesoph shrugged apologetically.

Isabel glanced again in the rearview mirror. Ahead of her was Dār Ta`izzah, a town of some thirty-six thousand due south of Qal at Simân. Behind her, the van was a diminishing speck on the horizon.

"He's still behind us."

"I know. We have to lose him."

"There's not much chance of that here."

Dār Ta`izzah spilled before them in a random cacophony of squat, adobe houses with flat roofs beneath the towering minarets of the town's several mosques. Jon held up his Blackberry, scanning for a signal. Disappointed, he dropped it in his lap.

"Guess it'd be asking too much to drop a microwave receiver in one of those things."

"Undoubtedly. If there's one thing I've learned about Muslims, they're fanatical about their mosques."

"Huh. Think we could use that?"

She glanced at him. "What did you have in mind?"

"Here," he said, handing her the *hijab* she'd worn earlier. "Put this on."

A moment later, he told her to pull the car to the side of the road as a man walked by leading a cart of vegetables drawn by a donkey. He rolled down his window and called out to him. The man frowned and came nearer.

Jon spoke to him quickly in Arabic, and after a moment, showed him his leg. The produce man's eyes widened when he saw the bloody bandage. Isabel stared in the rearview mirror as the van's dot grew in size.

"Hurry," she muttered.

Jon shook hands with the man, who turned and hurried toward the mosque. *"Allahu akbar!"* he called out after him. The produce man waved as he climbed the steps to the mosque.

He turned to Isabel. "Get us out of here. Fast."

"What did you tell him?"

"I told him the men in the van were terrorists, and they were coming to recruit the young men from the village to join the jihad."

"And that will stop them?"

"Slow them down at least. These people are farmers and craftsmen. They don't want anything to do with jihad. They'll keep them from entering the village, or force them to go around."

"And if you're wrong?"

"Then they'll be awash in recruits. Either way."

"Okay. So what now?"

"Just get us on the road to Aleppo and keep driving."

Sean stared ahead at the crowd of people gathered in the road. "What is this?" The men were waving their arms for him to stop. He was half tempted to crush the accelerator and plow through them, but instead he hit the brakes. The van skidded to a stop, sending dust flying into the crowd. The men surged around the van, all speaking at once, banging their open hands against the sides.

"What the hell?" Sean bellowed. "Tell them to get off!"

Yesoph unrolled his window, shouting at the crowd in Arabic. After a moment, he shook his head and rolled up the window. "They are telling us to leave their village. They think we are terrorists."

Sean grimaced and shifted into first. He pressed on the gas, pushing the van into the crowd. The shouts grew louder. Someone picked up a rock and smashed it against Sean's window. The glass broke into a crystalline spider web. Another one crashed into the windshield. Sean muttered an oath and unrolled his window just far enough for the muzzle of his Beretta.

"What are you doing?" cried Yesoph.

Sean glared at Yesoph. "Get them off my van or I'll shoot them off."

Yesoph's jaw tightened. Then he shouted to his men in the back. They picked up their Kalashnikovs and opened the side door, shouting commands to the angry mob outside. Yesoph climbed out with them, waving his arms furiously to drive the villagers away.

"Clear me a path," Sean hollered.

Yesoph directed his men in front, firing the AK-47s over the heads of the crowd, sending them scurrying out of the road. Sean depressed the pedal. The van lurched forward.

Rocks rained down on the roof and windshield, fragmenting the already shattered glass. He swore and smashed the windshield with the butt of his gun, breaking it loose from the frame and sending it sliding down the hood.

"Get out of the way!" he yelled, and hit the accelerator. He didn't see who it was that he hit, but Yesoph's shocked and angered glare told him it wasn't good. He hit the locks and kept accelerating through town. Yesoph would have to find his own way home. Sean kept one eye fixed on the GPS receiver, its blinking red dot receding ever further away.

"We have to get you to a hospital."

"I'll be fine."

"No, you won't. You're still bleeding. You've lost a lot of blood."

"It's stopped," he breathed. "And if we stop," long breath, "Sean will catch us."

His voice trailed off. She shook his shoulder.

No answer.

CHAPTER
42

He opened his eyes and stared quizzically at the depiction of a man being baptized displayed on the wall in front of him. It was a nice painting, done in the Florentine style, with dazzling and vibrant colors capturing the light and drawing the eye toward the center of the picture. The image in the center had to be Jesus, looking very pious and serene as he prayed in the water. Above him, a dove descended in a shaft of light from a cloud. Those gathered around the Christ were either gazing in wonder or looking away in anger.

Where was he?

Jon pushed himself upright and met a wave of nausea. He fell back to the bed and drew a long breath. Pulling his legs up, he examined his calf. A white bandage covered the wound, held in place by medical tape peeking out beneath several wrappings of gauze. He frowned. Where were his clothes?

He pulled off the sheet, not surprised to find he was completely naked in the bed. Taking a deep breath, he rose to one elbow and looked around. The room was built of plastered brick with a tile floor and wooden beams supporting the roof. Beside the bed stood a wooden end table and a straight back chair. A pair of pants and a shirt hung draped across the chair. Fresh underwear, a T-shirt, and socks lay folded neatly on the seat.

The initial nausea subsided. He sat up, breathing through the head rush that followed, then gingerly climbed to the floor. His leg throbbed with the movement. It wouldn't let him put any weight down. He stood on the other leg and leaned over to the chair, retrieving the clothes and tossing them onto the bed before pushing away from the wall and landing back on the mattress.

The room spun. He groaned and closed his eyes. When he opened them next, the room had settled on its previous orientation. He pushed himself back into a sitting position and got dressed, then tried walking again. This time he could hobble from one place to the next by bracing himself against the furniture and wall. The door stood at the far side of the room. He braced himself and lunged for it, nearly collapsing onto the floor when the door opened instead.

Isabel caught him in her arms. "You shouldn't be up yet."

"Hey," he muttered in greeting.

"Come on, let's get you back to bed."

"No. I'm fine. Just a little woozy. Really," he said when she looked like she'd protest further.

She shook her head. "You're as bad as Stephen."

"I'm beginning to think that's a compliment." He brushed a strand of hair out of her face. "Now, you wanna tell me where we are?"

Sean stared at the Aramaic church rising from the street below. Somewhere inside, the two Americans cowered, perhaps recovering from their narrow escape. Perhaps planning their next move. Going in after them would raise too much noise, and likely bring down the authorities on his head. It left him little choice but to wait. He pinched his lip. The red dot of the tracking device still pulsed red, but it hadn't moved in a day.

Had they slipped by him in the night? It was a distinct possibility, but only if they'd found Yesoph's transponder and switched vehicles. The transponder's signal began to fail when he neared town. It took him several hours of searching before he found it again, pulsating weakly before the signal vanished. Cheap Chinese electronics again. He'd seen the car in the church lot when he passed by on the street. He parked nearby, almost out of sight.

The church and street were too busy to risk going in alone and in broad daylight, but spending the day in a hot van with shattered windows and a decomposing corpse in the back was even less entertaining. He left the van at the corner to serve as a decoy, and took up position in a local rooftop restaurant across the street, paying off the help with a generous tip, and waited for darkness. The only problem had been when the restaurant closed. For that, a stack of money and prominent display of his Beretta proved sufficiently convincing for the owner to leave him be.

He had a commanding view of the street, and the building had only one entrance. It was disconcerting that should he need to flee, his exit strategies were somewhat limited. But the fact that he'd know if the owner chose to run or call the police ameliorated this concern.

The restaurateur had a car—an '85 Buick maintained with the same meticulous care with which he ran his business. Sean figured the money he'd paid him to keep quiet and leave him be was enough to cover it. He might even consider it a gift to Sean—a polite way of saying, "Please leave."

A door in the church opened. He raised his binoculars, peering across the street at the two forms that emerged. He rose in his seat, his hand reaching for the Beretta. The two people turned and ambled across the stone walkway toward the gate. He relaxed. It wasn't them. Just a couple of parishioners staying late for prayer. He checked his watch. In a few hours, it would be past sunset…time to go in after them.

"How did you find this place?" he whispered to her. She leaned in close.

"It was in Demetri's address book."

"Unreal. Do they know?" He left the rest of the question unsaid. She shook her head. They'd gathered in another room, what Jon assumed was the dining hall. Around the head of the table, the priests took their seats.

"You said the *Ektenia* for Brother Demetri?"

Jon smiled weakly at the monk, Brother Andraous, and said, "I did my best."

They nodded their heads in unison. "Our Lord is gracious and compassionate," said Brother Andraous, more to the others than to him. Jon took that to mean his meager prayer would have to suffice. The monk peered into Jon's eyes. "Brother Demetri was a dear friend. We received word of his mission two weeks ago. We were asked to provide him whatever assistance he might require, should he come our way." He held up a letter. "This letter was mailed or faxed to all our churches. We've been prepared for some time. I am saddened to hear of his death."

An image of Demetri apologetically taking the forged scroll from him flashed into Jon's mind. He bit his tongue. "I'm very sorry for your loss, Brother Andraous."

"I will inform the protus of his death. They will try to recover his body from the Turkish government."

"Lieutenant Kahil Çapanoğlu of the Turkish Gendarmerie may be able to assist you. He was in charge of the police when Demetri was killed. He is a good man."

Brother Andraous' eyes showed a growing respect. "Thank you."

"It's the least we can do. Thank you for, well, for patching me up."

"Your wife explained to us your association with Brother Demetri."

Jon blinked. *Wife?* He glanced at Isabel, who met his eyes with a pleading gaze. She'd lied to them. They were helping him. Taking care of them. Feeding them. Giving them a place to sleep. Gracious hosts in a country that still valued hospitality. And she'd lied to them, no doubt to secure their help. He felt sick at the thought. Would they have helped them if she'd told them the truth?

"I see."

"I regret we cannot do more for you."

"You've been more than helpful already, and we should be going. We don't wish to bring any trouble to you. We are in your debt."

Isabel touched his arm.

He stiffened. "Yes, Dear?" Great. Now he was lying, too.

"The man who shot you—the same one who killed Brother Demetri—he is still out there."

More lies. Undoubtedly because the truth was so complicated. "What are you asking?"

"We need help to escape him, to get back across the border into Turkey."

Turkey? Why did they want to go back there?

"So you want to ask them?"

"What choice do we have?"

He closed his lips. As much as he hated it, she was right.

Their entry into Syria had been a trick, but since then they'd watch the borders more closely. How else could they get across again, especially with that mercenary on their tail?

"Brother Andraous—"

"Say no more, my friend," Andraous said, holding up the letter. "We have anticipated your request, and as I've said, we are already prepared. You will carry to completion the work of Brother Demetri? Yes?"

He nodded. "We will."

"Then it is we who are in your debt. Allow us to repay you the kindness you showed our brother."

"How could we refuse? Thank you."

Brother Andraous nodded to his companions, who left quickly. He smiled at Jon. "We should get started right away."

CHAPTER
43

"You're mad at me."

He shook his head.

"Liar."

He stopped walking and looked at her. Isabel's eyes were cautious. Defensive.

"Alright. Maybe I am mad at you."

"Why?"

"Lying. These people are helping us. We're their guests, for crying out loud. I think they're entitled to the truth."

Her eyes were onyx. Lips set in a tight line. "Alright," she pressed her hand against his chest. "You want the truth? Tell them."

"What?"

"Go ahead. Tell them the truth. Tell them we lied to them to get their help. Tell them we're not married, but we've been sleeping in the same room or car together for several days. See what they say. And while you're at it, tell them about Demetri. Tell them how their 'hero of the faith' died stealing the scroll."

"He didn't steal it. I gave it to him."

"Whatever. Why not just give them the scroll?"

"Keep your voice down," he hissed.

A wry grin crossed her face. The hardness in her eyes deepened to a point, obsidian daggers puncturing his self-righteousness.

"Tell them you have no intention of turning over the autographs. Defend it in the name of scientific curiosity, or your supposed faith. Go ahead. Justify it any way you wish." He stared at her. She shook her head. "You're right, Jonnie. You are a hypocrite."

She turned on her heel and stalked away from him.

Hypocrite? He stepped quickly to grab her shoulder. She whirled on him, but he stuck his finger in her face.

"Listen, lady. I don't know where you get off, but I didn't make this mess. You did. And that doesn't make me a hypocrite just because I don't want to clean it up. I'm not your brother. I am not Stephen. I'm not willing to do whatever it takes just 'cus it's convenient."

Sean glanced at this watch for the third time in an hour. There'd been no movement at the church in the past three. Darkness was descending. He'd go in soon. He shifted in his seat. This was his first solo surveillance in years, and it was beginning to wear on him. He dearly wished for some Modafinil tablets to stay awake, but had to content himself with coffee. Ibrahim, the restaurateur, had brought him a carafe with cups about thirty minutes before. Sean noted the man's hands didn't shake anymore, a good sign. Ibrahim's initial fear had subsided, and he'd come to accept Sean as his guest, even if an unexpected one. His instincts as a host had taken over, and he would be compliant and deferential, making him easier to use. He turned when Ibrahim appeared in the door with a slight bow. Sean smiled slightly and nodded for him to approach.

"Ankm qd akmlt albn nym?—Are you done with your coffee, yes?

Sean set his cup down and thanked him in Arabic.

Ibrahim retrieved the tray and took a step back to the door. Then he waved toward the church and told Sean just what he thought of the infidels within it.

Sean almost laughed. *"Nym,"* he agreed. *Yes.* They were nothing but trouble. It was time to make his move. He thanked Ibrahim for his hospitality.

Ibrahim smiled toothily, the relief washing over his face so intensely he almost sobbed.

Sean stalked over to the steps and descended to the street. He chambered a round in his Beretta as he stepped across the sidewalk. It was time.

"So where are we going?" Jon asked as they climbed into the car.

"Your friend Leon said we need to go to Antakya. It's due west of here."

Antakya? "Antioch? Wait, when did you talk to Leon?"

"Oh." She handed him his Blackberry. "I called him while you were out. Took a picture of the scroll and emailed it to him. He translated it for us. Hope you don't mind." She said it with a noticeable edge. He took the Blackberry and checked the screen.

"You could've waited."

"Was there a reason to?"

"Guess not." He put the phone away. "Alright then. Where is the scroll?"

"I put it in Demetri's safe box." She tapped the box on the car's floor. "Leon said that would be best place for it."

A moment later, Brother Andraous poked his head through the driver's side window. "Brother Ouseph will drive you," he said. "He has family in Turkey, and often crosses the border to see them. Here," he handed them a pair of passports. "These will assist you in reentering the country."

Jon frowned at the passport. How did an Armenian church in Syria come to have access to forged passports? He gave Andraous a questioning look.

Andraous smiled. "Do not fear, my friend. Our forgeries are quite good. They look more authentic than the real thing, no? We Christians are a persecuted minority here in Syria. We take measures to protect our own. Especially when someone converts from Islam."

"You help them escape?"

"It is a death sentence for many. We help those that we can."

"So you lie to protect others?" said Isabel. Jon glanced at her.

Andraous shrugged. "You remember the story of Rahab the harlot? She lied to save the lives of the spies, and sent the men of Jericho another way. God protected her. If the truth will further evil, it must be withheld."

Isabel nodded, smiling smugly at Jon. He shook his head, thinking of pointing out the flaw in her logic. The situations were hardly commensurable. Instead, he turned and thanked Andraous. The monk spoke briefly to Ouseph, then tapped the hood of the car. Ouseph put the car in gear and drove forward. At that moment, the windshield shattered.

"Get down!" Jon screamed, throwing his body on top of Isabel. Two more reports rang out. Ouseph gunned the accelerator. The car lurched forward, blazing past a single man standing in the parking lot, firing at them. Jon caught a glimpse of Sean's face as the car sped past. Ouseph jerked hard on the wheel, throwing a hubcap across the street. The car fishtailed and left burnt rubber on the asphalt before disappearing down the street.

Sean stared after the retreating vehicle, seething. He crammed the Berretta into his belt, glaring at the church a moment before turning and looking back toward the restaurant. High on the roof, he caught Ibrahim's eye. The restaurateur had watched the whole thing. He kept his gaze on the man even as he crossed the street back toward the restaurant. Ibrahim retreated from the ledge.

In a moment, Sean burst through the door. Ibrahim's wife screamed as the restaurateur pushed to the front, his hands upraised in supplication. *"Allach' irchaem!—Allah, have mercy!"*

Sean pushed his shoulder against the wall and said in a near whisper, *"A'yt'ni siartk—Give me your car."*

"A'ytbr! Umn lk!—Take it! It is for you!" Ibrahim pulled a ring of keys from his pocket, dangling them out to him.

"Ashkrkm gzil alshkr," he thanked him. *"Wa lakemu a salaam."* He turned on his heel and left, passing his glance over the faces of Ibrahim's wife and daughter, huddled beneath their hijabs in the corner. As he banged through the screen door to the street where Ibrahim parked the Buick, he heard the shrill tongue-lashing of Ibrahim's wife, and the hollered defense of the restaurateur behind him. He closed the car door, shutting out the sounds, and started the car.

After driving a mile, he turned onto a side street and pulled out his phone. Beaufort picked up at the second ring.

"I lost them."

"Thought you'd be calling. This is getting to be a habit, my friend."

He smirked. Beaufort was growing predictable. Soon he would suggest a decrease in Sean's salary.

"What have you got for me?"

"Isn't that supposed to go the other way around? You're to bring something to me? I mean, that is what I'm paying you for, isn't it?"

"Dr. Munro and the woman have the scroll. I had them tracked from the basilica to Aleppo, but they've switched vehicles. Can't bloody well follow them if I don't know where they're going now, can I?"

Beaufort snorted. "I've noticed something, Sean, my boy."

Sean grit his teeth. There was no way he'd dignify that with a response. After a moment, Beaufort continued. "You're spending an awful lot of time lately telling me what you cannot do."

"You'll be giving me the sack then, are ya?"

"No. No, I don't think we need to come to that just yet. But I must confess I am rethinking our arrangement."

"Think all you want. But there's no way you'll be getting your hands on the scroll without the information I'm asking you for. Are you hearing me, Mr. Moneybags?" After a moment's silence, he added, "Tick tock, tick tock."

"Antakya. The Cave Church of St. Peter."

Another saint. It made sense. He hung up and started the car. He still had time to catch up and overtake them. And once the scroll was his, he'd take it to Beaufort.

It would be the last time he'd deliver anything to the man. He wondered what he could get for it on the black market.

CHAPTER
44

Kahil glanced up as Sergeant Bahar sat on the edge of his desk. He leaned back in his chair. This was unexpected. Around them, the office of the Gendarmerie busied itself with other crimes and concerns, largely ignoring the lieutenant since the incident costing Gani Sahin his life.

"Sergeant?" Kahil said.

"How are things at the office today?"

Kahil tossed the folder he'd been holding on the desk. It was one of many recovered from the late Dr. Kaufman's home. It landed amongst a pile of scribbled notes and phone messages awaiting his attention.

"Have we come to this, Bahar? You're mocking me now, too?"

Bahar smiled and shook his head. "No, Lieutenant. I come bearing gifts." He dropped an eight-by-ten photograph on Kahil's desk.

Kahil reached for it. "Beware of Greeks bearing gifts," he murmured. "Your father was Greek, wasn't he?"

Bahar stood. "Now you're mocking me."

Kahil looked at the photograph. It was a printout from a security camera at a border checkpoint. Bahar had circled two faces in the backseat of the car in red ink. Kahil lost all humor. "When was this taken?"

"An hour ago," the sergeant said, turning around. "Our new facial recognition software positively ID'd them, but not before they'd already passed through."

"And the man with them? The one driving?"

Bahar shook his head. "No idea. A number of vehicles crossed the border at this time. We can't pinpoint the timestamp of the photo with any particular name."

"I want the names of all who crossed over a half hour on either side of this timestamp."

Bahar smiled and handed a printout to Kahil, showing precisely that. "I guessed an hour, just to be safe. You'll also want this." He set a second photograph on the desk. Kahil picked it up. "Name is Sean MacNeil. Heavy on the terrorist watch list. Those bodies we recovered at the house were among his known associates. He passed through the same checkpoint not fifteen minutes after these three."

"You are a treasure beyond price, my friend."

Bahar smirked. "Someone should tell my wife. She keeps riding me for working these long hours."

"When you are awarded the Distinguished Service Medal for this, she will be grateful."

"I doubt it."

Kahil studied the list, finally stabbing his finger onto one name. "This one," he said. "This is the man they came through with."

Bahar glanced at the name. "Truly? How can you be so certain?"

"It is the only Christian name on the list. That monk, Demetri. He said he was working with them."

"Did he? I didn't realize he'd woken up."

"He came to yesterday. I was able to question him before——you know. Regardless, we find this man, we find the Americans."

He grunted. "It would be better if we knew where they were going."

Kahil nodded. He glanced at the folder on the desk, and saw his phone messages. There were four of them. All were marked urgent. He noticed now they were from America. He reached for the phone.

The voice on the other line said, "Detective Brown."

"Yes, this is Lieutenant Çapanoğlu of the—"

"Yes, Lieutenant. I was wondering when you would get a hold of me."

"How quickly can you get me the phone records of Dr. Munro?"

"I've already got them, actually. Ever since things started exploding over there, I've been following their movements rather closely. The last phone call was received at 9:43pm our time yesterday. A woman called and spoke to Professor Munro's graduate assistant, Leon Farris. He said something about the Cave Church of St. Peter. Sounded very excited about it, too."

"You don't say."

"Let me know when you're ready to bring this fellow in. I'll have warrants ready to serve stateside just as soon as you give the word."

"Very good, Detective," Kahil returned. "I will let you know soon." He hung up, picked up the folder of Stephen's notes, and strode purposefully to Captain Tabak's office.

Bahar remained seated on the edge of Çapanoğlu's desk. A moment later, the voices in Tabak's office grew louder, even as the noise in the Gendarmerie dwindled. All eyes became fixed on the captain's door.

The door flew open as a red-faced Kahil burst through, followed by the captain, his hands on his hips. Kahil stalked to his desk and started stuffing his things into his attaché case.

"What happened?"

"I've been suspended without pay."

"Why?"

"For digging into this again."

"Ah. I am sorry. It is my fault."

"No, my friend. This has been coming for some time."

"What are you going to do?"

"Captain wants me to pass all leads to Ahmet."

"Ahmet's an idiot."

"I know."

"Are you going to accept this?"

Kahil paused and looked at his friend. They'd grown close in the short time they'd known each other. Cut from the same cloth, his mother would've said. "What choice do I have? I'm off the case."

"But are you going to accept this?"

He smiled thinly. "Not a chance."

"So how do we find them?" asked Bahar as they left the building.

"I cannot ask for your help, my friend."

"You can't refuse it, either. You're suspended. I outrank you, now."

It was perversely logical. Kahil climbed into the passenger seat of Bahar's car. "We have to get to Antakya, and fast. They're going to Sen Piyer Kilisesi."

"That's over four hundred kilometers."

"Get us to the airport. I have a friend who owes me a favor."

Jon glanced out the window. The city of Antakya sprawled out before them in a mosaic of ancient walls and modern construction. Squat palms rose on the corners of busy streets crammed with cars, blue buses, motorbikes, and pedestrians. Cramped apartment buildings cast ungainly stares at either side of the Orontes River. The once graceful waterway was now sloped and scraped into little more than a smelly, oversized ditch. Every conceivable square yard of land between the mountains had been dug up, paved over, and converted into living space for the burgeoning population, and but for the walls and frowning stone, the city today gave little evidence of its twenty-three hundred year history.

Jon scanned the screen of his Blackberry, now fully functional with the modern communications available in Turkey. He frowned and tapped Isabel's knee. She eyed him suspiciously.

"St. Peter's Cave Church is the oldest known church in Turkey. Dates back to the first century. Some crusaders found it in the eleventh century and added to it. Capuchin friars rebuilt it in the 1860s at the request of Pope Pius IX. And the garden in front of the church has been used as a cemetery for centuries, as has the cave floor in and around the altar."

"Okay. So?"

"So we're not dealing with some place that is unknown and unexplored, like the *Domo tou Bibliou*. This place has received a lot of attention."

She started nodding. "Meaning it's unlikely we'll find anything there."

"Right. I'm just saying the scroll is an exciting find. As a canon, it would be the oldest in existence, assuming it's real. We might have to content ourselves with just that."

She pressed her lips in a thin line. "I'm not content. We have risked too much. Lost too much."

"I'm just trying to prepare for the worst. I'm still hoping for the best."

She shook her head. "How do you do that?"

"What?"

"Keep hoping, when you know the odds are against it?"

He put his Blackberry away. "Well, like you said, we've risked and lost so much already. But I think Someone meant for us to find this. Men who have been trained to kill have been hunting us, and the mere fact we're still alive makes me think Someone's watching out for us."

"You mean God."

"Yeah. As a scientist, I can study the facts and assess the odds. As a believer—and I am one—I can trust that God loads the dice."

She smiled. "Okay, yeah. I like that."

Sean didn't like it at all. He flipped on the turn signal and pulled behind the car. The bullet holes in the trunk and back window were clearer now, and against the light from the oncoming vehicles, he discerned three silhouettes in the vehicle. He'd spotted them leaving the border checkpoint in Syria just moments after he'd arrived, only five car lengths ahead of him. It had taken all his self-restraint to keep from blowing past the border guards and overtaking them immediately, but the pursuit that would have followed would've rendered his actions pointless, save for revenge.

He had something worth far more than that in mind. But the thought that somehow, something protected them kept nagging at his mind, no matter how many times he insisted he was just being paranoid.

Even paranoia was out of his norm.

He could hear William's voice chiding him, "We should just cut our losses and get out!" Sheer stubbornness kept him going. He felt like shaking his fist at the heavens, challenging them. Bring it on.

Bahar nervously pulled on the seat belt straps of the S-70A Blackhawk as Kahil's "friend" powered up the twin General Electric T700-GE-701C turboshaft engines. They started with a high-pitched whine as the four 16.36 meter rotors began to turn, but quickly grew to a dull roar.

He hollered to Kahil. "How did you manage this?"

Kahil shook his head and tapped the headphones. Bahar put them on and repeated his question into the microphone. Kahil grinned and looked at the pilot, a young man of twenty-eight years and bright blue eyes. Zeren Kartal glanced back and said, "His brother saved my life. Twice. I would do anything for a Çapanoğlu. Even if it means I will go to jail for this."

"Perhaps I can arrange for us to share a cell, eh?"

Bahar chuckled. "Don't take him up on it. There are some things too costly for even a life debt."

In a moment, the S-70A lurched into the air, climbing 3.6 meters per second and reaching a cruising speed of over two hundred and eighty kilometers per hour. Kartal said, "We should be in Antakya in little less than ninety minutes."

"Let's hope it's soon enough," Kahil replied.

CHAPTER
45

Ouseph pulled the car into the parking lot of the Cave Church of St. Peter. Before them sat a stone wall, a little over ten feet high, in which a single iron gate barred the way to the cave. Four simple lanterns glowed invitingly in the wall, but for all that, the parking lot was deserted and the gate locked.

Jon and Isabel climbed out of the car and approached the church, half-heartedly trying the gate before stepping back to assess their situation. On the other side of the gate, the pathway leading to the cave beckoned.

"Wait here," he said to Ouseph, then stepped around to the right. Here the ground sloped sharply downhill. By gripping the crevices in the rock, he inched his way around the corner until his fingers grasped the wrought-iron railing. With a grimace, he pulled himself up and climbed over the wall to land on the other side. He hobbled on his wounded leg, groaning. Moonlight filled the inner courtyard with a silky glow, and on the floor of the yard he saw the brickwork laid out in an intricate pattern. Against the wall on the far side stood a tall aluminum ladder. He grinned and limped over to it. In a minute, he'd have it over the wall for Isabel to climb up. As he reached for it, he heard a sound behind him. A moment later, Isabel swung her leg over the same fence he'd just scaled, and dropped safely down.

"I was getting the ladder for you."

She dusted off her hands. "No need. Come on, I'll race you to the cave."

"I'm wounded here!" he called to her retreating form. He shook his head and followed.

After a short walk down a well-marked trail, which curved along the southern base of the Mountain, they stood before the Cave Church of St. Peter. Known to the locals as *Sen Piyer Kilisesi*, legend had it that the Apostle Peter carved this ancient gathering place for believers with his own two hands, and that both Paul and Barnabas had preached there. Whether this was a cavern carved by the fisherman-preacher or not, it was doubtless an early meeting place for those followers of the Way whom the residents of Antioch themselves first called "Christians." The cave hid behind an enormous façade built by the crusaders, featuring three portals beneath tall arches of cut stone. Set high above each doorway, three embrasures allowed light to penetrate behind the stone and illuminate the chancel. The outer two openings were each a cross fitchée, like an eight-petal flower, above which sat an open circle. The center skylight was a more elaborate design, a St. Andrew's Cross with additional flowers carved above or below each point. The skylights were dark now, and only pale shafts of moonlight could penetrate the gloom within.

Jon went to each of the three portals, rattling the padlocked iron gates that denied them access, and shining his penlight inside, trying to see clearly in the darkness. The cave was locked securely. A warning sign in Arabic and Turkish informed visitors that the historical site was closed due to erosion of the cliff above.

"Locked," he muttered.

Isabel folded her arms and cased the front of the cave, looking amongst the grave markers in front before finally coming back to stand beside Jon, her hands on her hips now.

"There's nothing for it. We have to get inside."

Jon glanced around, then bent forward and retrieved a sizable rock from the yard. He hefted it above his head with both hands and brought it crashing down upon the padlock.

The padlock was relatively new and easily rebuffed his efforts. But the ancient gates were not built to withstand a sustained assault, and after so many centuries, they surrendered to his third and final blow by popping loose from their hinge mounts and sagging to the ground. He winced inwardly, regretting the result. He'd only meant to break the lock, not destroy such a marvelous historical treasure.

The damage was done. Jon pulled the gate free and swung it outward into the courtyard, then stepped into the cool blackness.

Sean turned off his lights and coasted to a stop. Ahead, he could see the single car he'd followed from Aleppo sitting in the parking lot. The driver had stayed behind, and was contentedly smoking a cigarette. He watched the pale ember pulsate with each inhalation. Dr. Munro and Ms. Kaufman must have already gone ahead.

He pulled out his gun and checked the clip, then retrieved the safe box from the back of the car, along with some flares. There was no way he'd let them get away with the scroll. Not after everything he'd been through. He shut the trunk and crept toward the parking lot.

God or no God, it was time to collect his due.

Inside the cave, Jon swept the beam of his pen light around the interior, illuminating the single stone altar in the front. On the floor, he could see the crumbling remains of a tile mosaic. Frescoes dating back almost two thousand years had once decorated the walls, but now they were faded to the point of oblivion, eroded by the loving caresses of the faithful through so many centuries.

Together they stole up to the altar and inspected it. In a corner toward the back sat a tiny fount carved into the rock. Jon searched all around it and inside, but came up empty and wet.

"Nothing," he whispered. His voice cascaded from the ceiling and walls, echoing "nothing" as if in hasty agreement. "Are you sure Leon said it would be here?"

"You could always dig out the scroll and read it yourself."

"Nah. I'll trust his work. Leon's too good to screw that up. We're missing something. Some clue as to where the scrolls are."

"Maybe that's why no one else ever found them."

"Yeah. Either that, or they were found a long time ago and lost again."

A single report from the Beretta, and Ouseph slumped forward in the car, his cigarette falling to the earth. Sean crushed it under foot and examined the locked entrance to the Cave Church. After a moment, he set the safe box down and stuck his gun in his belt. He started to climb around to the other side. He hoped there was an easier way back. He still needed the safe box. As he swung his foot up onto the railing, he heard the low throb of a helicopter looming overhead. He glanced up, watching the flickering lights of the aircraft pass closely above him.

"There!" cried Kahil, pointing out the entrance to the Cave Church. "Can you set down there?"

Zeren glanced out the windshield at the proposed landing site, then nodded. A few moments later, they were on the ground.

As they exited the helicopter, Kahil said, "You might want to call for some backup, friend."

Bahar nodded. His cell phone was already out.

Jon had started investigating the floor around the base of the altar when he froze. At first, he'd thought he'd heard a helicopter in the distance, then dismissed it when it stopped. But the sound of footsteps entering the cave was unmistakable. "Izzy!" he hissed. "The light!" She flicked it off.

A moment later, the cavern was filled with brightness and the crackling hiss of a flare.

"Dr. Munro! Ms. Kaufman! I know you're here. Come out now, and no one gets hurt."

Jon looked at Isabel. He mouthed the word "Sean!" to her. She nodded. He pulled off his glasses, holding them so the lens just barely peered around the corner of the altar. In the curve, he could see a figure moving toward his right, peering into the tunnel across the room. He put his glasses back on and motioned this to Isabel.

Together they crept around the side of the altar, trying to stay out of sight.

"You two are a most tiresome pair," Sean called out. "I have never encountered such challenging competitors in all my years."

He'd heard the helicopter arriving, and figured he only had moments before whoever it was came in through the front entrance. But that was all the time he needed. He worked his way toward the back of the apse, aiming his gun. Empty. He stepped around to the throne behind it. At that moment, Jon and Isabel sprang from the far side and dashed toward the tunnel. He turned and fired, his shot going wild and pinging off the stone with a loud crack.

Kahil and Bahar heard the gunshot as they approached the Cave Church. Exchanging a glance, they drew their weapons and dashed to the front. Light poured out from the cave. Kahil looked, then dove inside. Bahar provided cover. He ducked behind a column. A second later, Kahil appeared behind the other one.

Sean fired again, tripped over his safe box, dropping his flare, and then dashed down the tunnel after them. More rock splintered from the walls, provoking a yelp from the woman as they raced ahead. The tunnel continued to twist and turn, and more than once, Sean slipped on the wet rock, badly bruising his hand.

Jon grabbed Isabel and pulled her back into a narrow alcove in the rock. They pressed their bodies into the cave's wall, holding their breath. A moment later, a shadowy form dashed by, swearing and cursing the darkness that hid them. As Sean's footfalls retreated, Jon found himself staring at the image on the wall directly in front of him, a faded fresco, barely visible in the dim light from the tunnel's entrance. As he reached for it, Isabel yanked him back.

Two more forms appeared in the tunnel, weapons drawn, pursuing the mercenary as quietly as possible. When they were gone, she whispered, "Let's get out of here!"

He shook his head. Instead, he pulled out his penlight and flicked it on, casting the dim beam across the fresco on the far side of the alcove. Isabel stared at the image, gasping in recognition.

There on the wall, barely visible after nearly twenty centuries of age and neglect, was an image of Christ coming on the clouds in judgment, the sword coming out his mouth pointing downward at a sharp angle. The image was identical to the mosaic on the floor of the *Domo tou Bibliou*.

"This is it," he gasped. "This is the clue we had to see!" Jon followed the line of the blade down the wall to a small opening at the base of the alcove. He bent forward and shone his light into the gap, gasping in wonder.

He handed the light to Isabel and reached into the cavity, his arm disappearing up to his shoulder. Then he pulled it out again, holding onto a sealed earthen jar. "There's more," he said, reaching in again.

A gunshot broke the stillness, followed by three more. Isabel flicked out the light. In the darkness, they heard the sound of someone approaching. They held their breath. Quite suddenly, a flashlight's blaze dazzled their eyes.

"It's you. I might have known."

CHAPTER
46

"Lieutenant?" said Jon, clambering to his feet.

Kahil turned the light on himself so they could see. "Yes," he replied. "We got him." Then he collapsed against the wall. Isabel rushed to his side.

"He's been shot."

Jon scrambled to his feet, and with Isabel lifted the Gendarmerie officer to his knees. "No," he mumbled. "Help Bahar."

They glanced down the tunnel. "You first," Jon replied. "Let's get you to the chancel. We'll come back for Bahar. I promise."

Together they pulled the man along the tunnel's course back into the light, laying him down against the wall. "I forgot to tell you...."

"What?"

"You. Are under. Arrest." He cracked a grin, then closed his eyes.

"Lieutenant?"

He moved his hand, waving toward the tunnel. "Bahar."

Together they dashed back to the tunnel, scrambling through the darkness with Kahil's flashlight, calling Bahar's name. They found him in a large cavern close to the tunnel's exit. Water seeped from the ceiling and walls, flowing in tiny rivulets that caught and refracted the flashlight's beam, sending splinters of light back to them. Bahar was keeled over on the left of the path. His breathing was labored and each gasp brought a liquid gurgle from his chest.

Isabel gave Jon a worried look. "We have to get him to a doctor."

Jon nodded, and together they lifted him up. As they did so, another sound broke the cavern's stillness.

"Help...me."

As a threesome they turned, the wounded Bahar unconscious between them. Jon shone his light toward the sound. Sean lay about twenty feet away, pressing against his leg, his gun still in his hand. Blood seeped from the leg wound, staining the ground a dark crimson. His eyes were narrow slits, pleading.

Jon looked at Isabel. She shook her head. "No."

"We have to help him."

"No, we do not. We have to help this man here. He's the good guy. You don't help the bad guy. You just don't."

Jon gave Isabel the flashlight and pulled free of Bahar's shoulder.

"Jonnie!"

He crossed over to Sean and undid his belt. "We're all bad guys, hypocrites and all, but God loves us anyway." He looped the belt around Sean's leg and pulled it tight. Sean grimaced, but did not cry out. Jon picked up the gun and stood. "We'll come back for you. I promise."

"Thank you," Sean whispered.

He returned to the wounded Bahar, whose head lolled about as they lifted him up again. Together they turned and limped him back to the church. They set Bahar down with a grunt, next to Kahil. Jon turned back to the tunnel. "I'm going back for Sean."

"Jonnie...."

"He's still a man. He needs our help."

She said nothing. He turned to go. When he reached the tunnel's entrance, he heard, "I'm sorry."

He looked back at her. Her eyes filled with pain and fear. He smiled calmly. "It's alright," he said, and disappeared into the tunnel.

The way was more difficult with just his penlight, and once or twice, he thought he heard footsteps behind him. His leg throbbed with every step. He passed the alcove where the autographs waited. His heart fluttered. Soon, he told himself. But first things first.

After several minutes, he reached the cavern where they'd found Bahar. The beam from his penlight dwindled. The batteries were wearing down.

"Sean?" His voice reverberated from the walls and ceiling. "Sean, my light's going out. If you can hear me, try to make some noise." He held still, letting the echo of his voice fade into the dark. There was no sound now, save for the distant trickling of water on the rock.

This would be harder than he thought. He inched his way forward now, measuring his steps carefully in the brown halo of his flashlight's beam. He could barely see the rock formation just ahead, but he recognized it. He'd found Sean just beyond it. He pushed by the stalagmite and stopped. There on the ground, scarcely reflecting his light, was a pool of blood. There was no sign of the mercenary. He took two more steps forward before realizing what had happened.

Sean was gone.

He stood there dully for a moment, then shook his head. Sean's fate was not in his hands. He turned and went back the way he came. The light from his penlight was almost gone now. He reached the alcove of the scrolls and stared in disbelief. The jars lay on the ground, shattered and empty.

"No," he whispered, then louder, "No, no, no, *no!*" He dropped and thrust his arm into the hole, reaching, straining for any remaining jars.

Empty.

He straightened and sat on his knees, staring at the fragments on the ground until his light winked out and darkness enshrouded him.

There was only one explanation, too dreadful to consider.

Izzy.

She must have taken them. But why? Unless….

He rose to his feet, stumbling through the black toward the exit. There might still be time to catch her, if—

He broke through the tunnel's entrance into a blaze of flashlights and drawn weapons.

CHAPTER
47

"They just let you go?" said Leon.

Jon sipped his tea. "No. Not exactly. I spent the night in jail, of course, and had to answer a barrage of questions before I was even allowed a phone call. I must say, the American consulate did a stellar job of getting me out of there."

Michaels snorted, pacing in the corner of Jon's office.

"Think about it from their perspective," Jon said. "I entered their country illegally. Twice. I was involved in no less than three different terrorist events in the capitol city, let alone Antakya. And we won't even talk about Syria. I think, in the end, they were just glad to get rid of me."

"Well, it was downright stupid of you, if you ask me," Michaels blurted.

"Everything we did made complete sense at the time."

"What happened to Kahil and Bahar?"

He took another sip. "Last I heard, they were recovering from their wounds in the hospital. Kahil was forcibly retired, I think, and they suspended Bahar, pending a formal investigation. I wish I could have helped them."

"And what about the autographs?" said Michaels. "What's happened to them?"

He shook his head.

"And the scroll? The one in the *Domo*?" said Leon.

"Izzy has everything. I think."

"And you haven't heard from her?"

"Not one word."

Michaels slammed his fist on the table. "Jonathan, I'm sorry. I should have listened to you. I should not have sent you after this. You were obviously not the right man for the job."

"Is that why you hired Hamid?" He took another sip of tea, watching his boss' eyes turn furtive.

"What? What are you talking about?"

"Stephen was turning over a new leaf. He wanted to turn the scroll over to the Turkish authorities. Do things properly for once. But that's not why you hired him. You weren't interested in helping Stephen's reputation. You wanted to exploit it. And when he wouldn't play along anymore, you found Hamid. You told me you had a man watching him. As soon as Stephen realized what he was up against, he hid the scroll. You had to have known Stephen tried to contact me. All my mail is on the university's servers. You would've easily known. You sent that assassin after me, and sent me to Stephen, hoping to use me to lure out the autographs."

Michaels' mouth hung open. He closed it slowly. "You'll never prove it. You think anyone in the university will believe you? I'll have you out of a job before the week is out."

"Why'd you do it, Tony?"

His eyes narrowed. "How can you even ask that? That scroll is worth far more than your life. Surely you can see that."

"Oh, it is, but not for the reasons you think…. Heard enough, Detective?"

Michaels' eyes widened. Detective Brown opened the door and stepped inside, followed closely by Officer Hagel. Michaels' stared furtively between them and Jon. Jon opened his shirt, revealing a wireless microphone taped to his chest.

"Yes, Doctor. I believe that'll do."

A minute later, Brown led Doctor Anthony Michaels away from the office in handcuffs. Jon followed them to the door and shut it firmly behind them. Leon sat in the corner, shaking his head. Jon took off the wire and set it on the desk.

"What was that all about?"

"Betrayal," Jon replied. His tone was dark. "Once I realized who was behind this, I cut a deal with the Turks. That's why they let me go."

"Wow."

"There's just one more thing," Jon said. Leon looked up at him, bewildered. "How did Sean know we were going after St. Simeon? Only two people knew where to find us. Izzy. And you."

He stared at him, his arms folded.

"What?"

"You're the only one who could've known we were going to Simeon's church, or to St. Peter's cave. I just want to know why."

"What, so you can have me arrested like Dr. Michaels?"

"No. This is personal. Just between you and me. Why'd you do it?"

Leon bit his lip. "Alright, fine! I did it! You want to know why? 'Cus Mark Beaufort paid me to, that's why. Do you have any idea how much a doctorate costs these days? On a teacher's salary, I could never repay it."

"I thought as much. You're fired. Detective?"

A moment later, Jim Brown opened the door again. "Wondered why you took that thing off."

Leon stared at Jon. "Oh my God. Is that thing still on?"

Jon nodded, finishing his tea.

"I didn't mean for anyone to get hurt. I didn't know they would do that. I never wanted—I'm sorry."

"Let's go, son," said Brown.

"I'll be speaking to the Board about having you expelled. Cut a deal with them, Leon. They'll want your testimony against Mark Beaufort."

Brown shook his head. "Mark Beaufort ain't going to trial. He was found dead last night in his apartment. Double tap to the chest. Single gunshot to the head. Nine millimeter. Execution style."

"Sean MacNeil," Jon muttered, shaking his head. "Sorry, Leon. You're on your own."

"Dr. Munro!"

"Goodbye, Leon."

Brown and Leon left, closing the door behind them. Jon set his empty cup on the desk, staring at the equally empty office. So much had happened. He had nothing to show for it, and no one to share it with. He frowned, steeling himself against the hurt building in his chest.

The phone rang.

He studied it, then picked it up on the third ring. "Hello?" There was silence on the other end. Finally, he said, "Izzy?"

"Hello, Jonnie."

He licked his lips. "Where are you?"

"It doesn't matter."

"Are you okay?"

She chuckled lightly. "I'm fine. It's good to hear your voice."

"Yeah, you too."

"Well, I won't keep you. I—"

"Why did you call me?"

"You're a good man. I'm sorry I called you a hypocrite."

He cut to the chase. "You have them, don't you?"

"Yes."

"You took them when I went to help Sean."

"I did."

"And that's why you apologized in the cave."

After a moment, she said, "It is."

"Why did you do it?"

"Do you have to ask?"

"You're going to sell them?"

"Of course. I already have offers from six different countries."

"You should give them to a museum."

"There are museums interested. Among others."

He sighed. "So why did you call me?"

"I thought—I thought you might like to see them. You could study them. Validate the claim."

"Thus ensuring you get full price for them."

"That too. I thought it might be nice to see you again. But I know you won't do it. You said to me that we're all bad guys. But you try so hard to be good."

He shook his head. "Do I?"

"Yes. I think so."

"But what does it profit a man to gain the whole world, and lose his soul?"

"What?"

"It's something Jesus asked. It's in those scrolls you're so keen on possessing and selling to the highest bidder."

She said nothing.

"You really should read them."

"I know. Goodbye, Jonnie," she said, and hung up.

He stared at the phone. Somehow, he had to find a way to reach her.

EPILOGUE

Six Months Later

Demetri set down the phone and turned to the protus. "It is done," he said. "We can collect the scrolls from our contact in New York." He rolled away from the phone, positioning the wheelchair to face the head of the monastery. The doctors gave him even odds of walking again, but he trusted more in His Lord's power to heal.

"And what of the seller?" the protus asked.

"She has no idea. Our anonymity is protected."

"Excellent." He took a sip of tea, and then said thoughtfully, "how much did it cost us?"

Demetri cocked his head. "Does it matter?"

"No. But like all things, I must concern myself with the realities of our existence in this sphere."

"Well, I'm sure you'll be able to recoup the investment. With the scrolls at Mount Athos, there are many who will come to see them. The offerings alone should be enough to sustain you."

The protus nodded, and then smiled wistfully at him. "And what of you? Are you confirmed in your decision?"

"I am, Father. It is no longer time for me to be here. My ghosts no longer haunt me. I have no more need to run from the world."

"Where will you go?"

"Wherever my Lord commands. I should like first to go to Romania, and see my family again. And then? Who knows."

"Go with God, my friend."

Demetri smiled. "Always."

YOU MIGHT ALSO ENJOY:

AFTER THE CROSS
by Brandon Barr & Mike Lynch

Colton Foster, once hailed as a renowned expert in Latin, Hebrew and Greek, had his reputation destroyed when a shadowy antiquities dealer outwitted him with master forgeries from Solomon's Temple. Years later, his career and self-respect still in pieces, a team discovers an 800-year old letter in Istanbul and his life takes a pivotal turn. The job of translating the letter, purportedly revealing the hidden cross of Jesus, is his for the taking, and with it a chance to redeem himself.

Mallory Windom is smart, beautiful, and skilled at getting what she wants. A linguistic prodigy with a dark history, she trusts no one, an important skill in the black market antiquities trade where she regularly sells her expert talents to the highest bidder. When she's asked to join the same research team as Colton, she eagerly accepts, seeing it as a ticket to the legitimacy she craves.

As Colton and Mallory hunt for Christianity's most prized relic, mysterious forces seem bent on stopping them at every turn. In a race against time and hired mercenaries, Colton and Mallory's search leads them to an ancient town in Israel. They soon discover that the most important struggle of their lives is not around them, but from within, testing their beliefs, their ethics, and their growing love for one another.

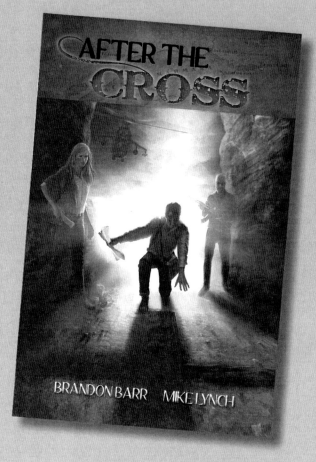

CHAPTER 1

May 22nd, present day, Constantinople Library excavation site, Istanbul, Turkey

A solitary figure emerged from the shadows, darkness draping him like a smooth leather glove. Dressed in black beret and fatigues, Emel Dwayat's profile was indistinguishable from the mouth of the ancient portico. He pulled the AK-47 held tight in his hands closer and slipped towards the flicker of movement under the eastern roof of the Constantinople Library. Despite his muscular frame, he maneuvered nimbly down the remnants of the 1600-year-old corridor, keeping to shadows as he crept towards the point of motion. He cursed the day he'd agreed to work for a woman—and an English woman at that.

Dwayat scanned the eastern roof, lying half-exposed, rising from the ground like the bones of a giant derelict. The size of the structure and multi-leveled trenches recently carved out by the dig team made a direct line of sight all but impossible. Securing the place was a joke. The grounds were littered with runs and hiding holes so intricate, he would have needed an army to protect it. Complicating the defense further was the English archeologist's notion that 500-watt spotlights mounted in the middle of the excavation would deter looters.

Nothing could have been more ridiculous. Dwayat had warned Dr. Lewis countless times those infernal lights would do more harm than good, that his

5

eyes worked better in darkness where he held the element of surprise, but his advice had not been taken.

Ironic, he thought. She hadn't hired him because of his ruthless reputation; rather, he'd impressed her with his knowledge of ancient Latin and Greek. Maybe he should have simply shot that large brimmed hat off her head instead of schmoozing her with a recitation from Virgil's *Catalepton*.

"Errare humanum est," he growled under his breath.

Silence was still his friend, if darkness wasn't. He squatted behind a patch of the library's scorched roof. Among the music of distant crickets came the quick patter of rubber-soled shoes running on sand—the insects went quiet.

Coming to his feet, he pressed his AK-47 against his shoulder and searched for movement. The dark green foliage skirting the excavation's ridges rustled softly as a series of freshly dug archways glowed painfully under the glaring spotlights. Otherwise, silence. Nothing.

The crickets' music bleated again.

Dwayat reached for the two-way radio piece in his ear. "Hassam," he whispered in heightened Turkish, "the Devil is out tonight."

Static crackled in reply. "You're not hearing things again?" asked a voice in his earpiece.

Dwayat frowned at Hassam's playful tone. His counterpart was an indolent, inexperienced young man, his job nothing more than an easy paycheck. Dwayat had little tolerance for such fools. In this line of work, it was either kill or be killed; it was not uncommon to find a guard's throat slit in the morning, and artifacts long gone. He himself bore the scars of three knife fights and a bullet wound in the leg.

"If I catch you asleep tonight, Hassam, I will carve my name in your chest. Do you hear me?"

His radio fell silent. The message had been received.

✛

Malik al-Hassam rose from the slab of marble where he'd been resting, brushing off the ever-present dust that filled the halls of the half buried Constantinople Library. He readjusted the beret just above his eyebrows.

A quick thumb against his lighter and a cigarette glowed to life in his mouth. Hassam bent down and picked up his rifle, figuring he'd do his required rounds, and then find another place to sit where he could hear the old fox coming.

Metallic clanking sounds shuddered down the corridor. Crouching low, he tossed the cigarette from his mouth and slipped his finger around the trigger.

Hassam offered a quick prayer to Allah for protection, and then navigated the lightless passageways towards the source of the noise. He neared a junction leading north to the records hall. Dozens of charred but recognizable manuscripts had been discovered there, though most had been reduced to cinders when the Ottoman Turks set fire to the library in 1453.

The opposite hall led to the heavily seared corridor with adjoining alcoves for private reading; and at the corridor's end, the newly unearthed chamber of the priests was littered with charred remains, save two bookshelves that had miraculously survived the flames. A soft light flickered against its walls.

Hassam fingered his earpiece. "Dwayat, there is someone down here. Where are you?"

Dwayat hissed with excitement. "Cut them off. I'll come down from the western entrance. Whichever way they go, we'll be waiting for them."

A wrenching nausea assaulted Hassam's stomach as he turned the corner. Dwayat panted from his earpiece, "And Hassam, don't forget to switch your safety off."

Hassam cursed silently as he brought up his weapon and flipped the switch near the trigger. He looked forward again and crept along the hallway of alcoves, carefully placing each step. Ahead, the frantic motion of a small flashlight dashed about the corridor. Hugging the wall close, he slid forward, his automatic pointed at the mottled gray entrance. For a moment, the flashlights moved out of view, then suddenly they went dark.

Hassam froze, his heart pounding. A man's panicky voice said something in an unfamiliar dialect. The voice cut short, and an unchecked pounding of feet echoed off the stone floor. Two shadows flew from the priests' chambers straight for him.

The deafening roar from Hassam's AK-47 pierced the hallway. His gun arched back and forth in quick stuttered waves. The weapon's discharge flamed a pulsating orange light against the stunned faces of two black-cloaked men. Searing pain bit Hassam in the arm, driving him backwards, and he sprang into an alcove.

He tried to control his breathing and remain quiet as warm blood flowed from his right bicep.

With stunning brightness, a light glared to life outside his hiding place.

Dwayat's harsh tone came from the corridor. "Hassam, you jackrabbit. Come out of your hole."

When Hassam stepped into the muted light, his partner was standing near one of two bodies. Dwayat's flashlight swept through the area until it hesitated on a shiny metal box partially obscured by one of the dead men's hands. Hassam knelt beside him without speaking, his body trembling, gunfire still ringing in his ear.

"Sir," he finally sputtered, "I've been shot."

The old fox glanced at his bloodied arm and laughed. "These men have no guns. You shot yourself you idiot. One of the rounds must have ricocheted off the wall."

Hassam ran his fingers along the injury. "I've had worse."

His attention returned to the two dead men. Dwayat slipped the metallic box from under the man's lifeless fingers, then blew away a thin layer of dust, revealing a seal imbedded into the silvery surface. Even a superficial look at it told him this artifact was important.

Hassam cast a glance at the man and then back at the box. *Important enough to die for?*

"They came for this," Dwayat concluded as he stared at the inscription. "Curious. It's as if they knew where to look."

Hassam fixed his gaze on the two men. "But that doesn't make any sense. This place has been buried for hundreds of years. How could they know what was here?"

"I cannot say." Dwayat studied the inscription a second time. "The writing here is Latin. Very old."

His partner squinted at the symbols. "How can you tell?"

"Years of observation and study, Hassam. Unlike you, I do not spend my time idly. I watch. I listen." Dwayat pointed at one of the dead men's chests. "If you were smart, you would have at least learned to shoot by now. Look at the pockmarks you made all over the walls. It's a miracle you hit these men at all."

Hassam pressed closer. "What does the inscription say?"

"It's some kind of royal crest. Whom it belongs to, I'm not certain. There aren't any names. But do you see that word below the crest? VERITAS. Truth."

Curiosity settled into Hassam's gaze. "Let's look inside."

With a nod, Dwayat unlatched a gold clasp and flipped the top open. Inside, a partially folded parchment lay in the shadows. With a delicate touch, he lifted it from the box.

Even in the dim light, a single name jumped off the page.

"Imad ad-din al-Isfahani," Dwayat whispered, as though he feared to say the name aloud.

Hassam stared in disbelief. "Al-Isfahani was the advisor of Saladin the Great." He pointed at the document with an accusatory finger. "Why would this be in a library of the infidels?"

"Shut up!" commanded Dwayat, scanning the parchment.

As the minutes passed, Hassam watched fear edge into the hollows of his partner's face until, finally, his patience broke. "Can you read it?"

Dwayat put a finger to his lips, his eyes never wavering from the mysterious words.

Hassam felt a growing dread and glanced at the two men, their cloaks half-covering their lifeless bodies.

The old fox's breathing grew shallow and his eyes drifted up from the letter. "The Devil has indeed come to Istanbul tonight."

Hassam glanced at the parchment, then back at the two bodies. "Why do you announce the Devil's presence? These men are dead; if the Devil was here, he is gone."

"No!" Dwayat took in his surroundings. "The Devil remains."

He refolded the parchment and placed it back inside the silver box, and then a look of horror studded his face.

"What is it!" demanded Hassam.

The room throbbed with silence. Dwayat's eyes were far away, held by something terrifying.

Hassam sensed another presence in the room, ghost-like and evil. An urge passed through him to claw at Dwayat's face—to viciously club him with his gun.

"Speak!" he hissed.

"A map," said his partner softly, staring into the night. "The letter is a map."

"To what?"

Dwayat slowly withdrew from the spell he'd been caught in. His eyes locked with Hassam's. "A map to the Cross."

"What are you talking about? What cross?"

Dwayat licked his lips. "The letter refers to the cross of Yeshua, and al-Isfahani's involvement in its survival."

"A map...a map to the Cross? From the first century?"

"Yes."

Hassam's eyes drifted down, the pitch-black ground grabbing his sight like a magnet. "The Cross," he muttered, "of the prophet Yeshua. Allah save us all."

AVAILABLE AT